LET ME OUT

AMANDA BRITTANY

B

Boldwood

First published in Great Britain in 2025 by Boldwood Books Ltd.

Cover Design by JD Smith Design Ltd.

Cover Images: Shutterstock

A CIP catalogue record for this book is available from the British Library.

Paperback ISBN 978-1-83617-186-7

Large Print ISBN 978-1-83617-185-0

Hardback ISBN 978-1-83617-184-3

Ebook ISBN 978-1-83617-187-4

Kindle ISBN 978-1-83617-188-1

Audio CD ISBN 978-1-83617-179-9

MP3 CD ISBN 978-1-83617-180-5

Digital audio download ISBN 978-1-83617-183-6

This book is printed on certified sustainable paper. Boldwood Books is dedicated to putting sustainability at the heart of our business. For more information please visit https://www.boldwoodbooks.com/about-us/sustainability/

Boldwood Books Ltd, 23 Bowerdean Street, London, SW6 3TN

www.boldwoodbooks.com

For Karen Clarke and Joanne Duncan
My partners in crime.

PROLOGUE

SIX WEEKS AGO

Elliot

The painful thud against my chest forces me to the cliff edge. Stumbling, earth crumbling under my boots, I try to get my balance, but it's never going to happen. My body arcs backwards over the ridge. I cry out, arms flailing, grabbing air with useless fingers, fear fracturing all hope as I fall, eight words jabbing my brain:

I should have stayed away from Sycamore House.

PART I

1

NOW

Annie

'How did I get here?'

This is my latest thing. Talking to myself. 'I don't mean physically,' I go on, voice muffled by the duvet over my head. 'I know how I ended up *here*, alone at thirty, in a flat in Greenwich with a mould problem that aggravates my chest. Basically, I can't afford anything better in London on my salary. Junior doctors just aren't paid enough.' So, when I say how did I get here, I mean mentally. Though, it has to be said, physically I'm not in a great place either. My gym membership expired in 2015, and the closest I get to healthy eating is the strawberries in my breakfast jam.

I drag myself from under the zigzag-patterned quilt, and prop my head against the headboard, quitting the cute cat reel I've been watching on my phone.

'Sertraline will take a while to take effect, Annie. But hopefully you'll feel better once it does,' the GP said a couple of weeks back. Then, with a sympathetic tilt of her head, she whizzed the

prescription digitally over to Boots, not seeming to realise that for me to walk across town to the chemist was an ordeal in itself.

I'm still waiting for the tablets to work. To bounce back to my former self. The self who liked socialising. Who loved her job. Was with a man she thought she'd spend the rest of her life with. But right now I feel lethargic, my brain foggy, too numb to cry. Perhaps that's it. Perhaps that's the effect the doctor was going for. Well, if it is, I don't like it.

I glance at the digital clock on my bedside unit. 11 a.m. Sleep is weird. From the moment I hit the pillow, whatever time I go to bed, I lie awake, seeing every hour pass by – bold, red, fluorescent numbers taunting me. Then, around 7 a.m., my body decides it's finally time to doze off and takes me on a journey through vivid, bizarre dreams. But it doesn't matter. I haven't got to get up. I'm signed off pending a chat with the mental health and well-being team. I'm not going to lie, it's lonely under this black cloud. It's pissing it down in my flat, leaving puddles of sadness everywhere.

I pick up the mug on my bedside unit. Take a swig of coffee. It's cold. Of course it is – I made it five hours ago. An unpleasant odour of Not My Cat's latest visit invades my nostrils. The previous tenant put a flap in the door, which means my neighbour's moggy often pops in to use my yucca's plant pot as a toilet. I need to seal the flap, but sometimes the furry feline comes over late evening simply to snuggle, and I like that – need that – and the yucca doesn't seem to mind that much, its leaves only a tiny bit brown around the edges.

I read a paragraph of my latest download on my Kindle. Put it down again. I should shower. It's been three days. But I need an injection of hot caffeine first, and maybe a chocolate muffin.

Back to the question. How did I get here? Well, I think an

accumulation of things brought me to this point. An affair. Not mine. I would never cheat. Except at board games as a child. No, it was my ex's affair. Though apparently, according to him, it was my fault. I never gave him enough attention, always put my job first. OK, so he was right. But he could have said something. Talked to me rather than crawling into bed with someone else. 'Would you have listened, Annie?'

A move from renting a lovely two-bed terrace in Finchley to this hellish hole I'm in now followed. In good news, Brenda came with me. (Not that my ex ever liked her much. Not a cat lover.) In bad news, Brenda died two weeks after we broke up. She was sixteen. I'd had her since a kitten. I wept for weeks.

On top of that, the last five years have been exhausting at the hospital, and despite thinking I'd come through it reasonably sane, BANG! Six weeks ago, a young woman came into A & E after having a fit. We found inoperable tumours on her brain. I held it together as I told her, despite her eyes growing wide and glassy as I broke the news, her mother sitting beside her, gripping her daughter's hand, chin crinkling. I'd dealt with these kinds of things many times, sadly, but somehow this was different. Don't ask me why. Why this girl tipped me over the edge. Why my body reacted to her pain, why my eyes filled with tears. Why I completely broke down sobbing, soaking my scrubs.

I've judged myself over and over, so no one else needs to, and I'm really not proud of how unprofessional I was. Since then, anxiety has got me by the throat, and it's squeezing and squeezing, not letting go – it's killing me.

OK, so my life isn't ruined, I tell myself on a daily basis. I'm just going through a hard time right now. Lots of people struggle with their mental health. It is what it is in today's world. Things will improve. The whole thundering heartbeat, tears, the desire to lock my door and never go out again – not helped at first by my pager going off in the middle of the night, or the calls from A & E being diverted to my phone by those who had no idea I'm a crumbling wreck – will eventually dissipate. I simply need time to get things back on track, and then I'll return to work, and everything will be sunshine and daisies once more – well, back to normal at least.

I struggle off the bed, pull on my giant yellow hooded blanket and make my way out of my bedroom – almost tripping on the hem as I head for the kitchen and the coffeemaker. As I trudge across the hallway, I spot an envelope on the doormat, recognising my mother's flowery writing instantly – the way she dots her *i*'s with hearts. I bend to pick it up, letting out a groan like a man in his nineties. The letter smells of incense – smells of Mum. I rip it open, and a handful of tiny gold fairies flutter to the floor – the kind of confetti you sprinkle on tables at parties. I pull out the letter, read her words, my heart sinking.

> *Your brother's been in a serious accident. Please come home.*

2

Snow speckles the windscreen. Wipers swipe glass. A stream of white beams race towards me, ghost lights in the darkness, making me disorientated.

I'm not coping too great travelling alone down to Devon. Even when I'm on top of my game, driving any distance is right up there with the thought of skydiving or having a tooth extracted.

'I hate driving,' I say to nobody. 'And I particularly hate motorways. Bring back the horse and cart, that's what I say. Clip clop. Clip clop.'

I hate that I'm going home to Devon to face the unimaginable. *'Hate's a strong word,'* Mum had said when I told her in no uncertain terms that I hated falafel.

I glance at the cream envelope on the passenger seat. Mum has never liked talking on the phone. Never embraced the internet. *'It will be the downfall of civilisation,'* she said when friends were getting AOL. She's a letter writer. Whatever the news. However traumatic. You'll find out via a tired looking postman wearing shorts.

The driver in front's brake lights flash on, followed by hazards. I brake too, tyres skidding on settled snow. My yucca takes a tumble on the back seat. (I couldn't possibly have left it. It would never have survived Not My Cat.) I manage to stop before slamming into the Volvo, heart thudding. There's a jam up ahead. Blue lights flashing in the distance.

I set off three hours ago, fully aware of the forecast. I knew it would be dark before I reached Ridgewater. That in my present state of imbalance it wouldn't be easy. But I had no choice. I tried calling my mother before I left. She has a landline. She didn't pick up. I asked her a long time ago why she still has the phone Dad had installed yet never uses it. She answered, '*Just in case.*' In case of what I have no idea. To be clear, Mum doesn't function like everyone else.

I turn down the CD player. Yes, CD player. I understand Bluetooth, know it's not some sort of dental problem, but, like Mum with her letters, I prefer something tangible. Something I can pick up and hold and say, *That's my music choice and I will always have it – even if AI takes over the world.* People think I'm weird, say I'm probably the only woman of thirty who doesn't use Spotify or whatever. But I don't care. I can't change who I am.

The traffic moves, slowly at first, then I'm up to twenty miles per hour and passing the accident. I don't look. I never look. If I look it makes it real.

Mum doesn't know I'm coming, because of the whole not picking up the phone thing, so I'll catch her off guard. *Surprise!* But then she will surely know I will respond to the heart-breaking news about Elliot.

Elliot is my older brother, and despite him being Mum's favourite (he insists he isn't, but he is) I've always loved him.

He's been living in the Scottish Highlands for the last twelve years, is thirty-one, unmarried.

According to Mum's letter, Elliot's accident was six weeks ago, and I'm trying not to feel hurt that she's only just told me. Her letter was short. A couple of lines telling me the tragic news that my brother is paralysed and hasn't spoken a word since he was found at the foot of a cliff at Ridgewater Cove. The same place Giselle Bancroft was found dead twelve years ago.

I take a deep breath. Did he fall? Was he pushed? Did he jump? No, not Elliot. *Surely not Elliot.*

I indicate to pull off the M5 at the next junction, dropping down the gears as I reach the roundabout. Less than an hour now to Ridgewater. Thank God, I'm exhausted.

I'm about a mile into twisty, dark roads, driving through a tunnel of trees, bowing branches heavy with snow, when the heat in the car begins to make me drowsy, my eyelids droopy. I turn up George Ezra and buzz down the window, letting in a flurry of snow. I consider pulling over, getting out to stretch my legs, but the area's remote. 'No one would hear me scream,' I say, pushing my foot down on the throttle, tyres skidding.

When I finally pull up outside the house where I spent so much of my childhood, and yank on the handbrake, I'm beat. I flop my head against the steering wheel and close my eyes, needing a moment before I face what's behind the heavy oak door of Fairy Cottage. Mum named the place. She believes in fairies. When Elliot and I were children, she would point them out to us at the bottom of the garden and, being young and brimming with imagination, we were sure we could see them too, dancing across the grass, leaping onto logs and mushrooms. Mum's convinced they warn her of all things bad, protect her and our family. I wonder where they were when

Elliot had his accident, when Dad died, when a domino effect of dreadful things happened to me.

When I started secondary school, I learnt quickly that telling anyone about the fairies was a big fat no. When I told my best friend Natalie Ford about them in confidence, it spread across the classroom like a bad smell, with the more popular girls finding it hysterical. It had never occurred to me before that my mum might veer towards eccentricity at best, have a mental disorder at worst – because I was sure I'd seen the fairies too, hadn't I? But then maybe I'd wanted to please Mum, and my imagination had done the rest. They had felt real to me.

'They're dragonflies,' my brother often said.

After that, I tried to understand why Mum's belief in them was unequivocal, unshakeable. She told me how it's only the flower fairies that visit, but there are other fairies: tree fairies, water fairies, house fairies and so many more she had yet to meet, her eyes lighting up as she spoke of them. She explained how many people believe but are afraid to speak out for fear of appearing a little crazy. *'But to believe means you are at one with nature, the beautiful world we live in – that you believe in miracles.'*

Despite her words, I never spoke of my mum's beliefs again.

Now I open my eyes, straighten, rotate my aching shoulders. 'Let's do this.'

A slice of amber light escapes through a gap in the curtains. Mum has always had double-lined curtains, to keep the heat in and evil out. Smoke billows from the chimney. A cosy real fire will be roaring in the grate.

I haven't seen Mum for about a year. The last time was with Elliot when we had lunch in Covent Garden. But I could only spare a couple of hours as I was due back at the hospital. I feel guilty about that now. I should have spared more time for them both.

I take a deep breath before swinging open the car door and stepping onto settled snow. Pulling my calf-length coat around me, I stand for a moment. It's been twelve years since I was last here. Since I left for London to train to be a doctor. Another swirl of guilt that I've never once visited Ridgewater weighs me down.

I breathe in the cold sea air, my eyes drawn to the dark sky, the fuzzy half-moon. A memory floods in: Elliot and me racing down the nearby track, wearing swimmies and flip-flops, towels around our necks, itching to get to the beach and down the slope into the salty water. We had good times at Ridgewater Cove. Elliot had known the place so well. How did he end up at the bottom of a cliff?

The only other property close by is Sycamore House, a rambling detached, which, as a child, I believed looked like something out of a scary movie, but now all I see is tragedy. Red brick walls holding in the pain of Giselle's death. My neck prickles as I sweep my gaze across the silhouette of the building. There's a light on in a downstairs window, but the rest of the sprawling house is in darkness. I squint. Someone is looking out, and I wonder if it's Margot Bancroft, if she still lives there. After the tragic death of her teenage daughter, I wouldn't blame her if she was living a thousand miles away.

I grab my yucca plant from the back seat, attempting to brush out the spilt soil onto the snow, and take my holdall from the boot. Swinging it over my shoulder (the bag not the yucca) I trudge towards the front door of Fairy Cottage, pausing before I knock, as memories rush in: the loss of my father, Giselle's tragic death.

I think of Elliot so helpless inside, and a desire to jump back in my car and drive away propels me backwards, a flutter of panic dancing in my chest.

But the door opens, the heat of the cottage reaching out like a warm embrace. And there she is: Florence Blake. Tall and willowy, hair the colour of cherries, piled messily on top of her head, her purple dress, long and flowing, meeting fuzzy bootie slippers. She looks younger than her sixty years, my quirky, bonkers, beautiful mother.

'Annie,' she says, stepping onto the snowy doorstep and drawing me into a hug.

'Elliot will be so glad you came.'

3

I put down my holdall and plant before removing my ankle boots.

Mum closes the door behind us and puts across a draught excluder. As I hang my coat on the crowded rack, I spot her gardening jacket and Elliot's woollen trench coat. I swallow hard trying to hold back tears. The last thing Mum needs is for me to break down as soon as I arrive.

She touches Elliot's coat, presses the sleeve against her nose. 'It's strange,' she says. 'He went out in it on the morning of his fall but wasn't wearing it when he was found. It turned up on the doorstep a few days later.'

'Who left it?'

She shrugs and beckons me towards the bottom of the stairs – a small square area, made even smaller by a pile of clean clothes in a linen basket waiting to go up. 'He'll be glad to see you.'

I would have been here sooner if you'd called me when it happened.

I press my hand against the wall to steady myself, legs like liquid as though they might give way in a moment. The thought of seeing my brother incapacitated sends shards of pain throughout my body. 'I need a moment. I need to know what happened.'

'Of course you do. Let me get you a warm drink, you must be exhausted from the journey.' She makes her way into the kitchen, ribbons of red hair falling from her loose bun. 'Sit yourself down. I'll put the kettle on,' she adds, gesturing towards the lounge door.

I enter the warm room, taking in the tangled smell of the roaring fire and burning incense sticks. Nothing much has changed: *Alice in Wonderland* artwork on the walls, crystals and fairy ornaments on every surface, a shelf crammed with books that range from theories on the afterlife to mythical creatures and witch trials. An incredible wooden carving of the Green Man, made by Elliot many years ago, hangs above the fireplace. Crowded on the mantelpiece below are photographs of Elliot and me at varying stages of growing up, but no pictures of Dad. Not any more.

'Sit, please,' Mum says, appearing once more after what must have been five minutes but feels like seconds and placing steaming mugs on the cluttered coffee table. She turns and touches my cheek with rough hands. 'You look tired.'

'I am. It was a long journey.' *And I'm dosed up with antidepressants,* I don't say. It feels insignificant to what's happening here. She never knew about my ex anyway, and I'll spare her the loss of Brenda.

Rubbing her lower back, she drops down onto the throw-strewn sofa with a groan, picks up an un-puffed cushion with a hedgehog on it and places it on her knees.

'Is your back OK?'

'It's giving me gyp, if I'm honest. Elliot's a dead weight.' She shakes her head. 'Oh God. Sorry, that's not what I meant to say at all.' She pauses for a moment, as though rearranging her thoughts. 'He has to be repositioned regularly, and his carer comes a lot, but I don't like to think of your brother in one position for too long; he'll get pressure sores.'

'You need to be careful.'

'Yes, well, he's my boy, and I'll do what I can.'

'You could injure yourself, even hurt Elliot. It takes two to roll a patient. Let the professionals do it.'

She nods as though she knows I'm right. She's so pale, dark rings around her big, Irish eyes. Not that she has an Irish accent; her parents travelled across the Irish Sea in the sixties, living in East London until she was five, when her mum died. After which she relocated to Bedfordshire with her father and two brothers. She has often told me how she became quite the tomboy with no female role models in her life.

'How is he?' My voice trembles. 'How's Elliot?'

'Sit,' she repeats. 'Please.'

As I perch on the edge of a wing-back chair, she shakes her head, tears filling her eyes. 'He was found at the foot of the cliff down at Ridgewater Cove by a dog walker.' She runs a hand across her neck. 'Miraculously, there were no broken bones, no internal injuries, but, as I said in the letter, he's paralysed and hasn't spoken.' She tugs at the loose skin around her neck. 'He'd taken to walking down to the beach a lot while he's been staying. He'd been low. Not himself at all.' She wipes a tear from her cheek and picks up her drink.

I cover my mouth with my hand, holding in a sob. 'Have you any idea why?'

She nods. 'His shop up in Scotland went into administration. He lost the apartment above too – his home.'

'Oh, God. He loved that shop.'

'It was his life.' She shakes her head, puts down her tea without taking a sip. 'It seems his business partner—'

'He has a business partner?' *Why didn't I know? Why didn't he tell me?* But the answer is obvious. My job always came first, taking priority over everything: my brother, my mum, my ex... even my well-being.

'*Had* a business partner,' she says. 'Christer. He made some silly investments then took off when it all went pear-shaped. Left Elliot in a right old mess.'

'Bastard.'

'I agree, but Elliot didn't blame him. Everyone makes mistakes, he said.'

'But he took off!'

'Guilt, I'm guessing. Your brother has always been too kind-hearted. Too forgiving. I'd have strung the chap from the rafters by his bits.'

My smile at her attempt at humour lasts seconds. 'When did you find out?'

'I met Elliot in London a couple of months back.'

I take a moment, a heaviness settling on my shoulders. 'You didn't think to tell me you were meeting?'

'We did.' Mum's face morphs from sadness to disappointment. 'You couldn't make it, remember? Something important at the hospital.'

My mind flashes back. There was always some reason why I rarely met up with my mum and brother, even when they came into London.

'He broke down that day, so upset about the shop. I told him to come home for a while. He was hesitant at first, but he needed a roof and someone to care for him. I know he isn't a fan of Ridgewater, and, like you...' Her eyes meet mine, pools of sadness once more. 'Well, he hadn't been back for years. But I knew he needed time out. He may be thirty-one, but he needed his mum. He'd been here a few weeks before his accident, attempting to get his life in order.'

There's a long silence where I want to ask more questions but can't seem to cobble my words together. I pick up my mug, wrapping my hands around it, the heat comforting. But I don't drink.

'They've done scans, blood tests, the lot,' Mum says, cutting through the quiet. 'But found no reason for his paralysis, no reason why he's not speaking. In fact, they've suggested it could be psychological.'

'Psychological?' A fine family we are: *You don't have to be crazy to live here, but it helps.* My pulse quickens. Depression can be genetic. Were we both preprogrammed to feel so down? 'So, if it's psychological, he can get better, right?'

'They're hopeful.' Mum presses her knuckles against her mouth, a tear rolling down her cheek.

It doesn't surprise me that Elliot had been low – anyone would be after losing their business, after being let down by someone they thought they could trust. It isn't the first time he's suffered with depression. When Dad died twelve years ago, he never really got over losing him, made worse by Mum banning our father's name in the house. And when Giselle died a month later and Elliot was questioned by the police, it compounded his depression, and even though her death turned out to be accidental, he never fully got over the fear of being questioned, the looks as he walked through Ridgewater. And then things took a positive turn. He entered one of his wood carvings into a competition and won, collecting his award and prize money at a grand ceremony in Scotland. He fell in love with the Highlands, where he opened his shop and never looked back. Until now.

I finally take a sip of my drink. Wince. Mum always makes strong tea. I stare at her for a moment. Her head is down, loose tendrils of hair falling about her face as she stares into her mug.

'The specialist called his condition conversion disorder.' She looks up, her eyes meeting mine.

'I've never heard of it.'

She shakes her head. 'Call yourself a doctor?'

Her comment hurts. 'Yes, but I don't specialise in psychological disorders.'

'Well, basically, there's no explanation for Elliot's symptoms. No known medical condition, no neurological disease to explain them.'

'So, what? They can't find anything wrong with him?'

'Exactly. Yet he's paralysed and hasn't said a word since the accident. Silent for six whole weeks. It's agonising seeing him like that.'

Tears fill my eyes. 'How the hell are you going to cope with this?' I whisper to myself.

'Sorry? Did you say something?'

I shake my head. 'It's nothing.'

'Are you OK? You don't seem quite yourself.'

'I'm just worried about Elliot, is all.'

'Of course.' She leans forward, taps my knee. 'We all are.'

Another sip of strong tea. 'Will he know me?'

'There's no reason to think he won't. No reason to think he's not fully aware of what's going on around him. And they're hopeful his symptoms will disappear as quickly as they came. The neurological physiotherapists come regularly, making sure he keeps his muscle strength, so as soon as he's well again, well...' She's trying to sound upbeat. She's doing a crap job of it.

'That's good,' I say.

'Yes.' She shrugs. 'Well, I hope so. Though this could go on for months or more.' Her fake optimism has left the building.

'How can this be happening?' My voice breaks, and I put down the drink I've barely touched, slopping tea onto a wildlife magazine. 'Sorry,' I say.

'Don't worry about that.' Mum's never been overly house-proud, though the cottage is clean. Lived in, that's what Mum says.

My body starts trembling. I take a deep breath, attempting to keep myself in check, worried Mum will realise I'm completely useless, that I've brought yet another burden to her door.

'Natalie Ford knocked last week.'

I'm glad of her change of subject, though taken aback that my once best friend would come to Fairy Cottage.

'Natalie? I thought she left Ridgewater years ago.'

'She did. Moved to Hertfordshire with her parents, if I remember rightly. She's been back a couple of months I think.'

'With her parents?'

'They're dead.'

'Both of them?'

'Her father died several years ago – a brain aneurism – her mother more recently after several years of battling cancer.'

'That's awful.' I struggle with my emotions. I didn't like Natalie's parents. They controlled their daughter through her teenage years, made her life hell. 'So, how is she?'

'She seemed... I don't know... agitated. And I don't mean to be unkind, but she looked very different, and not in a good way. Far too thin.' She touches her hair. 'And all that pretty blonde hair she had in her teens. Gone. Chopped off. Dyed black.'

I try to conjure up the image but can't, still seeing the beautiful young girl I spent so much time with. 'What did she want?'

'She wanted to speak to you or Elliot. I told her you were in London doing whatever you do in London—'

'Being a doctor.' *When I'm not having a breakdown.*

'And that Elliot had been in an accident and was not up to seeing people right now. She didn't even ask how he was.'

'And you've no idea why she wanted to see us?'

Mum shrugs. 'She gabbled on about hoping you might remember something that happened years ago, not making herself clear.'

Natalie left Ridgewater with her parents when we were eighteen. The same year my father and Giselle died. My once best friend had stopped speaking to me and Elliot before she left, would turn and walk the other way if she saw us. We never knew why. Only that her silence had followed a drunken night in Sycamore Wood. I approached her once, asked her why she was ignoring me, if I'd done something to upset her, but she ran from me as though I was the Devil. If she couldn't bear to talk to us back then, why now?

'Anyway,' Mum says, 'she's a receptionist at the vet's in Ridgewater. I noticed her when I took one of the hedgehogs down there the other week. The little chap had come out of hibernation, and before you say it, I know that can happen' – *it's not what I was going to say* – 'but I wanted to make sure he was OK.'

'And was he?'

'Was he what?'

'OK? The hedgehog?'

'Yes, all good.' Mum curls a straying hair behind her ear. 'You should go up and see your brother. Pull off the Band-Aid.'

I shake my head. I don't want to see him, not yet. It will make it real. I don't want it to be real. *Please don't make me see him. Why do I feel like I'm ten years old?*

She puts down her tea too, rises and, taking my hand, pulls me to my feet. She's a good five inches taller than me, and I feel small against her, despite being five foot five.

'I'm not sure I can,' I say. But she's giving me no choice, she's pulling me across the room, out into the hallway, where she stops, her sad eyes taking her up the stairs. I stand beside her, taking in the worn carpet, the banister in need of a paintjob, the pictures of flower fairies.

'He has a main carer – lovely Michael, who comes in three times a day, often bringing an assistant with him to help with washing and repositioning, that kind of thing,' she says, finally moving, keeping hold of my hand as I follow. 'They suggested Michael live in. Here at Fairy Cottage. But I didn't want that. Some days it's like Piccadilly Circus with doctors, nurses, physiotherapists, you name it, popping in and out. But I prefer that to Elliot being in a hospice or staying in hospital. I couldn't have that. I couldn't have him all alone. Not my boy.'

We stop on the landing, a smell of disinfectant of some sort and another lemony scent reaching my nostrils.

'I do everything I can, Annie.'

'I know you do, Mum.' I place my hand on her arm. 'He's lucky to have you.'

'I'd like to have a stairlift fitted so he can come downstairs, and they've talked about an electric wheelchair. But it all feels so long term...'

'Well, let's hope he gets better quickly so he doesn't need either.'

'Yes, yes, let's hope so. It wasn't easy for the health team to get him up here, with all his needs, and I wonder now if I should have put him in the dining room.' She's waffling, struggling to keep her voice even, seeming to delay us entering his room now we're up here.

A sliver of light peeps from under the door. A ceramic sign with a little red tractor says 'Elliot's Room'. My heart races, my body aches. Once I see him, there's no going back.

Mum pushes open the door and leads the way, reaching back for my hand and squeezing, tugging me inside.

I let out a gasp. I should have known what to expect. I've treated bedbound patients many times, but this is my brother, and I'm totally unprepared for what I see.

Growing up, everyone said my brother and I looked alike: the same dark hair, the same blue eyes as Dad's, Mum's slim, sharp nose. But as we grew into teenagers, he would keep his hair cropped short and was always more tanned than me, and our similarities became less. Today, as he lies so still in a specially equipped bed, he looks nothing like me. But then he looks nothing like the Elliot I know either. He's so still. So pale. So lifeless. I place my fingers against my lips, holding in a cry. I can't go to pieces. I need to convince Mum I'm strong and here to support her. Support Elliot.

She hurries across the sterile room and sits down on one of the plastic chairs beside him, holding his hand, but I can't move from the doorway, my eyes roaming the room that was his as a boy. A large washable rug covers the carpet. On one wall there are still the framed posters of Marvel heroes he put up in his teens, but his CDs and DVDs, his Pokémon bedspread, his *Harry Potter* and *Goosebumps* books are all gone.

'Annie's here, love,' Mum is saying close to his ear, and my eyes return to my brother. My beautiful, helpless brother.

There is life in his eyes, and he opens his mouth as though to speak. But whatever he wants to say is locked inside. *'They've done scans, but found no reason why he's paralysed, why he's not speaking.'*

'Elliot,' I say, far brighter than I feel, taking a step forward.

It's the drip, the catheter, but particularly the feeding tube that gets to me. The memory of him stuffing his face with burgers and pizzas. Laughing as he knocked back a bottle of lager. *Oh, Elliot.*

Mum sees me looking. 'It's hopefully temporary,' she says, patting the seat next to her.

I move towards him, sit down next to Mum, the chair creaking into the quiet.

'Hey!' I stroke his arm, glancing at Mum, begging her with my eyes to fill the silence, because if I speak, I will sob. Can you feel your heart when it breaks? I think you can.

'It's snowing,' Mum says, answering my prayers. 'Remember that giant snowman you and Annie built when you were about ten?'

'And I cried when it melted,' I say, finding my voice. 'And you said that the snowman was magic, that he would be back next year.'

There's no response from Elliot, and his eyelids flicker down. *Sorry, we're closed.* If I stay a moment longer, I'll lose control of my emotions, I know I will.

'I'll talk to you again tomorrow, Elliot,' I say, getting to my feet.

Mum picks up a Dan Brown book. 'I'll stay a while.'

'Does he like Dan Brown?' I ask, imagining him listening to a genre he might not enjoy, unable to protest. Though I'm pretty sure he's asleep.

'It was with his stuff.' She nods towards an empty holdall by the window. 'Though he may well have read it.'

I glance towards the corner of the room. The wardrobe door stands ajar, a red and black checked shirt pokes out. Imagining him wearing it as he carved his wooden figures makes my stomach twist. My eyes move to some Pokémon stickers from his childhood on the cupboard door. Impossible to remove.

'You'll need to make up the bed in your old room,' Mum says, as I make my way towards the door. 'Sheets, pillowcases and a quilt cover are in the airing cupboard.'

As I leave the room, I glance back just once to see her open the book and begin to read. She loves her son so much. But then, what's not to love? My brother has always been the best.

4

I trip on the hem of my hooded blanket, launching myself into the kitchen, my hands stuffed in giant pockets.

Mum turns from igniting gas under the kettle and grabs her chest. 'Oh, my word. You startled me. You look like a monk.'

'Since when do monks wear yellow?'

'A duck, then. A giant yellow duck.'

I smile. 'Daisy or Donald?' My eyes land on a lonely blueberry muffin on the worktop. 'Is that going begging?'

'For breakfast? Annie, you need to look after yourself. Have granola, fruit, Greek yogurt?'

I don't recognise any of these words. 'Maybe later,' I say, biting into the muffin.

It felt odd spending the night in my childhood bedroom, the bed so much smaller than I remember. The snowed-in silence in this almost isolated part of Ridgewater feeling strange after the hustle and bustle of London. I struggled to get any sleep, but then that's nothing new. Last night all I could think about was Elliot in the next room, so still, being fed through a tube.

Mum's gaze takes her out through the window, and I move in next to her. Some of the snow has gone, and a watery sun brightens the area. The garden is deliberately wild in places. It's a beautiful view, even more so from the upstairs windows where you can see Sycamore Wood, and Ridgewater Cove in the distance where rough waves hit against the shoreline.

'The fairies will be out today,' Mum says. 'I've seen two this morning; they adore the winter sunshine.' She looks at me. 'Did you look in on Elliot on your way down?'

I shake my head, flick a crumb from the corner of my mouth. 'I'll go up later.'

Truth is, when I passed his bedroom five minutes ago, I felt a surge of panic, couldn't face opening the door. I know I have to. That he can hear, think, and that he already knows I'm here, and if I don't go in to see him, he'll believe I've abandoned him, that I don't care.

Once we're holding a mug of coffee each, and I've quickly swallowed down my sertraline tablet without Mum seeing, we head into the lounge and sit down.

'I've watered your yucca,' she says.

'Thanks, but there was no need. It only needs watering every ten days.'

'I know.' *Of course you do.* 'But it looked so dry.'

To be fair, it's probably been more like two weeks since I gave the poor thing a drink. 'Thanks,' I say again.

'It smells a bit funny. I've put it out back in the lean-to.'

'OK.'

'It may need a change of soil. I can do that.'

'Wear gloves.'

'Always do.'

We're silent for a few moments, but my mind races on, and I say, 'Why did you wait so long before telling me about Elliot?'

I'd promised myself I wouldn't ask, but now I'm here, I can't help myself. Elliot's accident was six weeks ago; why didn't she pick up her landline and call me?

'If I'm honest...' She moves a cushion onto her lap like a shield, her eyes meeting mine. 'I wasn't sure you would come.'

'What? Why?'

'You haven't been to Ridgewater since you left all those years ago. Your studies, then your work, always taking priority.' She breaks eye contact. 'If we didn't come to London, we would never get to see you.'

I tense. She's right. When I left Ridgewater my only thought – my only dream – was to become a doctor. I don't know, maybe I felt I needed to prove something to Mum, to myself. *And look how that's turned out.*

'I'm here now, aren't I?' I sound snappier than I intended.

'Yes, but for how long?' She takes a sip of her drink. 'You're always so busy.'

'I can stay a while.' I have no intention of telling her why, that I've crumbled under the pressure of a job I'm sure she never thought I'd succeed in. But then Mum was never impressed that I'd studied hard, that I'm Doctor Annie Blake with letters after my name. In fact, she was always more impressed that Elliot built her a hedgehog sanctuary in the garden, that he made wooden sculptures and grew vegetables and herbs. *The fairies love him.* I get it to some degree: Mum was so young when her mother died, only remembers being brought up by her father. She told me once how she would play football or tag in the street with her brothers until the sun went down. That she always thought of herself as 'one of the boys' when she was young – perhaps a daughter felt alien to her.

I dangle my arm over the side of the chair, and she reaches over and touches my hand, her eyes glistening.

'The consultant explained that the fall is the reason Elliot's like he is,' she says, 'but the fact he was low prior to that made it easier for his brain to succumb to trauma. Antidepressants are being administered through the drip.'

I need a change of subject. Anything to push away the thick black clouds hovering above us. 'I noticed lights on at Sycamore House last night. Does Margot Bancroft still live there?'

Mum flicks a tear from the corner of her eye and pulls her hand away from mine. With a brusque tone, she says, 'Why would you bring *her* up?'

'I just wondered, is all.' OK, perhaps I should know better than to discuss Margot with Mum. It was at Sycamore House that Dad died twelve years ago of a heart attack. His death was a terrible shock, though not completely unexpected. He'd had a heart condition for some time, and during the months prior to his death he'd been working from home, Skyping his lectures on theoretical physics to his university students. What was a shock was that he died in Margot's lounge half-dressed. Margot broke down at the time, confessed they were having an affair. Claimed she was desperately sorry. Begged Mum to forgive her. She never has.

I've never believed she was having an affair with my dad. I'm not quite sure how to explain his state of undress, or Margot's confession, but he wasn't the type to stray, plus he was ill at that time. And, despite the fact he believed that everything could be explained by mathematics or physics, and that fairies were fantasy, my parents, Richard and Florence Blake, were soulmates. They would stay up late listening to vinyl LPs – Fleetwood Mac or Genesis – talking and laughing. They shared a love of wildlife. Dad, a keen birdwatcher, would sit in his study for hours with binoculars, recording the birds he saw in

Sycamore Wood or along the rocky coastline. I often caught my parents holding hands on their nature walks or grabbing sneaky kisses when they thought Elliot and I weren't looking. Yes, I'm convinced my father wasn't having an affair with the glamorous Margot Bancroft. Whatever the reason for his visit to Sycamore House that day, it wasn't that.

Dad's death happened a month before Margot's teenage daughter Giselle was found dead at the bottom of a cliff at Ridgewater Cove. The irony that Elliot was found in the same place hasn't escaped me. At first, there was talk that Giselle's untimely death was suicide, then came the suggestions that it was murder. In the end the coroner ruled it as accidental. Mum never did offer Margot her condolences, said the fairies had told her that she'd got her just desserts after having an affair with my dad. That the winged creatures believed there was evil in Sycamore House and Margot was a wicked woman. It didn't help that on the morning Giselle's body was found the police came knocking on our door, questioning Elliot about her death.

'If you must know,' Mum says now, taking a gulp of her coffee. 'Margot still lives there. I avoid her, and so should you.'

I was wary of Margot as a child. There was something about her. She was like a beautiful queen in a fairy tale, and I was never quite sure if she was as wonderful as she seemed. If perhaps she was hiding another side. If she might turn into a wicked witch.

Once we've finished our drinks, I rise to my feet. 'I'm going to walk into Ridgewater, Mum,' I say, surprising myself. Has the desire to venture outside really returned? Are the tablets starting to work? Or is it more to do with the fact I won't bump into work colleagues or my ex? 'I need a breath of fresh air.'

I leave the lounge and head up the stairs for a shower. As I pass Elliot's room, I place my splayed palm against the door and breathe deeply. 'I'll see you when I get back,' I whisper, bashing down a surge of guilt, attempting to convince myself that if I don't take care of my own mental health, I'll be no use to my mum or brother.

* * *

Despite the pale sun brightening the area, there are still patches of snow, and my car is iced over. I pull on my woolly hat and gloves and set off past Sycamore House.

It looks as it always has: gothic, rambling, magnificent. An incredible house steeped in tragedy. I hurry by with my head down, the thought of having to talk with Margot making my skin prickle. 'Please don't see me,' I whisper, risking a glance at the row of upstairs rectangular windows – heavy wooden shutters closed at every one.

I pull my gaze to the unmade road in front of me, quickening my step. I'm almost passed when I hear her voice. *Crap!*

'Annie!' she calls, and I turn to see her on the doorstep waving. She must be in her late forties, early fifties by now. Slim, willowy. Wide-legged cream satin trousers and a cashmere sweater making up her attire. Her dark hair is scooped up into a perfect bun, and even from this distance I see her scarlet lipstick. 'How lovely to see you, darling. It's been years.'

Twelve, I'm tempted to say. *Just after Giselle died. After my father died in your house.*

'I'm heading into town,' I call, despite part of me feeling I want to run back to Fairy Cottage and never leave.

'Knock on your way back, please,' Margot calls as I go to step away. 'I've made cake.'

I want to say I can't. That I'm busy. But she has the ability to make me feel like a child with her cut-glass English accent and stiff, strong exterior. And there's something else drawing me to her. The teenager who lost her father still needs to know if they really were having an affair.

'OK,' I say, raising my hand, before turning to continue on my way.

5

I walk over the rickety bridge that crosses the pretty river, feeling strangely OK that I'm out in the wild. It's as beautiful in Ridgewater as it was when I was young, and there's something about the clear sea air that's helping me think coherently.

I pass my old junior school on the left. I loved it there as a child. From the time I was in Year 3, Elliot and I would walk the two miles from Fairy Cottage each morning and run home again at the end of the day, rucksacks banging against our backs, shoelaces undone, navy jumpers tied around our waists whatever the weather.

Thoughts of Giselle creep into my head. The way she was home-schooled by her mother. I remember, at the time, wondering what that must be like. I know now she would have been lonely.

I'd been Giselle's only friend between the ages of five and eleven. We would play together, though I was always restricted to the garden, never permitted into the house, not even to pee – and sometimes I was pretty bursting. I recall looking through the windows as a child, seeing the old lady, Joan – Giselle's grandmother – drifting about behind the unblemished glass like a phantom, giving me the creeps. I asked Giselle once why I wasn't allowed inside, and she said simply, 'I love you, Annie, you know I do, but Mother says you are always grubby.' She'd taken my hands then, pointing out my palms caked in mud, my nails embedded with dirt. 'She and Grandmother like everything sparkly clean, and, well, you're not.'

Giselle was never allowed to venture down to the sea, or into Ridgewater. Margot was strict about that too. 'The world is a dangerous place,' Giselle told me once. 'That's what my mum says.'

When Giselle developed an awful skin condition, just after her eleventh birthday, she stopped playing outside. I was told by Margot that Giselle couldn't be exposed to sunlight without her skin flaring up. I've thought about that over the years and still, despite my medical training, have no idea what was wrong with her.

From then on, I only saw my friend waving from her bedroom window when I walked by. I felt for her desperately, but was also relieved, which makes me feel mean now. Giselle was still happy, at eleven, to play with toys and what I thought were the most sinister looking Victorian dolls I'd ever seen. At the time, I was beginning to want more than the restriction of playing in her garden and struck up my friendship with Natalie Ford – one of the pretty, popular girls in my class.

I reach the second-hand bookshop where I'd spent so much time as a child searching for Jacqueline Wilson novels. I'm after *Goosebumps* books today, the ones Elliot enjoyed as a teenager. That's what I'll read to him.

I push open the door, instantly recognising the musty smell of used books. I was a prolific reader until I started training to be a doctor and feel a pang of sadness that I've rarely found time to read fiction over the last twelve years, often downloading a book onto my Kindle with good intentions but never finishing it. There's a sign for a full-time assistant on a noticeboard near the door and I imagine for a moment working here. How, instead of the pressures of A & E, my only concern would be keeping the shelves stocked and discussing books with customers. Of course, it would mean a huge drop in salary, and the waste of years of hard work – but then what is that next to the price of my sanity?

I find a couple of R. L. Stine classics for Elliot and pick up a Kate Atkinson for me. Getting lost in the pages, blocking out my runaway thoughts, could be what I need right now. I pay before heading for the vet's on Clifton Street. I need to talk to Natalie, find out why she came to Fairy Cottage. Why she wanted to speak to me and Elliot. Why she's broken her silence after all these years.

* * *

'I'm afraid Natalie isn't in this morning.'

The girl at the counter at the vet's is young and frazzled and has a handful of paper towels. Behind me three dogs, two cats in baskets and a gerbil are waiting to see a vet. One of the assorted animals has peed on the floor. The puddle must belong to one of the dogs as it's far too big for the gerbil.

'She only works Saturdays.' The girl stares at me through round-rimmed glasses. 'Is there anything else I can help you with?' She's trying for polite but not fully pulling it off.

I shake my head. 'I haven't got any animals. Not right now. My cat died.'

'I'm sorry to hear that.'

'And Not My Cat is not my cat, and she's in London anyway, and pretty healthy going by her... never mind.'

The girl clenches her paper towels, eyes wide. I understand her bewilderment. I'm not sure why I felt the need to share my lack of pets, but then I'm really not myself.

'I don't suppose you know where Natalie lives?' I say. 'I'm an old friend, just back in the area.'

'I'm afraid I can't share that information. It's confidential. And I really should—' She gestures to the puddle.

'No, of course. Go ahead.'

'I can tell her you called by.' She's moving out from behind the desk.

'No, it's fine. Thanks for your help.' I turn, take a step forward, slip on the pee and skate a short distance before getting my balance with the help of the back of a wheelchair where a man sits, a ginger cat on his lap. A doodle of the Labrador variety decides it's a game and bounds towards me, wagging its tail and jumping up, leaving pee paw prints on my coat.

'Jasper!' a woman calls, getting to her feet and tugging the dog away as a feisty Jack Russell barks.

'Mitzi?' A vet in green scrubs has appeared, and the man in the wheelchair heads across the room towards her.

I leave quickly through automatic doors, the cold air hitting me like a smack in the face. I should see the funny side, laugh at myself, but instead I race around the corner of the building out of sight, and cry. No, this is not crying. I'm sobbing. My body heaving as I fumble in my pocket for a tissue. Oh God, I need to get my act together. Elliot will be OK. I know he will. I need to be strong and positive – for him, for Mum. I take a deep breath, dab my face with the screwed-up tissue and step out of hiding, swiftly heading for the cottage.

* * *

Margot is looking out of a downstairs window of Sycamore House as I walk by with the books tucked under my arm. Within moments she opens the front door and dashes down the path with flamboyant flourish. 'Annie, darling!'

We meet at the wrought-iron front gate, and she kisses both my cheeks, a strong smell of powdered make-up and heady perfume catching in my throat. 'It's so good to see you, dear. You haven't changed a bit. The same penchant for jeans, I see. And all that long, straight hair. Have you never thought of lightening it a little? Or putting it in rag curlers – you would look delightful with a few curls.' She places her hand on my arm, her nails beautifully manicured a deep shade of red. 'Can you spare a few minutes? I would love to talk with you.'

I can't think of an excuse without being rude, so follow her up the path like a dutiful child, throwing glances at Fairy Cottage, praying Mum doesn't see me enter Sycamore House with the woman she believes was my father's lover.

6

It feels strange entering Sycamore House. Odd to be welcomed inside, after being banished as a child.

I remove my coat, which smells faintly of dog pee, and hang it on the heavy coat stand. Despite the rectangular side window that looks out over the road, the hallway is dimly lit.

'Boots, dear.'

'Sure.' I bend to unlace them, slip them off and place them by the door.

As Margot guides me towards the lounge, my neck prickles. There's something unsettling about this house. Perhaps it's the full-length portrait of Giselle on the wall by the stairs. She looks to be about six. Blonde, wavy hair cascading past her shoulders. Dressed in a pink tutu. I try to look away, but Margot follows my gaze, her eyes now pinned to the picture.

'Beautiful, wasn't she?' She fiddles with her necklace, which spells out her daughter's name. I recall vaguely that Giselle was wearing it when she died. 'She would have been the prima ballerina I could never be... had she lived.'

'She was such a sweet girl,' I say, because she was. 'We were good friends.'

'Yes, yes you were.' Margot opens a door and beckons me through to the lounge. There's a cumbersome TV in the corner, an old VHS video player beneath. Giselle's on the screen, her giggle tinny through old speakers, making my neck prickle once more. This is too much. It's as though I've stepped into a museum: the Museum of Giselle Bancroft.

Two sets of French doors lead into the garden where the twin swing-set we played on as children sits abandoned. A layer of snow has settled on the seats. Grass is higher in some places than others. Nettles have control.

'I had a gardener for a short while,' Margot says, her lips twitching. 'He didn't last. I keep meaning to hire another. Though I rarely step out there these days.'

My eyes flitter around me. I've seen this room many times from the outside looking in. The carpet is the same cream-coloured shagpile – as clean as it was years ago. Plastic covers seal the cushioned three-piece suite, still there from when it was first bought, I suspect. Every surface gleams. A smell of polish in the air.

A dark wood coffee table, with ornate legs, is laden with cakes. Some balance on a three-tier stand, and a carrot cake, oozing with buttercream, sits on a fine-china plate. She must have known I would be tempted inside, which makes me feel vulnerable.

'Sit down,' she says, and I meet her eyes. She does look older, I realise now, lines spreading from heavily made-up eyes. OK, so it's been twelve years, but I'm sure it's more than that. The death of her daughter would have taken its toll. 'Would you like a cup of tea or coffee with your cake? Homemade lemonade?'

'I'm OK, thank you.'

'Nonsense.' She flicks her hand, like she's batting away a fly. 'I'll put the kettle on.'

As Margot drifts through the door towards the kitchen, a light breeze from one of the French doors moves my hair. It's slightly ajar, and I look outside once more. A fence creates a barrier between the garden and Sycamore Wood. A gate leads to the tall, dense trees. A place I hung out in my teens with Natalie.

I pull my gaze back inside the room and sweep my eyes across a floor-to-ceiling bookshelf full of the classics. Giselle told me when we were six or seven that she'd read every Dickens and was now reading Thomas Hughes. I thought she was amazing.

I pull my eyes from the bookshelf and across the many framed photos of Giselle on the walls and displayed on every surface, some as a baby, some as a toddler, some as a little girl. Many are of her practising ballet. It was her grandmother who encouraged it. Giselle once told me, as we swayed back and forth on the swings, that her legs ached all the time, that her grandmother wouldn't let her rest until she had mastered the latest step perfectly. She said she didn't mind. That she wanted to be the best. Wanted to please her grandmother. But I wasn't so sure, she always looked so pale.

There are a couple of photos of Margot with Giselle, but none seem to show the grandmother.

'Mummy, watch.' It's Giselle's voice coming through the speakers. On the screen she's cartwheeling across the lounge. Her blonde hair in old-fashioned curling rags. She looks to be about eleven – a time when I no longer saw her, though there's no sign of her skin condition, maybe staying inside was keeping it at bay.

'Don't get your clothes ruffled, dear,' a younger version of Margot calls. 'Don't forget Uncle Joel is visiting, he's back from Canada, and I need to do your hair. Make you look beautiful.'

Uncle Joel? I don't recall Giselle having an uncle. Though I guess I never really knew anything about her life.

'Here you go.' Margot places two delicate porcelain cups, mine only half-full of tea – as though she fears I will spill it – onto saucers on the low table in front of me. My heart sinks. I don't want half a cup of tea – I don't want any tea at all. And I don't want cake. But still I sit down on the plastic-covered armchair, hearing it squeak under my weight.

Margot hands me my drink, and a small cupcake balanced on a tea-plate. My hand trembles as a surge of panic that I might drop crumbs makes me even more uneasy. I want to scream at six-year-old me who wasn't welcome here to take a hike, and for thirty-year-old me to get some bloody backbone. Margot sits down on the sofa opposite me, her legs elegantly crossed, her little finger raised as she takes a sip of tea.

'I was just thinking about how Giselle couldn't go out in sunlight,' I say, trying to sound nonchalant. What was actually wrong with my friend that she couldn't come outside any longer?

'Why?' Margot's forehead furrows.

'Oh, I don't know. Being back here, I suppose. Thinking about her.'

'Mmm, well, it was truly awful for her. For both of us.'

'So, what was wrong with her?'

Margot licks her red lips, her eyes veering to the TV screen. 'Xeroderma pigmentosum, a severe reaction to sunlight.'

I know what it is. 'Odd.'

'Why?' Her staring eyes are back on me.

'From what I know about the condition, there are normally

earlier symptoms, is all. I don't recall Giselle having sunburn, when we played out together.'

'Well, she did,' Margot says, and her sharp tone tells me I've crossed a line. 'You weren't here, putting cream on those awful blisters.' She leans forward with a jolt, her eyes still fixed on mine. 'Childhood memories aren't always accurate. They can bend and stretch to suit our own narrative.'

'Of course. Yes,' I say, trying to pour water on the fire I've created. 'You're absolutely right.'

'So how have you been?' Margot asks after a pause, leaning back once more.

'Not so great.' My voice breaks. 'I'm guessing you've heard about my brother's accident?'

She nods. Takes a bite of cake. Chews. Swallows. 'A friend told me. Very sad, you must all be devastated. He can only be in his late twenties, am I right?'

'Thirty-one.'

'Really? Where do the years go? Though I should have known. Giselle would be thirty now. Like you.'

I nod, batting down a surge of emotion, attempting to pull my eyes from her gaze.

'Your mother must be suffering as I suffered.' She swipes a crumb from the corner of her mouth. 'Nothing worse than a child going before a parent.'

'He's still with us. Elliot. He's still with us.'

'Yes, but to be permanently paralysed, unable to speak. Sorry, I didn't mean to remind you.' She waves a hand, as though chasing away her words.

'We've been told it's psychological, that he'll hopefully be OK.'

'You have?'

'Conversion disorder.'

'Hysteria?'

I bristle.

'I would have thought the fall would have done a lot more damage.'

I shift to the edge of my seat. 'I should probably go.'

She leans forward, presses a hand against my knee. 'No, stay. Please. Ignore me. I'm just concerned, that's all. I know your mother won't have anything to do with me, but I care. Really, I do.'

I remain seated, conscious once more of the plethora of photos of Giselle. It's as though the little girl I once knew is in the room with us. Watching me.

'I'm so sorry about what happened to Giselle,' I say after a few moments. It's the first time I've ever said it. In the weeks following her death, before I left Ridgewater, Mum watched my every move. I liked to think at the time it was more to do with a young woman dying in the neighbourhood, that she worried about me, rather than making sure I kept away from Sycamore House.

I attended Giselle's funeral, sneaking in at the back of the crematorium. The place was rammed with Ridgewater residents who didn't even know Giselle – but then nobody did but me, and I'm not sure I really knew her. Certainly not at the time of her death. Elliot and his mate Seb came with me, none of us able to keep a limb still, the fact it was Giselle in the coffin at the front impossible to believe. The most vivid memory for me was seeing Margot break down sobbing and being almost carried out at the end by the celebrant and the landlord of the Fox.

Margot takes a sip of her tea, her eyes not straying from mine. 'You and Elliot left Ridgewater soon after Giselle's death, didn't you?'

'I left to study—'

'To be a doctor?'

'Yes. My dream at the time.'

'And how's that working out for you?' She says it as if she's aware I'm on sick leave, but she can't possibly know. 'Are you enjoying being a doctor?'

I don't want her to know my business. 'I'm taking a sabbatical, to support Mum and Elliot.' I turn away from her, my shoulders aching from sitting so rigidly.

'What a good daughter and sister you are. Your mum and brother are lucky to have you.'

I run my hand across my neck, restless. Margot seems strange somehow – stranger than I recall – but I remind myself that when your only daughter dies tragically at the age of eighteen, you can't expect to come out of it unscathed. I finish my tea in three greedy gulps, thankfully without spilling it, and put the empty cup and saucer on a coaster. 'I need to get back.' I rise to my feet. 'Mum will wonder where I am.'

'You're not a child, Annie.' She rises too. 'You don't have to do everything your mother tells you.'

'Yes, I know. But she needs me right now.'

She nods. 'Of course she does. Well, it was lovely to see you after all this time.' She presses an ice-cold hand against my cheek, and stares at me long and hard. I struggle to move, weighed down by her touch, her power.

She finally removes her hand, and I make my way into the hall, where I glance towards the wide staircase leading to the first floor.

'The top half of the house is closed off,' she says, catching where I'm looking. 'The place is too big for just little old me. To heat it all would be extortionate, what with the ridiculous price of fuel these days. Giselle's old schoolroom is now my ground-floor bedroom. It suits me.'

We reach the front door, and I pull on my ankle boots, the laces taking forever to tie. 'Well, thank you for the cake,' I say – though I didn't touch it.

'You're welcome.' She opens the front door. 'And please do come and see me again. It's lonely here on my own.'

I hear the echo of my mother, *'There's evil in that house.'* But I'm sure she's wrong. The only thing within the walls of this vast place is a woman still grieving the loss of her daughter.

As I walk down the path, I look back just once to see her on the step, her long, slim arm raised high in a wave. I should have spoken to her about my father, but it was all so tense. I kick myself at the wasted opportunity.

I'm relieved when I'm out of her eyeline. That is until I spot someone in the trees at the entrance to Sycamore Wood. Whoever it is, they're tall and slim, dressed in black, hood up, a scarf covering their face. They're lingering suspiciously, and I shudder, stopping for a moment to take a deep breath. I'm tempted to head towards them and get a better look, despite my thudding heart. But before I can, they slip into the trees, disappearing from view.

7

THIRTY-FIVE YEARS AGO

From the edge of his bed, the mattress hard beneath his long, slim limbs, Joel stared at the closed attic door. Would his mother appear before he could escape? Her bumps and bulges squeezed into her musty, tweed suit, silver-grey hair cut short and sharp, face full of disappointment, eyes giving away her fury.

She was almost sixty now, though as formidable, controlling and cruel as she'd ever been. Joan Bancroft had single-handedly made Joel into a crumbling, disturbed teenager, who lashed out at the world every chance he got.

He dreamt once of killing her. A ghoulish, crazy nightmare that stole from his subconscious, rapid eye movements frantic behind closed lids. In the dream he broke down her bedroom door, and, as she bathed in her luxurious freestanding bathtub, he shoved her head deep under the bubble-filled water. He saw his hands, long fingers – piano fingers his sister Margot called them, though he'd never played – pinned to his mother's skull, holding her down, watching as the life drained from her. Just as she'd done to him. His hatred for his mother controlled him, his fear of her all-consuming.

There was a knock on his bedroom door. Not Joan. He hadn't heard his mother's heavy footfalls on the stairs, and anyway, she would never knock. She'd caught him once masturbating. Said he was sick. Threatened to have his genitals removed. Joel still lived in fear that she might fulfil her promise.

The door eased open and Margot poked her head round. 'She's gone out,' she said, stepping into the small room, which smelt of mould and mouse droppings. Not that he'd ever seen a rodent – perhaps if he had he would have felt less alone.

'If you're going, it needs to be now,' his sister said. 'You can't be here alone with Mother.' She dropped down beside him on the bed, straightening her pink dress. Margot always looked so elegant with her long legs and arms, her willowy body. A beautiful, talented ballerina. Margot was two years older, and she tried so hard to steer Joan's anger away from Joel. It sometimes worked. But his sister was leaving soon, Mother had found her a place at a prestigious ballet school in London. And Margot was right, he needed to get away now.

He had little to take with him. A couple of carrier bags, already packed, that's all.

Margot thrust a wad of money into his hands. 'Take this.'

'Where did—?'

'It's Mother's. She'll never miss it.' It was true, their mother stashed money everywhere, forgetting where she'd put it half the time. Margot drew in a breath. 'Have you thought about a passport?'

'You think I need to go abroad?'

'Eventually, yes. You need to get far away from Sycamore House. You can apply for a passport when you're eighteen.' She handed him his birth certificate. 'I found it in Mother's desk drawer. Just find somewhere to stay until then.' She kissed his cheek. 'I'll miss you.'

'I'll miss you too.' And he would. Margot couldn't always stop the cruelty. But she was always there for him. Picking up the pieces.

'I'll be leaving shortly after you,' she said. 'A taxi is coming for me.'

'You will make it big, Sis,' he said. 'I know you will.'

She shrugged. 'And fulfil Mother's dream.' She touched his cheek, handed him a slip of paper. 'This is where I'll be staying in London. With all the other prima-ballerina hopefuls.'

'Do you really want this, Margot?'

'What choice do I have?'

'Just be careful, please.' He shoved his sister's future address into one of the bags and rose.

'You too,' she said.

8

NOW

Annie

I'm not sure why the figure at the entrance to Sycamore Wood still bothers me.

Whoever it was, they were probably out walking a dog, or taking a winter stroll, like my parents used to do. But I can't shake it, there was something odd, as though they were there for me.

I head into the kitchen. Glance out through the window. Mum is out there. The hedgehogs are hibernating, but, like when I was young, she checks on them daily. I pour a glass of water from the jug in the fridge, and, with the *Goosebumps* books in my hand, head upstairs for some alone time with my brother.

When I reach the top step I hear a voice I recognise coming from Elliot's room.

I make my way across the landing and peer through the crack in the door. Natalie, though looking very different to when I last saw her, sits beside my brother. Her lips are moving, but her voice is a muffled whisper. I can only think Mum must have let her in. I narrow my eyes, absorbing her skinny frame clad in black trousers and a hooded sweatshirt. My teenage friend is so pale, wax-like. Her eyes, bright, big and beautiful in her teens, are now puffy and shadowed. But most of all, her once long blonde hair is cropped short and dyed black, not in a quirky or trendy way; it's as though she's taken a pair of scissors and chopped it off in a rage.

I'm about to open the door, to come face to face with her for the first time in over twelve years, when she rises, her voice elevating. 'I'm so sorry, I shouldn't have come. I had no idea you were so—'

I swing open the door, making her jump. The look of distress on Elliot's face is palpable. 'What's going on?' I say. 'What are you doing here, Natalie?'

'Annie! I didn't know you were back in Ridgewater.'

Elliot's face twitches.

'You need to leave,' I say, my heart thudding. 'I don't know what you've been saying, but Elliot looks upset.'

'OK, yes, fine.' She grabs a crumpled canvas bag from the floor, tries to rush past me, but I take hold of her stick-thin arm.

'What exactly are you doing here?'

'Let go of me,' she says, trying to pull away.

I release her, knowing I'm overstepping. But how dare she upset my brother?

She straightens her jacket, as though I've rumpled it, and her dark eyes meet mine. 'I need to know what you and Elliot recall about that night.'

'What night?' But I know what she's talking about: the August before Giselle died in the October. The night Natalie took off through Sycamore Wood in a wine-fuelled state, leaving Elliot, his friend Seb and me behind sitting on a tree trunk in the darkness. The next day she stopped speaking to my brother and me. 'Something happened, didn't it?'

She stares, eyes glistening, then looks at Elliot, whose eyes are sealed. 'I need to explain, but not here, not now.' She takes off, racing down the stairs and, before I can give chase, she's out through the front door, the slam echoing in my ears.

I move further into Elliot's room and sit down on the chair she vacated. 'Hey, brother,' I say, squeezing his hand. I debate with myself whether to talk about why Natalie may have visited, deciding against it. He's clearly bothered by her turning up, and I don't want to upset him further. 'I've bought you a couple of *Goosebumps* books. Remember how you loved them in your teens?'

He opens his eyes but doesn't blink.

'As you know, I'm no actress,' I go on with a laugh he'll know is fake. 'But I reckon I can pull off the scary voices. But if it's too frightening for you, you'll have to find a way to let me know.' He doesn't react to my feeble attempts at humour, but even so, I take a deep breath and carry on. 'Are you ready for this?' I open the book and begin to read, trying to block Natalie from my thoughts, for now at least. But I know I have to speak to her. Find out what she wants, and maybe even fill the Natalie-shaped hole that was cut from my life twelve years ago.

* * *

Elliot

The slight quiver in my sister's voice, as she reads *Night of the Living Dummy*, makes me wish I could hold her in my arms and tell her everything will be OK. But then it would be a lie.

Things are far from OK. I fear for her. Fear for Mum. Fear for myself.

It took a while to calm my heartbeat after Natalie's visit. I'd known immediately when she entered the room that it wasn't Mum or Annie – or any of the stream of people who visit me: medical staff taking my blood pressure, my pulse, oxygen levels, the lot. And then there's Michael, singing as though I want to hear his renditions of Lady Gaga or Madonna as he and his assistant roll me on the air mattress so they can wash me, or heaving my body into different positions. *'We don't want you getting bedsores now, do we?' 'Just keeping you comfortable, my love.'* And I know Michael's constant singing is meant to keep me upbeat. That he's doing his best. But having a grown man wash my body... Well, it's humiliating, that's what it is. Sometimes I wish I had died from the fall. There wasn't that much to live for before, so God help me now.

'Elliot,' Natalie had whispered once she was close to my face. Too close. I recognised her voice from when she and Annie were friends. 'I'm so sorry,' she continued. 'I shouldn't have come. I had no idea you were so...'

Then Annie chased her away. *What did you want from me, Natalie?*

Now my sister is trying so hard to do the creepy voices as she reads, and I love her for that – my little sister, Doctor Annie Blake, who I haven't seen enough of over the last twelve years. I regret that now.

The book from my childhood is a welcome change from *The Da Vinci Code*. I've nothing against Dan Brown. Enjoyed the book, and the film. But the novel belonged to Christer, and I don't want to be reminded of the man who let me down.

'What made you come back, Elliot?' Annie says, pausing at the end of a chapter and placing her warm hand on mine, squeezing. 'Mum said you were down. I thought you were happy in Scotland.'

She knows I can't answer, but if I could, I would tell her, just as I told Mum, that my shop went into administration. But I wouldn't stop there. I would spill everything, how my heart was broken into a thousand pieces, that the sniffling boy inside of me ran home to his mummy – to Ridgewater – the place I'd escaped from all those years ago. *Pathetic.*

Annie moves her hand from mine and closes the book.

One more chapter, I want to say, but she rises and kisses my forehead. And as she heads towards the door, leaving me alone in this useless body, I scream inside.

Let me out. For Christ's sake, let me out. There's so much I need to tell you.

Annie

I make my way out through the back door, seeing Mum's still at the bottom of the garden, wind chasing her hair across her face. The same chilly air whips round me like a baby tornado as I pick up one of the many wooden figures Elliot's made through the years. It's about eighteen inches tall and is meant to be our dad. I brush snow from the hat and calf-length coat. Run a hand over the face, the beard, and smile as I put it back amongst the terracotta pots. Mum must know it's here, and I take heart that she hasn't removed it.

'Did you let Natalie in?' I call, making my way down the path.

'No. Why?'

'She was in Elliot's room, talking to him.'

'What? Oh God. She must have let herself in.' Mum has never locked the front door, insisting there's no need. *The fairies will keep us safe.* When Giselle died, and there was an initial fear she'd been murdered, I thought she might start turning the key in the lock – wished she would. But no, she still insisted nothing bad would ever happen to us. That her winged creatures would always protect us. I wonder, as my thoughts come back to Elliot, if she still believes that.

'I've been out here for ages,' Mum goes on, hastily pulling off her gardening gloves. 'Is he OK?'

'Pretty sure he didn't want Natalie there. I can't believe she just walked in. But he seems OK now. I've been reading to him.'

Mum looks towards the back of the house, drops her gloves into a wheelbarrow. 'I should check on him,' she says, leaving my side and running up the path without a backward look.

I stand for a while, rubbing my hands together to push away the cold. I can see the top of Sycamore House from here. The row of shuttered windows on the first floor. The attic room. And I wonder, not for the first time, what went on within those walls over the years. What it was like to be Giselle Bancroft.

9

THIRTY YEARS AGO

Margot, her dark hair swept up in a stylish bun, stared at Sycamore House from the opposite side of the road.

'Hush, little one,' she said, as the baby murmured – the tiny bundle held close to her in a corduroy sling, just five weeks old. Margot kissed the baby's fine, fair hair. She adored this child despite everything.

The two of them were hidden in the trees that flanked the country lane, but Margot knew she had to cross over. Face her mother. Face Sycamore House, a place she'd hoped she would never return to.

She looked down at herself, liked to think that despite what she'd been through she had never once neglected her appearance. Mother would be glad of that. *'The face you give to the public is everything. It's what they'll judge you on.'*

Today her pink dress was flared at the waist, her lips painted red. She believed she'd created a look of her mother's favourite ballerina, Margot Fonteyn. The dancer Margot had been named after. The dancer she'd spent her life trying to emulate. The dancer she knew now she would never be.

She was aware her mother would ask about the baby's father, and Margot would tell her that the man died. If she told her the truth, that she'd fallen for the owner of the private ballet school, that she'd been seduced by him, by his charm, his kiss, his touch... Well, her mother would never forgive her.

He'd told her to leave when he discovered she was pregnant. That a ballet school wasn't a place for a loose young woman. He gave her money. Told her to get an abortion. But she'd kept the baby, given birth alone in a bedsit. Her mother would be horrified if she knew the truth. Would tell her she was ruined.

But she wasn't ruined, was she? She had her baby, and little Giselle would make everything right. Mother would see in Giselle a fresh, new ballerina to live her sad life through.

There was no movement in the windows of Sycamore House. Though it would only be her mother inside – her brother Joel was long gone – and the austere woman would probably be in the lounge at the back of the house where she often sat reading.

Joel had written to Margot a few months back, said he'd made it to Canada, met someone – *Jackie* – said he was happy. That he wouldn't return to the UK until *the witch is dead*.

Margot took a long deep breath and stepped out from the safety of the trees, her heels clicking on the unmade road. She sniffed the baby's newness, breathing in the smell of Johnson's Baby Shampoo. 'I love you, little one,' she whispered as she walked up the path. 'I'm sorry it's come to this.'

Stepping closer to the house, passing the now abandoned folly on the right, where the groundsman and housekeeper once lived, she wondered, not for the first time, if she was doing the right thing.

But then she had no choice. She'd tried so hard to think of

another way. A tear rolled down her cheek and she wiped it away. She'd been so stupid thinking she could escape the claustrophobia of her childhood at Sycamore House.

Blue-painted shutters were pulled back on the first floor, curtains flapping in the light breeze. Downstairs a dull amber light shone from the dining room, despite the bright day. She hated this place. She hated her mother. But she had nothing. No one. What kind of life would that be for her darling Giselle? *Giselle.* The name was symbolic of Margot's fall from grace. The mess she'd made of everything. But at least at Sycamore House her baby would have everything she needed. She would be well fed, and Margot could be at home, play with her child. And once the baby was old enough, Margot would escape once more and give Giselle the freedom that she had never had.

A figure loomed in the window, dark, foreboding. *Mother. Joan Bancroft. A fearful woman. A tyrant.*

'You'll be safe here, little one. She was never cruel to me.' She kissed Giselle's head once more and, moving forward, whispered, 'She was only ever cruel to Joel.'

10

NOW

Annie

I'm not sure why, after dinner, I felt the need to get away from the cottage. Or what made me walk into Ridgewater, preferring to sit here in the One Trick Pony, a trendy bar in the town centre where the Fox used to be, rather than spend the evening with Mum.

I guess Mum and I are, to some degree, estranged. I love her, but although I've never blamed Elliot for being her favourite, I have to admit, buried under years of trying to accept that fact, I still harbour a fear of not quite measuring up however hard I try. And there's the sadness too, that she believed – and still believes – that my dad would have an affair with Margot Bancroft. My precious father idolised my mum. He was an amazing man who never preferred one of his children to the other, loving Elliot and me equally. I desperately wish Mum hadn't destroyed his perfect memory.

I push my stupid emotions to the back of my mind. Take a sip of wine. It tastes sour on my tongue. *What am I doing here?*

The tiniest spider crawls up the side of my glass. I'm ready to save it from an alcohol bath should it reach the top. I must look a sorry sight, hair flopped forward like some sort of ghost girl. I shudder. Maybe I shouldn't be drinking while I'm on anti-depressants. Maybe I need to go back to Fairy Cottage and crawl under a quilt and talk to myself. 'Enough with the self-pity.'

'You OK there?'

I turn towards the friendly voice, embarrassed that I'd said the words out loud. I'm greeted by concerned blue eyes, dark, wavy hair and a wide smile. The man is wiping down the table beside me, collecting up a couple of glasses. 'Tell me to mind my own business,' he goes on. 'But it looks like you're drowning your sorrows.' He tilts his head. 'I'm Tom by the way.' He sits down in a chair next to the table he's cleaning, and I realise, as I've sat here in my own world, the bar has emptied. 'Tom Brown.'

'Annie.' I push away my wine. The spider saves itself by skydiving to the wooden table and runs for freedom on his eight legs. My job here is done.

I'm not sure why I've told this man my name. A stranger. Maybe that's exactly why. Perhaps a passing stranger who doesn't know anything about me is just what I need right now. Back in London my friends were all connected to the hospital, and since my crash and burn I've avoided them. At first, they tried calling and messaging, but I'm ashamed to say I hid from them. Ignored them. But for some reason I don't want to ignore this man in his pale pink polo shirt with the bar's logo, and faded jeans. He's tall and slim with kind eyes. I look behind me at the bar. 'Do you work here?' *Of course he works here. He has the bloody logo on his polo, and he's cleaning tables.*

'Yeah, been here a few weeks now. Nice place, Ridgewater.'

'I was brought up here. Live on the outskirts.'

He gets up, asks if I mind him joining me at my table while it's quiet, and I don't mind. I don't mind at all.

'So, where do you live?' I ask him.

'I'm staying with family, a fifteen-minute walk away. Before that I lived and worked in London.'

'Me too. Surprised I haven't seen you around.' A laugh dies in the back of my throat.

Another smile plays across his lips, there's something almost childlike about him. 'It's a big place.'

'It's not as unlikely as it sounds. Where did you hang out?' I take a sip of wine; it's tasting better suddenly.

He shrugs. 'I worked long hours, then crashed and played computer games, or Dungeons and Dragons. Boring, right? And probably not what you were expecting.'

We talk for a while, and I actually feel like the old me. The one before my relationship broke down. The one before my meltdown. The one before my brother's accident.

'Have you moved from London permanently?' I ask.

He shrugs. 'I like living by the sea, so I'll be here for a while. I'm not sure what my plans are, quite honestly. I need to work out my next step.'

'Whereabouts in London did you live?'

He looks at me for a long moment, and I realise I'm bombarding him with too many questions. 'Highgate,' he says, finally. 'Just a room in a Victorian house.'

We talk non-stop for what must be half an hour, until the door swings open and a group of forty-something women fall into the door, followed by a young couple. Tom gets up to serve them, and I feel a vacuum where he was sitting a moment ago. It's clear he's going to be busy, so I get up, slip on my coat, raise my hand as I leave, not sure if he notices.

I order a taxi, and as I wait at the side of the road, quick footsteps approach. 'Hang on!'

I turn to see Tom running towards me.

'Can we swap numbers?' he says. 'It would be nice to keep in touch. I don't know many people in the area.'

'Sure,' I say, taking my phone from my bag. 'I'd like that.'

* * *

I sit in the back of the taxi, thoughts of Tom swimming around my head. I like him. He made me smile, which is exactly what I need right now, and I grin at the memory of him telling me his claim to fame is a YouTube video of him rapping the periodic table. He's so proud of his eight-hundred-odd hits. Although as I scroll down my phone, I can't seem to find his channel.

As the car heads down the dark road towards Fairy Cottage, I think how he appeared when I needed someone, and my paranoid brain begins to doubt him. 'Would a handsome stranger really make a beeline for you? You're a miserable wreck,' I say out loud.

The driver glances in his rear-view mirror, one eyebrow raised. 'You OK back there?' he says, as we pull up outside Fairy Cottage.

'Fine,' I say, though anxiety bubbles in my chest as I look towards the cottage we moved into when I was five years old. 'Totally fine.'

But I know I'm far from it.

11

TWENTY-FIVE YEARS AGO

Giselle stared through the dining room window of Sycamore House, her small hand pressed against the glass, a look of longing on her pale face.

The old folly had stood empty for so long, and now someone was actually moving in. Builders and decorators had been going in and out for a while, and Mother had said a family would arrive soon, but to actually see them so close up made her tummy flutter.

A girl of about Giselle's age skipped in circles, dark hair pulled back in a swinging ponytail. There was a dark-haired boy too. Taller than the girl.

Carrying a box, the boy followed a man with a beard through the open front door. They all looked so happy.

Suddenly the girl stopped skipping and looked towards Sycamore House. Giselle bobbed back – she'd spent her life so far inside those walls with her mother and grandmother, and apart from the postman, and people passing by on the way to Ridgewater Cove, she rarely saw anyone. She took a deep breath and looked back through the window. The skipping girl, who no longer skipped, smiled and lifted her hand in a wave.

Giselle waved back.

'She looks nice,' she said, turning to her mother, who was polishing the coffee table. 'She could be my friend.'

'Come away from the window, dear,' her mother said. 'Grandmother Joan will be taking you for another ballet lesson shortly.'

'Do I have to? My legs ache.'

'Nonsense.' It was her grandmother standing in the doorway, her arms folded across her tweed skirt suit. 'It's up to you to succeed where your mother failed, Giselle. Now get into your leotard and ballet shoes.'

* * *

Annie was spellbound by the girl at the window of the big house. So pretty, blonde curls resting on her shoulders, a white dress with more frills than she'd ever seen in her whole life.

'She looked like Shirley Temple.' It was Annie's dad, heading back to the van for another box, and glancing over at the house.

Annie screwed up her nose and shrugged, no idea who Shirley Temple was.

'Before your time,' he said with a laugh, as Annie ran to his side and picked up a small box of toys, a teddy falling to the floor. 'Before mine too, to be honest.' He smiled, tickled her and she giggled. 'Looks like you'll have someone to play with, at least.' He lifted a box full of books from the van, and Annie scooped up the teddy.

'Where do you want these, Flo?' her father called as they made their way up the path.

'The lounge,' Annie's mother said, appearing at the front door. 'This place is magical, Richard.' She clenched her fists to her chin. 'We're going to be so happy here, I can feel it.'

12

NOW

Annie

After a restless night, I struggle to get out of bed, the day feeling darker than the night. Rising feels impossible, my body wants to shut down.

There's a tap on the door, and before I can answer, Mum enters my room. 'The physiotherapist is here,' she says, opening the curtains. I pull my duvet over my head. *Go away.*

'Are you OK?' I feel the weight of her body sink into the mattress beside me.

'It's hard,' I say, as she pulls back the cover and strokes my hair from my sweaty forehead. 'I just want to stay here in bed and never get up.'

'I know.' But she doesn't. She has no idea I was a mess before I even arrived here, that I just want the ground to open and swallow me whole. 'But you have to be strong,' she goes on, patting the bed and rising. 'Now, get up, love. Nothing can be as bad as what Elliot's going through, and your brother needs you.'

I spend the morning reading to Elliot, until his carer arrives to take over. It's the first time I've met him. A man in his thirties with a wide smile, and a flash of purple in his otherwise dark hair. He presses a long finger against his name badge. 'I'm Michael.'

I introduce myself and hold out my hand for him to shake.

'Oh, come here, lovely,' he says, giving me a hug, which in theory seems an odd thing to do but in practice feels natural – and quite reassuring. He seems like the kind of man who hugs everyone. The kind of man you feel you've known all your life. 'You've been through hell with all of this, you and your mum. If there's anything I can do, you know where I am.'

I leave him to change Elliot's catheter, his words staying with me as I head down the stairs. It's halfway down that my phone rings. It's Tom from the bar, and I can't help the slight flutter in my stomach.

'Hey,' I say, answering, and taking the final stairs, before hovering near the coat rack.

'I was wondering if you fancy meeting up?' His tone is light. 'A meal, maybe.'

I can't. I have to put Elliot and Mum first. 'To be honest, I've got a lot on right now.'

'It's not you, it's me.' He laughs. 'No worries. You know where I am.'

'It's not that. I—'

'You don't owe me an explanation. It's fine.'

'No... I know. But once I've got a few things sorted, I'll give you a call, if that's OK.'

'Sure. I'll look forward to it. And... take care, OK?' He ends the call, and I breathe in, and out, before making my way into the kitchen.

'There's a letter for you,' Mum says, her tone soft. 'Hand

delivered,' she goes on, above the whir of the washing machine. 'I've put it on the coffee table.'

'Right. Thanks.' I leave the kitchen, my head still full of Tom, and enter the lounge. A white envelope rests on the low table. I drop down onto the armchair and pick it up, tearing it open. Seeing immediately that it's from Natalie Ford.

Dear Annie,

I'm sorry I rushed off. I'm not thinking straight at the moment. But I wondered if we could meet. I need to talk to you. I'll be at the One Trick Pony around seven this evening if you are happy to meet me there.

Natalie

I stare at the words, her writing familiar from when we were at school together. I have to meet her. I need to know what she wants. Why she stopped talking to Elliot and me after that night in Sycamore Wood. What's brought about this change of heart.

Mum appears and flops down onto the sofa, her eyes shadowed. 'Who was the letter from?'

'Natalie.' I fold it sharply, shove it back into the envelope. 'She wants to meet me tonight.' *At the One Trick Pony – where Tom works.*

'Are you going?'

'Maybe. I'm curious what she wants, I guess.' But Mum's eyes have glazed over, she's staring out of the window. 'Are you OK?'

She turns as though I've prodded her. Nods, and brings her watery eyes to meet my gaze. 'Elliot knows Ridgewater Cove so well, Annie,' she says. 'How did he fall?' A tear rolls down her face.

'I agree, it doesn't make any sense.' A vivid image of my brother lying unconscious springs into my head. My stomach clenches, and I rise, make my way to the sofa to hug Mum, and she takes my embrace readily. 'Let's hope he'll soon be able to tell us exactly what happened.'

13

TWENTY-TWO YEARS AGO

Elliot stared out of his bedroom window, *Harry Potter and the Philosopher's Stone* spread open on his bed like the wings of a butterfly. A bottle of half-drunk strawberry milk on his bedside table. He was watching the girls playing in Giselle's garden. He didn't want to join in, not really. Giselle was far too girlie. But it would be nice to be invited. He missed spending time with Annie. The two of them were inseparable before they moved to Ridgewater. Now they didn't play as much. OK, so he talked her into going down to Ridgewater Cove yesterday, and they played in the sea. It was great. Just the two of them. But today she'd been invited to Giselle's *again*. So off she went. Didn't even say goodbye.

They were on the swings. Annie going high. She was daring. More daring than Elliot. She always had scabs on her knees and elbows, or a twisted ankle, a dirty face. She was waving with both hands now, could see him at the window. He waved back and stepped away from the glass.

Seb would be round soon. Elliot liked Seb, who was in his class at school. They liked the same kind of things: trains and superheroes. He thought his friend's stutter made him who he was, hated that the other kids teased him. And Seb's troubles didn't stop at the end of the school day. He lived next door to the Shaw brothers in Branson Drive. They made his life a misery. Teasing him about his stutter was nothing compared to some of the things they did. Once, they dragged him into Sycamore Wood, tied him to a tree and left him there all night. And they often threw stones over the fence. One actually hit his mum when she was hanging out the washing.

Elliot tried his best to protect his friend. Threatened the Shaw twins a couple of times. But they weren't scared of anything. Their dad was on TV, and they thought they were great, living in their big house.

Seb's parents were kind but quiet. They always gave Elliot beans on toast when he went round to play. His dad owned the butcher shop in Ridgewater. His mum always seemed a bit sad. Seb and Elliot caught her crying once, and Seb said she was always upset, and he didn't know why, and that they should go upstairs and play with his train set.

Now the doorbell rang, and Elliot dived down the stairs.

'Seb,' he said, opening the door. 'Wanna play *Prince of Persia*?'

* * *

Margot filled the silver tray with three crystal glasses and a jug of homemade lemonade. The girls may only be eight, but her daughter deserved the best.

'That Annie girl,' Joan said creeping up behind her, wheezing in Margot's ear. 'She's not the kind of friend I would have wanted for my granddaughter. If Giselle was my child, I would put an end to their relationship.'

Well, she isn't yours. Margot picked up the tray. She wasn't quite brave enough *yet* to say the words out loud, but she was no longer afraid of her mother. Not like when she was young – a time when she would do anything Joan asked of her, frightened the woman would turn on her like she'd turned on Joel. The fear had still been there when she returned to Sycamore House eight years ago, but it had dissipated. Her mother was getting weaker. She was only in her late sixties, but she suffered chest problems, could no longer do much without getting breathless – she even struggled with Giselle's ballet lessons. In time, Margot would become the queen of Sycamore House, and her mother would fall. *Off with her head.* She just needed to bide her time.

Margot carried the tray across the lounge, slipped off her heeled slippers and pushed her feet into her outdoor shoes before stepping into the garden.

'Drinks, girls,' she said, continuing towards the table, ice bobbing in the jug of homemade lemonade.

* * *

Annie jumped off the red swing from a great height and dropped down knees first into the mud. She knew Mrs Bancroft didn't approve by the grumpy look on her face.

'Are you enjoying yourself?' She blew her daughter a kiss, her lips blood red.

Giselle jumped from the swing too, her blonde waves bouncing as she ran towards her mother and hugged her. She looked like a doll in her white frilly dress, pink ribbons tied in her hair. She was wearing a pretty necklace too. It spelt out her name. Annie wished her mum would dress her like a princess. But her hair was long and dark, and today, like most days, was pulled back in a tight ponytail with an elastic band that had come via the postman, wrapped around some letters. It would hurt when it was removed. *Why can't I be as pretty as Giselle? Wear dresses instead of dungarees or jeans.*

The girls reached the table where Margot had poured lemonade into glasses and cut a slice of cake for each of them. She used a handkerchief to clean Giselle's face, which, as far as Annie could see, wasn't dirty at all. There were lacy napkins, which Annie had learnt from watching Giselle that she needed to place on her knees.

'You look like a little urchin,' Margot said with a tinkling laugh, as Annie climbed onto a chair.

The woman said this often, though Annie had no idea what an urchin was. It couldn't be good.

'Your mummy won't be pleased if you go home dirty,' Margot went on. 'You'll probably get a scolding.'

She wouldn't. Her mum never minded, always out in the garden pushing her fingers into soil. She loved it when Annie and Elliot were outside with her, would tell them about the wildlife, the flowers and trees, and the magical land of fairies. Annie could still see fairies at the bottom of the garden, though Elliot said they were just dragonflies. He didn't believe any more, not since he turned nine and got all grown up.

Margot returned to the house and changed back into her slippers, and once she was out of sight, Giselle and Annie finished their lemonade then raced back to the swings.

'Where is your daddy?' Annie asked.

'Dead.'

'How did he die?'

Giselle shrugged. 'No idea. But I think he was very brave. I've got an uncle, though. I've seen a picture.'

'Annie!' It was Elliot, dangling out of their father's study window, Seb beside him. They looked tiny. His voice small. 'Mum says you've got to come home now.'

'OK.' Annie jumped from the swing and raced towards the French doors, hoping to take a short cut through the house. Though she'd never been allowed before. She so wanted to see inside. But Margot was suddenly there, blocking the little girl's way, arms folded.

'Not through the house, dear, you know that.' She smiled with her mouth but not with her eyes. 'We don't like dirt inside.'

'OK.' Annie tried to see through the glass. It was so clean. Perfect. 'See you tomorrow,' she called to Giselle with a wave, before racing to the side gate.

'Perhaps leave it until next weekend,' Margot called after her. 'Giselle has so much on with her ballet, plus we don't want fun getting in the way of her education now, do we?'

14

NOW

Annie

It's dark as I head down Ridgewater High Street towards the One Trick Pony.

In the years I've been away, Ridgewater has become a trendy place, with lots of arty-farty shops, boutiques, and coffee lounges with chairs and tables spilling onto the pavements. Not that anyone's sitting outside now. It's freezing, and the forecast promises more snow.

I pull my woolly hat lower, trying to warm my numb ears, my stomach churning as I peer through the side window of the bar at the dozen or so tables tucked inside, mostly full. I instinctively look at the bar staff. I can't see Tom. Perhaps he's not working tonight, and I feel a mixture of disappointment and relief.

My eyes fall on Natalie sitting alone, cradling a large glass of white wine, her head down. I have to go inside, talk to her. But it won't be easy. This was once my best friend. A best friend who suddenly cut me out of her life with no explanation.

A group of laughing teenagers pass by, reminding me of myself at that age.

From the age of eleven I'd hung out with Natalie, having abandoned Giselle. We'd laughed a lot back then – a stretch of seven mainly happy years, where we became obsessed with Robbie Williams and kidded ourselves that we danced like the Sugababes – Natalie doing a far better job of it than me. I was carefree before Dad died, before Giselle's horrific accident – before being a doctor took over my life.

15

NINETEEN YEARS AGO

Giselle often scratched at her skin, making it bleed. The bumps on her arms were raised and white, the rest of her skin red and inflamed. Her face, too, was puffy, itchy, stinging. Her mother said they were spoiling her prettiness. It would wake her up in the night. Sometimes she screamed and her mother came rushing into her room, put white cream on the welts to ease the pain. Mother said Giselle was allergic to sunlight. Had a condition with a funny name. That if she went outside, it would get a whole lot worse.

After a few months of staying inside, her skin improved. During that time Annie had knocked a few times asking if she was coming out. Giselle missed her, but her mother said she must say no.

'Can I come in then?' Annie had asked once. But Giselle's mother wouldn't allow it, even when Giselle cried.

Annie had a new friend. She was tall with long blonde hair. Beautiful. Giselle saw them often through her bedroom window. They didn't play like Annie and Giselle used to: with Sylvanian Families, pretend cookers and prams. Instead, they linked arms and giggled as they strutted by Sycamore House. Giselle didn't like Annie's new friend, whose lips were the same red as her mother's – she wished she would disappear.

They were outside now, at Fairy Cottage, leaning against the fence. Elliot and Seb, Annie and her new friend. A tear rolled down Giselle's cheek. She wanted to be out there. Be a part of it. Be normal.

It had been over six months since Uncle Joel visited. He'd left in a hurry after arguing with her mother, leaving Giselle a note with his address. *'If you ever leave Sycamore House, and you really should, this is my address.'*

'Time for your ballet lesson, darling.' It was her mother. It was just the two of them now, and Giselle had hoped the ballet would end when her grandmother went into a care home. But her mother seemed even more determined Giselle would be the ballerina she never was.

Mother said her grandmother was *'going funny'* and had to go. She visited her sometimes and always came back with a bottle of wine. 'To calm my nerves,' she would say.

'Maybe I could go outside when the sun goes in, after my ballet lesson?' Giselle said.

'You're eleven years old, dear. Far too young to go out after dark, and anyway, at night-time bad people come out; you're far safer inside with me to take care of you.'

Elliot felt for Seb. He was attempting to talk to Natalie as they stood outside Fairy Cottage, his stutter tying his tongue. She barely looked his way, and, OK, perhaps she was out of his league – he was a bit of a dweeb and there was no doubting she was pretty – but kindness costs nothing.

'Let's go,' Elliot said to his friend, unable to watch him making a tit of himself any longer.

'You're going?' Natalie's eyes widened.

'Things to do.' Elliot dragged Seb away. They would go into town. Elliot had some birthday money and wanted to get the latest *Call of Duty* for his Xbox.

As they walked, kicking stones, he looked at his friend. Seb's mum had recently taken her own life, and Elliot couldn't imagine what he'd been through. And it wasn't only the loss of his mum; his dad was losing it, had started behaving oddly. He would walk along the road for three steps, turn around and take two steps back, turn again and take three steps forward, and so on, making his journeys more of a marathon than a walk. Aiden Shaw called him the Turnaround Man, and it had caught on. The whole school was calling him that. It was hell for Seb.

The only positive in Seb's life right now seemed to be that he and his father had moved from their house in Branson Drive, away from the Shaws, and now lived at Willow Farm just outside of Ridgewater. At least Seb was left alone when he left school and could hide away without being taunted.

16

NOW

Annie

'I'm so glad you came,' Natalie says as I reach her table, holding a small glass of wine.

I slip off my coat, sit down and rest my elbows on the table, trying to catch her eye, curiosity pumping.

'You haven't changed, Annie.' She takes a gulp of wine, her hand clenched around the stem of the glass. 'Still pretty.'

I feel myself blush, unsure what to say. She looks different, so pale and drawn. 'You're wearing your hair short now,' I say after a pause.

She runs slim fingers through it. 'Yeah, I got a bit drunk and lopped it all off. Threw a dye on it.' Another gulp. 'Did you hear my parents are dead?'

I nod. 'I'm so sorry.'

'Yeah, well... it wasn't like we got on.'

My mind drifts to how strict they were. How controlling. How they couldn't cope when Natalie rebelled.

'Still,' she goes on, 'I'm left with all kinds of baggage I don't know how to handle. Guilt, for one.'

'Guilt?'

'I treated them like crap. What if they were only looking out for me? What if I'd listened?'

'You're grieving,' I say. 'Despite everything, they were your parents.'

She shrugs. 'Maybe. I guess I'm confused right now.'

I want to ask questions but feel she must lead. I wait for her to talk. Except she doesn't. Instead, she downs her drink in silence.

'You wanted to see me?' I say in the end.

But she's on her feet, cradling her empty glass. 'Another?'

'I'm good thanks.' I've barely touched my drink.

Within seconds she's at the bar, slamming the glass on the counter. 'Large white,' she calls to the barman who is serving someone else.

Once back, she takes a long deep breath. 'So, I'm guessing you'll want to know why I stopped talking to you and Elliot.' She closes her eyes briefly, as though she's fishing around in her head for the right words.

'I never understood why.'

She shakes her head. 'Maybe I should have turned to you, rather than...'

'Something happened that night, didn't it?'

'The night we drank too much wine and told ghost stories... yes, something happened. Something awful.'

I want to reach across, take her hand, but sense she'll pull away. That she doesn't want the feel of my touch.

'It turned out to be the worst night of my life. A night I've never got over, and I never will.' Her eyes shimmer with tears, but her jaw is tense. 'My only hope of feeling normal again is to find out the truth.'

I lean forward. 'What happened?'

She covers her mouth as if holding in the words, as though if she lets them go, it might break her.

'You don't have to tell me,' I say. 'If you'd rather not.'

She shakes her head, leans forward and whispers, 'I want to. I want to get the sordid nightmare out of my head. The horrific truth my parents never let me share. But they're gone now, they can't stop me telling you.' A tear rolls down her cheek, and she wipes it away with the back of her hand. Whatever happened, talking to me is bringing it all back, making her desperately sad and bitterly angry.

17

TWELVE YEARS AGO

Annie sat dead-centre of the brown Dralon sofa feeling like a giant gooseberry, her arms folded across her Robbie Williams T-shirt from his *Take the Crown* stadium tour.

She stroked the tabby cat curled next to her, trying to distract herself from Natalie sprawled on Aiden Shaw's lap, his hand roaming up the hem of her skirt, as Maroon 5's 'One More Night' blared out of a huge speaker. *Why the hell did I let her talk me into coming?*

'I need you, Annie,' her friend had said, and to be fair, Natalie had been there for her when her dad died.

'You know what Aiden's like,' Annie had said, trying to talk her out of coming. And Natalie knew exactly what he was like. But Aiden was gorgeous – the boy everyone at school fancied. Except Annie. She thought he was a jerk and was certain Natalie was only with him to impress the other girls in their class. *Look everyone, Aiden wants me.*

The Shaws' house in Branson Drive was large. The lounge-diner vast, though dated. A six-bed sixties detached with swirling orange and brown carpets throughout, and a fireplace that looked like a rock face. Natalie had told Annie that Aiden's dad was an actor who played the killer in a slasher film five years ago and a gangster in a long-running TV series in the US – where he'd been living for the last eight years – and was apparently returning in November for the seventh series.

Lance Shaw rarely lived in Ridgewater, despite inheriting the house from his parents. According to Natalie, he and his wife were divorced, but he'd agreed she could live in the house with their non-identical twin sons while he was in the US. Natalie told Annie that the woman moved to Essex when he returned this time, saying the brothers were eighteen now, and didn't need her any more.

A giant photo of the boys as babies was on the wall above a drinks cabinet, but there were no recent pictures.

Aiden's brother was a mystery. Annie had rarely seen him. He didn't go to their school. *'Mouse is a bit of a weirdo,'* Natalie had told her. *'Aiden said he used to go down to Sycamore Wood and flash his willy to dog walkers. Not only that, he once locked his mother in the shed and set fire to it. Aiden found her, and that's when Mouse was sent to a special school.'*

The cat jumped from the sofa and left the room, seeming to look over its shoulder in disgust at Natalie and Aiden still rehearsing for a porn movie.

Lance was sitting at his laptop at a pine table at the far end of the room next to a Welsh dresser ladened with dusty patterned plates. Handsome for a man in his forties. Clearly worked out. An older version of Aiden, Annie supposed. Natalie had flirted with him earlier. *Does she even know she's doing it?*

Suddenly Aiden pushed Natalie off his lap, and she thumped to the floor, looking over at Annie, who averted her eyes. *Kick him in the fucking nuts, Nat. He deserves it.*

'Need a piss,' he said, getting up and leaving the room adjusting his jeans. *Is that a gun in your pocket, or are you just pleased to see me?*

'Lance...' Natalie got to her feet, her voice swoony as she rested a hand on his shoulder. 'I noticed you have a couple of bottles of wine on the rack.' She took his hand and pulled him up and into the kitchen. Annie could see them both through the crack in the door, Natalie floating around him like a butterfly as he poured her a large glass of white wine. She would try this whole flirting thing with Elliot sometimes, but he wasn't interested.

Her friend took a long gulp of wine, leaning her slim body against the wall, one foot off the floor, pressing a heel against the orange tiles. Lance approached then – *for God's sake, Nat* – resting his arm on the wall above her head. Trapping her there. Not that she made any effort to escape. He touched her cheek, lowered his lips to hers.

'Where's Nat?' It was Aiden, zipping up the fly of his jeans.

She appeared, cheeks flushed. 'You OK, babe?' she said as he dropped into the chair and she flopped to the floor at his feet.

'I reckon you should meet my brother, Annie,' Aiden said with a smirk. 'He needs to lose a bit of weight, have a decent haircut, but there's definite potential there.' He burst out laughing. 'He's playing *Resident Evil*, but when he's finished, I'll introduce you.'

Natalie laughed too, took a gulp of wine. Then mouthed *Sorry* at Annie.

'I'm off.' Annie rose, reaching for her hoodie on the back of the sofa.

'Don't go.' Natalie got up. Tugged at her short skirt. 'Have a glass of wine. That would be OK wouldn't it, Mr Shaw?'

Not 'Lance' when Aiden's about.

'No thanks,' Annie said. She couldn't stay, but then should she leave her friend with these two horny men? 'Maybe you should come with me.'

Natalie shook her head. Got up to give Annie a hug. 'I'll call you later,' she said.

* * *

Natalie didn't object when Aiden took hold of her hand and yanked her towards the door.

'We're going upstairs, Dad,' he said, and Lance looked up from his laptop, ran slim fingers through his hair and grinned.

'Don't do anything I wouldn't do,' he said. 'And remember Mouse is in his room. He doesn't want to hear you two going at it.' He turned his eyes back to the screen in front of him. Laughed.

'I should probably go.' Natalie knew she'd been flirting with Aiden, with his dad, rebelling against her parents' strict upbringing. But was she ready for what her boyfriend had in mind? She was still a virgin despite what people thought. An idiot. She should have gone home with Annie.

Aiden pulled Natalie into the hallway. And before she could stop him, he kissed her softly on the lips. He had the most beautiful eyes. A royal blue that seemed almost unnatural. Annie thought they were contacts, but Natalie was certain they were for real. And he was a good kisser. He winked at her, and with her hand in his, she followed him up the stairs, knowing it was a mistake before she reached the top step.

* * *

Annie was relieved when Natalie called her saying she'd dumped Aiden, though she was worried for her in equal measure. He wasn't used to girls ending things with him and had a temper – she'd seen it when some boy dobbed him in for selling weed on school grounds, saw him draw a knife on the poor lad, slashing his arm so badly he needed stitches.

Natalie explained how, when Annie left the Shaw house, she'd gone up to Aiden's room. That she'd told him no – that they hadn't been together long enough. But he'd pushed her forcefully onto the bed, laughing as though Natalie was joking. She'd caught her forehead on his bedside cabinet. It was painful, but it was as though he didn't even notice – or care. She'd struggled to fight him off. His hands everywhere.

'He said I was a prick-tease,' she said now as they sat in the Fox, the noise of the pub swallowing her words. 'Said I led him on by going up to his room. Perhaps I did.' She shook her head. 'I know I'm a flirt.'

'Stop blaming yourself,' Annie said. 'You did nothing wrong.'

She shook her head, her chin crinkling. 'I just keep wondering what might have happened if the floorboards on the landing hadn't creaked. If Aiden hadn't gone out there, yelling, hammering on his brother's door, calling him a pervert. If I hadn't taken that chance to get out of there.'

'Everything will be OK.' Annie wished she could believe her words. But she knew what Aiden was like. *He won't like being dumped.*

Natalie's eyes skittered across the crowded pub. 'Shit!'

'What is it? What's wrong?'

'It's nothing. I just thought I saw...'

'Who?' Annie followed her friend's gaze towards the

crowded bar. The huddle of punters waiting to be served. 'Who did you see?'

'I thought it was Aiden's dad, but I can't see him now. I'm imagining things. Going crazy.' She placed her pink phone face down on the pub table, her hand trembling. 'I've put it on silent,' she said. 'I don't want Aiden ruining this evening.' Her eyes glazed with tears. 'I don't know what else to do. He keeps blasting me with calls and texts. It's not because he wants me. It's because he can't bear it that I don't want him.'

She looked so pretty in a short white dress, but despite her heavy make-up, the bruise where she'd banged her head was visible. Annie placed her hand on her friend's, struggling to find the right words to console her.

The young women entwined fingers. 'Don't think about it, Nat. Just keep away from him from now on. He's a nightmare.'

'Here you go.' Elliot was carrying a tray full of drinks. White wine for Natalie and Annie, a pint of lager for him, a red wine for Seb.

The Fox was rammed. Some band – *pretty good for local* – was crammed into the corner playing cover versions of well-worn songs. Elliot handed Annie her drink, Natalie hers, and her smile said it all. She'd had a massive crush on him for years – but it would never come to anything, he wasn't interested. Natalie was beautiful but firmly in 'little sister's friend' zone. She was also rebellious and daring. Whereas Elliot was easy-going. In fact, if he was any more chilled, he'd fall over. It would be a match made in hell.

Elliot put the other drinks on the scratched round table and discarded the tray on the windowsill behind them before sitting down. Elliot and Annie didn't normally hang out in the evenings. Yes, they'd always been close, but he tended to do his thing – mainly sculpting wooden animals – and she did hers –

reading up on all things medical. So it was nice to be out together.

'They're not bad,' Elliot said, nodding towards the band now playing 'Hotel California'. 'A mate of mine went to school with the lead singer's cousin's friend.' He laughed. 'How's that for a claim to fame?'

Natalie threw her head back in a laugh that summed up her adoration.

Elliot glanced Annie's way, discreetly rolling his eyes. He knew about her friend's crush – it was hard to miss.

Seb was pushing his way through the crowd, his man bag over his shoulder. He was nineteen, five foot nine, thin and wearing a black hoodie and jeans. He had always been a gentle sort of a guy who still struggled with teenage acne, and his effort to grow a beard, perhaps to cover his poor skin, had only half-worked, and looked more like bumfluff.

Elliot mentioned once that he wondered if Seb was gay, as he certainly didn't seem especially interested in women, but then neither did Elliot. Apparently, after a heart-to-heart one drunken night, Seb told her brother that he was simply nervous around women, though recently he'd got friendly with an Australian girl online, who was coming to the UK. He was hoping when she saw him in person, she wouldn't run a mile. It was sad how little confidence he had in himself. He was a nice guy.

Seb dropped into the vacant seat and took a huge gulp of wine.

'Band's good,' he said, stuttering slightly. 'Not quite the Eagles, but not bad.' He took another gulp, and Annie felt for him. He didn't look at Natalie once. Learnt through the years she didn't have much time for him. In fact, she was probably the kind of girl who might have teased him at school. She had a kind side, Annie refused to believe otherwise, but sometimes her desire to be popular took over. A few years back Natalie had spotted Giselle at an upstairs open window wearing a frilly white dress. She had begun talking loudly, *'Christ, what a weirdo. Why were you ever friends with her, Annie?'* There was no doubt that Giselle had heard.

The more drinks they consumed, the more relaxed the evening became. Eventually people got up to dance, and Natalie dragged Elliot to his feet. He wasn't a great dancer and looked awkward as she danced flirtatiously around him – using her best Sugababes moves. He kept throwing Annie looks that clearly cried *Help.*

'I think she likes him,' Seb said close to Annie's ear. He was slurring slightly, the alcohol bringing him out of his shell, halting his stutter. 'But he's not interested, can't she see that?'

'She's had a thing for him for years. You know that,' Annie said. 'I don't think she'll give up until he tells her to sod off – and he'll never do that. He's too kind.'

The door slammed open, and Annie recognised the cocky stance of Aiden Shaw, cringing as his dark eyes scanned the noisy pub, looking for Natalie.

'Crap!'

'You OK?' Seb asked as she leapt to her feet and raced towards Natalie to warn her.

'What's up, my lovely friend?' Natalie said, pulling Annie into a drink-fuelled hug.

'He's here!'

'Who's here?' Natalie smiled at Elliot, who looked relieved to have stopped dancing, though not so relieved when she stroked a finger down his cheek. 'You are so, so handsome,' she said.

'Listen to me, for God's sake!' Annie cried. 'Aiden is here.'

'Oh God.' Her blue eyes scanned the room. He was heading her way, pushing through the throng of drinkers. 'Oh God!' she cried again, seeming to sober up.

Aiden was suddenly there, towering over Natalie, gripping her arm. 'What the hell?' he said. 'A text, for Christ's sake? You end it with a fucking text?'

She attempted to pull away from him, but he dragged her crying across the bar, barging between startled people. The dancing had stopped. The music had stopped.

'Hey!' Elliot was right behind them. 'Leave her alone.' Elliot was tall, but not particularly broad, looking small against Aiden and his muscles.

Aiden stopped and turned. 'And what the hell are you going to do about it?'

Suddenly, Seb was standing next to Elliot, picking up an empty pint glass as a weapon, though Annie wasn't quite sure how he would use it. Annie joined them, her heart thudding.

'What is this?' Aiden snarled. 'The Three Musketeers?' But he let go of Natalie, and she raced to hide behind Elliot, nestling into his back, holding him. 'Fine,' he said. 'But this isn't over. Nobody makes a fool of Aiden Shaw.' He looked around at the confused, worried faces of the punters. 'What the hell are you all looking at?' he yelled at the silent crowd, before leaving the pub, the door slam behind him.

18

Natalie was disappointed by the bell announcing last orders. She didn't want the evening to end. Elliot had been so brave standing up to Aiden. He'd saved her. He'd even danced with her. No, she mustn't go there. He saw her as a sister. That's what Annie told her. But then what did she know?

'We could get wine from the offie,' she said, leading the way out of the pub and onto the pavement outside, the warm air hitting them – despite the late hour. It had been a hot August day, and the straps of her dress dropped from her shoulders, revealing her tan. She flicked her eyes towards Elliot, hoping he was looking, but he was chatting to Seb. 'We could go to the clearing in Sycamore Wood,' she continued. 'Light a fire.' She looked pleadingly from Elliot to Annie, not catching Seb's eye, not bothered whether he came or not.

'I'm up for it.' Seb looped his man bag across his body, alcohol clearly giving him confidence. 'Though I'd better call my dad.' He took his phone from his pocket. 'He'll only worry if I'm late.'

'I thought your dad had lost the plot?' Natalie wished she

could take back the words. The flash of anger in Seb's eyes distorted his features, and Elliot was none too happy. 'Sorry,' she said, pulling up her dress straps. 'I shouldn't have said that.'

'You OK, mate?' Elliot said, resting a palm on his friend's back.

'For fuck's sake!' Natalie's cheeks flamed red. 'I said I'm sorry. It was only a joke.'

'You think the fact my mother committed suicide and my dad is suffering is funny?'

'No! No, of course not. Look, can we forget I said it?'

'Fine,' Seb said. 'But seriously. You need to think before you speak. The world doesn't revolve around you.'

Natalie wanted to retaliate, but there was a warning look in Elliot's eyes. Perhaps she was simply jealous. Whatever Seb's father was, he cared about his son. Her parents would never worry in the same way. When she was younger, they had controlled her. The way she dressed. The way she thought. She was around eleven when she started to rebel and now she didn't know how to stop – it had got so out of hand, she knew that. Her father had told her more than once that he prayed for her forgiveness every night. That she needed to repent or she would go to hell.

'Well, I'm in for a drink in the wood,' Annie said, shoving the tips of her fingers into her jean pockets and rising back and forth on her toes, clearly trying to defuse the tension. 'The night is young and so are we.'

Seb stepped away, phone pinned to his ear as he told his dad where they were going. That he would be home in a couple of hours.

'Elliot?' Natalie said, raising her eyebrows. 'You coming with us?'

'OK, why not?' But he was keeping his distance from her,

and her heart sank. 'We could tell ghost stories round the fire, I s'pose.'

'No way,' Annie said. 'Your ghost stories scare the bejesus out of me. Remember that story you told me about Fairy Cottage being haunted?'

Elliot laughed. 'And you lay awake at night worried a ghost in white would appear at the end of your bed.'

'Then you came in the bloody room with a sheet over your head.'

They grabbed a couple of bottles of wine from the off-licence, and as they spilled back onto the street, Natalie stopped. 'He's over there,' she said, her heart picking up pace. 'Look.'

Aiden was sitting on a bench in the town square swigging from a bottle, elbows on knees, legs splayed. He was with an overweight lad with straggly dark hair and an out-of-control beard.

'He's with his brother,' Natalie said. 'I've never met him, but that's got to be Mouse.'

'We should go,' Seb said, ending his call to his dad and glancing at the two young men.

'He goes to a special school,' Natalie said. 'Been there for years. Aiden told me how he chased him round the house with a knife a couple of years back.'

Annie linked arms with Natalie. 'Let's get out of here.'

The group looked back a few times as they moved on, heading for Sycamore Wood. Relieved that Aiden and his brother didn't follow.

* * *

Giselle heard the laughter first. Sat upright in bed. There it was again. Outside. She swung her legs round, tiptoed to the window.

Annie and Elliot were out there with their friends, swigging from bottles, having fun as they passed by, seemingly oblivious that she still lived there, trapped within the walls of Sycamore House. Her first and only friend had forgotten her.

Giselle looked over her shoulder at her dimly lit bedroom.

Mother was asleep in the next room. The room that was once her grandmother's before she went to the care home. A room that still smelt of Joan Bancroft's heavy perfume, the powder she always wore. The powder that would crack on her cheeks when the woman bent to kiss her.

Surely Mother wouldn't notice if Giselle went outside. If she danced through the wood like a fairy. It was dark so her skin wouldn't flare up. She could sit just out of sight of Annie and her friends, watch, pretend she was with them.

She pulled on her slippers, her white gown. She wouldn't go for long. She would be back before her mother stirred.

* * *

Annie led the way to the clearing, where surrounding tall sycamore trees reached up to the night sky and dry earth beckoned. Elliot lit a small fire, more for atmosphere than warmth.

They sat in a row on a trunk of a fallen tree, swigging wine, passing the bottle to and fro.

'These woods are haunted,' Elliot said, a mischievous glint in his eye, and Natalie moved in closer to him.

Annie knew he was about to tell the story of the girl in white who drifted through the trees at midnight. Her eyes skittered across the area, flickering flames creating jumping shadows, sending a sliver of fear down her spine. It was almost midnight. She snatched the bottle from Seb, took several gulps, her head swimming.

'It was a few weeks back that I heard the crying—'

'Except he didn't because it's not true,' Annie snapped trying to stop the moment, defuse the fear.

'Let him finish,' Natalie said, eyes glued to Elliot.

'Then I saw her, a white, misty shape drifting through the trees, barely six feet away from where I stood, frozen to the spot.' He shuffled forward, stirring the silence. 'My heart raced as I realised it was a young woman, though there were no discernible features, only a white shape, with long, flowing hair.'

'Oh my God!' Natalie cried. 'What did you do?'

'What part of "it's not true" don't you understand?' Annie said, rolling her eyes.

Elliot laughed, but continued, clearly enjoying the effect his story was having. 'I felt a sense of dread as I watched the spectral figure glide through the trees, hearing her wail, the night air turning to ice.'

'Oh my God,' Natalie repeated, her voice high-pitched, over excitable. 'You're so utterly brave—'

'Yes, because it's pure fantasy.' Annie was irritated, the wine turning on her. She got up, walked to the edge of the clearing. Blinked. There was someone out there. A judder of white dashing through the trees. A creep of fear travelled down her spine. 'What was that?'

Elliot looked up. 'What?'

She returned to the log. Had she imagined it? 'Nothing. It was just—'

'A ghost?' Elliot laughed, took another gulp of wine.

'I saw a ghost once.' It was Seb. He had been silent until now. Invisible.

'Do tell,' Natalie said, perhaps making up for her cruel words earlier and resting her head on Elliot's shoulder. He instantly moved away from her.

'Go on, mate,' Elliot said to Seb.

'It was just after my mum died. I must have been about eleven. I woke to find her sitting on the edge of my bed.'

'God, that's awful,' Natalie said.

'No, no it wasn't. I wasn't afraid. She looked so real, but I knew she couldn't be.' There was no sign of a stutter, but his voice was cracking. 'I'd been to her funeral a few days before.' He lowered his head. 'She told me to be good. That she would always watch over me. That she would always love me.'

His story changed the mood. This wasn't a ridiculous scary story. This came from the heart.

'She wanted you to know she will always be there for you,' Elliot said, resting his hand on his friend's arm.

And then Natalie chose that moment, of all moments, to make her move on Elliot. Her lips locked on his as she pressed her palms against his cheeks.

'Hang on!' he said, pulling away and grabbing her wrists. 'Listen, you're a great mate—'

'Mate?' she cried, jumping to her feet. 'Elliot, can't you see how much I love you?'

Love? Though to be fair, everyone loves everyone when they're pissed.

Annie rose, too, as Natalie started to cry. She pulled her friend into her arms. But Natalie tugged away and took off into the darkness, darting through the trees.

'I'm going home!' she yelled.

Within moments, Seb was on his feet. 'Should we go after her?'

'Probably.' Annie staggered a few steps, realising she'd lost all coordination. 'Except I'm very, very drunk.' She dropped down next to Elliot.

'I didn't mean to upset her,' he said, thrusting his head into his hands.

'We've all had too much to drink.' Annie put her arm around his shoulders. 'Things will look better in the morning.'

'I'll go after her,' Seb said, picking up his man bag. 'Try to catch her up, make sure she gets home OK.'

'Good idea.' Annie watched him go, feeling like a terrible friend, before returning her eyes to Elliot.

'I should have told her from the off I wasn't interested,' he said, lifting his head from his hands.

'You did.'

'Did I? I don't remember making it clear. What a mess.' He shook his head. 'I like Natalie, but—'

'Shall we get back to the house?'

'You go ahead,' he said. 'I need a few minutes to put out the fire.'

But Annie knew it was more than that. Elliot was a sensitive soul. He would hate that he'd upset Natalie. He needed time to think things through.

'OK,' she said, stepping away. 'But don't be long.'

19

NOW

Annie

I wait, hands flat on the table, my eyes locked with Natalie's.

'I was attacked.' She chokes out the words as though they've been caught in her throat for years. 'Raped. Left for dead in Sycamore Wood.'

'Oh God.' This time I reach out, shock ricocheting through my body, but she snatches her hand away, stares for some moments before picking up her wine, hovering the glass close to her dry lips. 'Why didn't you tell me, Nat?'

'I couldn't. Not back then. But now... Do you remember how I ran off into the wood?'

I nod, my body tense.

'I was drunk. We all were. It was so dark, every part of the wood looked the same, as I ran unable to find my way out. I heard footsteps, thought it was you. Turned and called your name. Whoever it was got closer, the footsteps louder, faster.' She sucks in a breath. 'They shoved a hessian bag over my head, pulled me to the ground. I've never felt such suffocating fear.' She lets out a cry, and two young men at the next table look over, then back at their drinks. 'I need to know who attacked me,' she whispers. 'I need to know.'

'I'm so sorry,' I say, unable to think of the right words. I feel useless. 'Have you talked to someone, a counsellor or therapist?'

She shakes her head. 'I haven't told a soul. Only my parents at the time, and now you.'

'Oh God, Natalie. I wish I'd known. Did you see him?'

Another shake of her head, as a tear streaks down her face. 'It's all a blur.'

'There's nothing you remember?'

'I heard something that night... I just wish I could remember what.' Another shake of her head. 'And there's something else I can't quite reach. But whatever it is, it hasn't come back to me in twelve years.'

'What can I do?'

'You can help me.'

'Yes. Anything.'

'If I can find who attacked me, I can at least stop looking over my shoulder... I can report them, get justice.'

I'm not sure how easy it would be to get justice after so long, but I feel for her desperately, and want to help her in any way I can. 'Why didn't you say something at the time? You should have told the police, me. I was your best friend.'

She takes another gulp of wine. 'My parents swore me to secrecy, said if anyone knew what had happened it would bring shame on them. They said by dressing like a tart and staying out late... I'd been asking for it. That it was my own fault.'

'My God.' I hadn't liked her parents, knew they were Victorian in their thinking when it came to their daughter, but this was unforgiveable. 'That's just not true.'

'I know that now. But I blamed myself. Told myself if I'd listened to my parents, it would never have happened. Plus, I had no idea who'd attacked me.'

'If you'd gone to the police, you could have—'

'Stop!' she yells. The bar staff look over. 'Don't you think I know that?' she says, reducing her words to a whisper. 'Didn't you hear me? My parents took control. I was a wreck, a mess, a scared young woman. When they suggested we move right away, I jumped at it. Certain I would be able to put the awful experience behind me and move on. But it didn't work out like that. The fear never left.' She's crying now, burying her head in her hands.

'I'm so sorry,' I say, tears in my words. 'I didn't mean to upset you.'

She looks up. 'You didn't. Whoever forced themselves on me that night is to blame for everything. And I need to find out who it was.'

'And you think that's possible?'

'Yes. Elliot and Seb were there—'

I throw my body back against the chair, gripping my neck. 'Christ, you can't think it was Elliot?'

'He was questioned about Giselle's death. It could be connected.'

I don't want to lose sympathy for Natalie. She's been through hell. But to accuse my brother! 'Giselle's death was an accident. There's no connection.'

'But the police questioned him—'

'That was routine, before the coroner ruled it as accidental.' My heart pounds, I need to keep calm. This has nothing to do with Elliot. Breathe. Natalie can't possibly think my brother is connected. He would never do something so awful. But I can't help the sudden flash of memory: I left him that night, sitting alone on the tree trunk in the middle of Sycamore Wood.

'I honestly don't know who it was,' she says, bringing me back to the moment. 'I don't think it was Elliot, or Seb for that matter. But try to understand how much I need to know who it was that ruined my life. Put yourself where I am for a moment.'

I stare at the mess that was once my stunning, confident friend and spot the scars on her skinny arms – not an attempted suicide, these are self-harm. Seeing me looking, she pulls down her sleeves. How can I put myself where she is, even for a moment? What she's been through is unimaginable.

'I just need a friend right now,' she says.

'And I'm here for you.'

She leans forward, her eyes glistening. 'Then help me, please. Help me find him. The man who took away everything.' She lowers her head, silent for a moment. 'Would you believe I still feel dirty after all these years? Ashamed. A victim.'

'No, not a victim.' I place my hand on her arm; she doesn't pull away. 'A survivor.'

She clenches her fists, raises her head and looks deep into my eyes, then, in a whisper, she says, 'Do I look like a fucking survivor?'

I fumble for something to say, but she beats me to it. 'Help me.' She's begging me now, her palms pressed together. 'I need to talk to Seb. To Aiden and his brother. They may not have attacked me, but they might remember something that will lead me to who did.'

'You can't want to talk to Aiden, surely?'

'That's just it. I do. I want to look him in the eye, look Seb in the eye. Because I'll know when I find the man who crushed the young woman I once was.'

'But Seb was as gentle as a lamb; he would never hurt

anyone.' I look at her long and hard. 'You've been through a terrible trauma. Maybe—'

'Don't for Christ's sake suggest I need psychiatric help.' She shakes her head and leans back in her chair, draining her glass. 'I don't need therapy, if that's what you were about to suggest.' Her jaw clenches. She puts down her glass with a thud, twists her fists into tight balls. 'I need justice.'

But I don't hear the word justice, I hear the word revenge.

'Are you prepared to help me, Annie, or am I doing this alone?'

Back at Fairy Cottage, I head straight to my room and bury myself under the duvet, sobbing quietly for fear Elliot or Mum will hear. My teenage best friend was attacked by an unknown man twelve years ago and said nothing, instead blaming herself. My body shakes as my sobs get more ferocious. 'Oh, Nat, why didn't you tell me at the time?'

It's as my sobs turn to small bursts of pain, I wonder if anyone would notice if I never got out of bed again.

PART II

20

Kerry steps out of the blistering sun into the relief of the air-con at Sydney Airport. The rapid repeat of her mum's phrases, as they make their way across departures, making her feel as though she's twelve years old, not twenty-three. She gets it. They said goodbye to Kerry's older sister Fi at this very airport almost thirteen years ago and she hasn't been seen since.

'You will be careful?' her mum says. 'Please say you'll be careful.'

'I will, Mum. Please stop worrying.' Kerry's not prone to worrying, but if her mother doesn't stop soon, she may turn around and run for home. This is huge. Massive. Travelling to the UK alone. She needs her mum to say everything will be fine.

'Don't go anywhere remote.'

'I won't. I promise.'

'And keep an eye on your sugar levels.'

'I will.' She's been diabetic since she was seven. She knows the ropes.

They make their way to the cafe in departures and order coffee.

As they drink, time ticks by. Kerry will need to go through customs soon, board her flight, leave the soaring temperatures of Australia's summer and head for the bitter chill of the UK's winter. She's heard there's been snow in Ridgewater.

Her mum leans forward, touches her cheek, and Kerry smells the familiar alcohol on her breath.

'I really wish you would change your mind,' her mum says. 'I don't know what you hope to achieve.'

I hope to find out what happened to Fi. I wish you'd understand that.

'I'll be OK,' she says for the millionth time, finishing her drink. She flicks her blonde bobbed hair behind her ears. She looks nothing like her older sister. She's smaller. Curvier. Though they share the same blonde hair and blue eyes just like their father's, and they've both inherited his personality. Strong. Capable. Unlike their mother. 'You must stop worrying, I'm a big girl.'

'It doesn't make you invincible.' Her mum's voice is weak, her hands tremble. Her hair, greyed prematurely, is cut short. Lines on her tanned, leathery skin are deep.

'I will be careful,' Kerry promises once more.

Her mother's hazel eyes shimmer, but there's something else. Something missing that had been there for so long after Fi went missing. Hope. She thinks Kerry is wasting her time. She thinks Fi's dead.

It hadn't been easy at ten years old to see her mother crumble, eventually morphing into the shadow of the woman she once was. Even Kerry's dad left in the end. Could no longer cope with the long, painful silences. The waiting. The nothingness. The drinking.

He did all he could when Fi disappeared. Spent months in Europe travelling France, Germany, Italy and Spain – all the places on Fi's meticulously thought-through itinerary. He returned to Australia a broken man when he didn't find her. He lives in Adelaide now. Remarried with a six-year-old son. A cute boy. Blond. Tanned. Kerry's only met her half-brother once. Though her father sends endless photos. In fact, she hasn't seen her father in years. Her choice. It's not that she doesn't love him. She does. She just feels he abandoned her and her mother.

But she hasn't let it beat her. She stands strong, determined. Her sister wouldn't have wanted her to go under. Her beautiful, intelligent sister who taught her to swim wild in the sea, to never judge people by appearance and that you can never have sunshine without shadows. And that's how Kerry found her sister's abandoned travel blog a couple of months ago. She was doing yet another search of the internet for clues to her sister's whereabouts when something made her key in 'Sunshine and Shadows'. And there it was in the search, a travel blog of that name.

Her mother doesn't fully believe it's Fi's blog, despite Kerry's certainty. It covers all the areas Fi had travelled before she vanished, on the dates she would have been there, the last one being France, a few weeks before they lost contact. But it isn't the post that is making Kerry jump on a plane to the UK, it's the conversations Fi – *if it is Fi* – had with another blogger called The Wooden Man. The first time he turned up on the blog was when he commented on her post about St. Malo:

> Amazing! You should come to the UK, Devon is beautiful – I recommend Ridgewater.

Fi had responded:

Sounds great. I've just googled, looks lovely.

At first, Kerry thought that's where the conversation had ended, until she clicked on The Wooden Man's blog, a site devoted to his home town of Ridgewater. There were lots of comments by Fi on his posts, and one particularly caught Kerry's eye:

I'm heading to the UK, will be in Ridgewater by the weekend. Hope to meet you in person.

The Wooden Man had replied:

Direct message me. We can meet and I'll show you round. My email address is in the 'About Me' section.

The Wooden Man appeared to live in Ridgewater and seemed proud of his home town, but that was about it: no photos of him, no sign of his real name. He continued to post for another six months – but there were no more comments by 'Sunshine and Shadows' and no more posts on what she suspected was her sister's blog.

'I have to do this, Mum,' Kerry says now. If there's any chance this was Fi's blog, she has to go to Ridgewater. Ask questions. 'It's the first lead we've had in years.'

'Please don't get your hopes too high. If our Fi is alive, she would have found a way to contact us. I know she would.'

The flight times on the information board are ever-changing. Kerry must get through customs in the next twenty minutes. 'I have to go,' she says rising to her feet and picking up her carry-on bag.

Her mum gets up, takes her daughter tightly in her arms as though she may never let go. 'I wish I could come with you,' she says. She suffers from angina, but Kerry knows it's more than that. Her mother has always been afraid of flying. When Fi first went missing, she refused to go with their father to France to search for her. Even at the age of ten, Kerry couldn't understand why her parents didn't go together. Why wasn't finding Fi overriding her mother's fear? But the truth was, she simply wasn't strong enough. And later, Kerry often found her mum crumpled at the bottom of a cupboard or wardrobe when she came home from school, buried under heaps of clothes sobbing into the teddy bear Fi had as a child.

'I'll FaceTime you,' she says, trying to pull away from her mother's grip, her thoughts on the twenty-four-hour journey ahead of her.

'Every night? Promise?'

'Of course.'

'I need to know you're safe.'

'I really must go.'

Her mum wraps her arms around her once more, tears trawling her face. But Kerry fights her own tears, refusing to let them meet her eyes. She needs to start as she means to go on. Strong. Determined. There's no doubt this will be the hardest thing she's ever done, but if anyone can discover what happened to her beautiful sister, she can.

21

Annie

'One more chapter?' I say, but Elliot lies so still, eyes closed. I rest *House of Shivers* on my knees, glance over my shoulder at the door standing ajar.

'I saw Natalie last night,' I say.

He twitches, though I'm not sure if it's a reaction to my words, or his condition.

'Do you remember that night we all hung out in Sycamore Wood telling ghost stories?' I place my hand on his arm. 'Well, she said something happened to her. Something awful.'

His eyes remain closed. He doesn't stir. And I know I can't tell him the details, that it would betray Natalie's trust.

'I thought I saw someone that night dressed in white.' It had come back to me in the early hours. 'Do you remember?'

The door swings open. Michael.

'Hello, lovely Elliot. How are we this merry morning?' He flutters his fingers at me. 'Good morning. How's our boy been?'

'Much the same,' I say, my sad tone clashing with his sparkle.

'I'll cheer him up with a bit of a song. He'll like that.' He smiles as I walk towards the door. 'Could you put the hot water on, please?'

I leave the room, head down the stairs and, once I've flicked on the boiler, I make my way into the garden.

I sometimes wonder what Mum finds to do out here when the weather's so cold, and most of the ground is iced over. But she's not working today. She's sitting on the bench at the foot of the garden, wrapped in Elliot's thick woollen coat, wearing a brightly striped bobble hat. I make my way down the long winding path towards her.

'Annie,' she says, rising and fiddling with the bird feeder. 'I've been chatting with the fairies. They've been flitting here, there and everywhere this morning. I think their wings are cold.'

If it wasn't that Mum has believed in fairies since we arrived here, I would worry. Although there's no doubting her fantasies got worse when Dad died. '*Away with the fairies,*' Elliot used to say, attempting to make light of it.

'I don't suppose you fancy a walk?' I ask. 'Michael's here, and I haven't been down to Ridgewater Cove in so long.'

She looks up at the bedroom window, to where Michael is sitting on the windowsill, a book in his hand. 'OK,' she says. 'I haven't seen the sea in some time. It will clear our heads a little.'

And I'll be able to see where my brother fell.

22

The sea is calm, frothy waves hitting icy sand. It's beautiful here. Quiet. Tourists tend to use the main beach. Not many know about Ridgewater Cove.

But the peace, the momentary serenity, doesn't last, as I look towards the cliff my brother fell from. 'Where was he found?'

Mum points towards a section of cliff, to the soft sand beneath. It's only metres away from the jagged rocks that took Giselle's life.

'Shallow water softened his fall to some extent.' Mum's voice wobbles. 'Though it's a miracle he missed the rocks.'

I look up, see the bench near the edge that's been there for years. He must have been at the far end of Sycamore Wood. What was he doing there?

'He was found just after noon.'

I don't know why; I'd always imagined it being dark. 'How long had he—?'

'A few hours they think. Thank goodness it wasn't cold.'

Mum and I sit on a rock side by side, Elliot's coat flapping at her ankles. We're silent – not awkward, just quiet – my mind travelling back twelve years to Giselle's body being found at the foot of the same cliff. An accident. Misadventure, that's what the local papers called it.

'There's something I need to tell you,' Mum says, worry in her tone. 'For a while now, someone has been hanging about the cottage. A grey-haired man.' She shudders. 'I don't know who he is, but he seems to be watching me.'

I consider her words. 'I think I saw someone too,' I say. 'He disappeared when I started to approach.'

'It must be the same person.'

'Should we call the police?'

'Yes. Next time we see him – though I doubt there's much they can do.' A beat. 'Did you meet up with Natalie last night?' Mum says, eventually.

I nod, knowing I can't tell her about Natalie's terrible experience. 'She's changed a lot.'

'I told you, didn't I?' She fiddles with her gloves, tugging at the wool, finally pulling them off and stuffing them in her pocket. 'You must have had a lot to catch up on.'

'We did, yes.'

Another short silence descends.

'Mum, what do you remember about the night Giselle died?'

'Giselle?' She turns to face me, narrows her eyes. 'What's brought this on?' She rises, heads towards the sea, and I follow, my boots sinking into the sand as I go. 'It was a long time ago.'

'But you must recall something as tragic as that.'

We've reached the water's edge. Standing together we stare out at the silver-greys and blues of the sea and sky.

I wasn't home the night Giselle died, so have no actual memories of my own. But I know what happened. Margot realised her daughter wasn't in her room and went searching for her. Found her body on the beach at the foot of the cliff. Margot was hysterical by the time the police arrived.

I recall the aftermath: police knocking on our door the following day, their cars parked up along the lane. The taping off of the route leading to Ridgewater Cove.

'I remember seeing Giselle from the lounge window,' Mum says, bringing me back to the moment. 'It was a shock, as I hadn't seen her outside for years. As you know she couldn't go out in daylight with her skin condition, but it was dark, so I assumed, at the time, that was OK. I thought she was carrying a bag but, if she was, they didn't seem to find it.' She shrugs, slips her arm through my elbow, and we start to walk by the sea, a cold wind getting up, stinging our cheeks.

'Giselle was wearing a long white dress and a white fur jacket. I couldn't see her clearly but noticed how her hair caught in our porchlight as she passed, golden, sweeping curls down her back, just like it was when she was little.' She bites her lip. 'She looked to be heading into the woods.'

A squawking seagull swoops low, startling me, then continues on its way. 'Did you see anything else?'

She shakes her head. 'I only noticed Giselle because I was pulling the curtains across at the time.'

'Didn't a dog walker see her that night?'

'Yes.' Mum stops, pulls off her boots and socks, steps into the frothy water, paddling. 'Ah! So cold!' She tiptoes out again, her feet turning pink. 'Why all the questions?'

'Do you remember who the dog walker was?'

She shakes her head, curls her toes into the sand. 'I can't recall. As I say, it was a long time ago. But I remember he said at the time that he saw someone else hanging about. Someone in a black hoodie, hood up. He couldn't give much of a description though – didn't even know whether it was a male or female.

That's why the police came knocking, asking if we'd seen anything – and, of course, when they saw Elliot's black hoodie on the peg, they asked who it belonged to, asked to speak to him. This was before her death was ruled accidental. As you know, it gave Elliot quite the scare.' She stops, tugs socks over damp, sandy feet. 'You were in town at the time.'

'Mmm, waiting for Natalie in the Fox. She never showed up.' Nothing new there, she was always unreliable.

Mum bends and picks up a shell, holds it against her ear. 'I've always thanked the fairies that the coroner declared her death accidental. If they hadn't, Elliot may have been questioned further. Or worse.' A shake of her head. 'You hear of all these miscarriages of justice.' She turns the shell over in her hands, trancelike, her tone sombre, small waves splashing her legs, dampening her socks further.

She pulls on her boots, and we make our way back. As she tugs her gloves from the pocket of Elliot's coat, a piece of paper flutters to the floor, before being chased away by an excitable wind. 'Get that, please, love. I wouldn't want to leave any litter.'

I race after it, pick it up, and shove it in my pocket.

I recall most of what Mum's just said about the night Giselle was killed, though I'm not sure I fully took it in at the time, so preoccupied with what my future held. Part of me can't help drawing a connection between Natalie's attack so close to Giselle's accident. Both young blonde women. Would the police have made more of Giselle's death had they known what happened to Natalie? Was the person in the darkness wearing a hoodie the night Giselle died connected to her death? And what was Giselle doing in Sycamore Wood? Could the hooded stranger have attacked Natalie too? I shake my head. Am I being ridiculous? But I can't ignore the feeling that something may have been missed the day Giselle died.

23

I stand at the kitchen sink washing up a couple of mugs.

I've agreed to meet Natalie at the cafe on the High Street at half eleven. '*We can sort out our plan of attack,*' she said last night, which made me uneasy. Questioning possible rapists isn't something anyone would be comfortable with, and I'm not sure what we can find out all these years later. The fact that, to my knowledge, no other attacks have been reported in Ridgewater since seems odd too. Unless whoever did it moved away. *Elliot moved away.*

I wring out the dishcloth with too much force, lay it over the taps, as Mum always does, and dry my hands. It's time to walk into Ridgewater. I make my way to the front door and shrug on my coat and woolly hat. 'I'm going out!' I yell up the stairs to where Mum's cleaning Elliot's room, not sure if she hears me.

I step into the cold morning and hurry past Sycamore House, muttering to myself, my emotions see-sawing. Most of the frost has cleared, though my cheeks tingle, my fingers numb by the time I reach town.

Natalie, tall and willowy, stands next to a sandwich board

advertising all types of coffee and declaring that friendly four-legged friends are welcome with well-behaved owners, a metal bowl full of water by the door proving their statement. Natalie, in black Doc Martens and a khaki-coloured parka, matted fur around the hood, lifts a hand in a half-hearted wave. I wave back. It's hard to believe we were so close as teenagers; it's as though I'm stepping out towards a stranger. I wonder if I even know her any more. But then how well did I know her back then?

It's as we're shuffling into the cafe's window seat that I spot Tom on the pavement opposite. He's passing a B & B, making his way towards the small Tesco's. My stomach gives a little flutter. 'I will call you,' I whisper.

'Sorry?' Natalie says, and I return my gaze to see her drop her black-cased phone face down on the table with a clatter.

'Nothing,' I say. 'I saw someone I know, is all.'

She winds her way towards the counter, glancing back and saying, 'I'll get the drinks in,' clearly not interested in who I saw. I imagine her head is crammed with plans to track down potential... what? Witnesses? Suspects? A fizz of anxiety – this all feels wrong. I wouldn't be equipped for this at the best of times, and surely neither is Natalie, who has been through the worst experience anyone could imagine without support.

I glance again through the window at the pretty street with its boutiques and art shops and I know I should go back to Fairy Cottage, support Mum and Elliot, and that Natalie should be seeking help for her trauma, not searching for her attacker. Her goal to find him – come face to face with the man who ruined her life – can only end in disaster, surely.

'Cake?' she calls from the counter. 'Blueberry muffin?'

I shake my head. I do have a weakness for cakes, but I'm not hungry, my stomach's churning. 'Just a mug of tea, thanks.'

* * *

Natalie thumps my tea down in front of me, spilling some onto the table. I grab a napkin and mop up the brown liquid. She sits down, scratches her scalp.

'There are things. In here.' She bangs her head, as though the action will open it up, and all the evidence will spill out. 'Things hiding just out of sight. I'm hoping once we start picking off the layers of that night, things will come back to me. But at the moment I have nothing.'

'This must be so awful for you.'

'It's crap times a thousand.'

I pick up my tea, take a sip. 'Where do we start?'

'Well, we saw Aiden and his brother that night hanging about.'

'We don't know for sure it was his brother, do we?'

She shrugs. 'It must have been.'

'And you're really OK with seeing Aiden again?'

'I'll do anything it takes to find out who attacked me. And I need to talk to Seb Blair. He might remember something.'

Truth is, I haven't had any contact with Seb for years, and I'm pretty sure once Elliot moved to Scotland, he lost contact with his friend too. I noticed, when I walked by earlier, that his father's butcher shop has been replaced by a branch of White Stuff. Trying to find Seb may be impossible, particularly with the ever-changing faces of Ridgewater.

'I'll ask my mum if she knows where Seb is now,' I say.

She pulls a small silver flask from her bag, splashes clear liquid into her coffee. 'No need. I've been through the files at the vet's.'

'What?'

'I thought it was the best way to see if either Aiden or Seb still live in Ridgewater – obviously only useful if they've got a pet.'

'Well, I guess so, but surely the files are confidential.'

'I don't care. Let them sack me. Let them report me.' She takes a long gulp of her coffee, and I notice how dilated her pupils are. 'Anyway, they won't do any of that because they don't know. And, more importantly, Seb has a dog, and he still lives in Ridgewater.'

'OK, well that's promising, I guess.'

'It's a cockerpoo. One of those cute dogs everyone seems to have these days. It's only ever been in for vaccinations, and that was long before I got a job there.'

I can't help thinking she won't have a job there for much longer if they catch her dipping into private files. 'And Aiden?'

'Still lives in Branson Drive – got a cat according to the records – or his father has, and if Aiden's moved out, Lance Shaw is bound to know where his son is. But let's visit Seb first. He lives at 46 Railway Street.' She takes another gulp of her coffee. 'Drink up, we need to pay him a visit.'

My stomach turns over once more as I blow steam from my tea. Natalie is eager to get this visit over with, but the thought of seeing Seb after so long is making me super-anxious. Especially with the questions Natalie has in mind.

* * *

'What are we going to say to him?' I say as I follow Natalie down the road, struggling to keep up with her long strides.

'First, we'll ask him what he remembers about the night it happened.' She sounds brusque, as though she's a police officer dealing with a case that has nothing to do with her.

'Well, we know he went after you. Said he was going to make sure you got home OK.'

She stops, and I slam into her back. 'He went after me?' She turns to face me. 'You never told me that.'

'I never got to tell you anything at the time, you wouldn't speak to me, remember? And I had no idea what happened to you. Anyway, I've only just remembered. He didn't want you to walk home alone and took off after you. But it doesn't mean—'

'No, you're right. It doesn't mean anything. But he may have seen someone or something. Something he thought meant nothing.'

And then it hits me. 'Like a ghost.'

'A ghost?'

'I saw something that night. Something white, juddering through the trees. Except then I doubted myself, thought I'd imagined it. What if—?'

'It's definitely worth putting in the file.'

'File?'

'Yes, I've got a file.' She continues past the deserted park, where swings creak in the wind, and turns the corner onto Railway Street.

I have no idea what to say.

The road is made up of pretty Victorian terraced houses, one side crammed with cars, the other striped with double yellow lines. A sporty-green Mini catches my eye, parked outside number forty-six.

The bay window of Seb's house has wooden slatted blinds. A metal gate opens onto a short, black and white tiled path leading to the front door. Natalie wastes no time in ringing the bell, and a dog – the cockapoo, I suspect – goes frantic behind the door. I hover behind Natalie, still unsure of what she's going to say – how she's going to cope – and I'm beginning to wonder what the hell I'm doing here.

An attractive woman in her thirties, blue-eyed with dark hair tied back in a sleek, shiny ponytail, answers, a toddler in a Bluey sweatshirt perched on her hip. The cute doodle is behind a stairgate across the lounge door, barking, leaping so high I wonder if it's going to spring over in a moment and out through the front door.

'Hang on.' The woman closes the door on us for a few moments. 'Bingo is quite the little monkey,' she says on her return, the dog still barking behind a closed internal door. 'What can I do for you?' She's well-spoken, highly made-up, her clothes – a figure-hugging tracksuit and trainers – look to be designer.

'My name is Natalie Ford, and we're looking for Seb Blair.' Natalie's tone is sharp, abrupt. She's not coming across well.

The woman narrows her eyes. 'Can I ask what this is about?'

'We knew Seb when we were teenagers.' Natalie attempts a smile at the toddler, who buries her face into her mum's shoulder. 'We're back in the area hoping to track down a few old friends for... a reunion. We had some great times with Seb.'

'Seb didn't like school,' the woman says. 'I can't imagine him being interested.' The little girl squirms and the woman hitches her further up her hip. 'Anyway, he's in his workshop out back and doesn't like being disturbed.' She puts the child down, takes hold of her small hand. 'If you leave your number, I'll get him to call you.'

Natalie looks at me and back at the woman. 'Is there any chance you could let him know we are here?' she says, pressing her palms together. 'Please.'

The woman seems indecisive. She fiddles with the little

girl's blonde topknot for a few moments, before saying, 'Well, if you tell me your names again, I'll tell him you are here. Let him decide.'

'This is Annie Blake,' Natalie says. 'And I'm Natalie Ford.'

The woman closes the door, leaving us on the step.

'Do you think he'll talk to us?' I say, moving from foot to foot, full of anxiety and a desperate urge to run.

'If he's got nothing to hide, he will.'

'So, if he comes to the door, we can cross him off our list?' The fact I've created a list of suspects in my head bothers me.

'No,' she says. 'It could be he'll speak to us because he needs to put his cover story in place.'

'He can't win, then.'

The door swings open. To say the last twelve years have been good to Seb would be an understatement. His stance alone oozes confidence, and that beard he was attempting to grow when he was younger, well he's managed it, and it suits him, dark and close shaven. Wood shavings are caught in his brown hair. Even his skin is clear of boyhood acne.

'Seb,' I say, struggling to keep the bewilderment from my voice. *Is it really you?* 'How are you?'

He pushes up the sleeves of his checked shirt, revealing firm arms, tasteful tattoos, and I find myself noticing how tight it fits across the shoulders. *Jesus, Annie, quit with the ogling.*

'Annie,' he says, stepping out of the doorway, and air-kissing my cheeks. 'I heard about Elliot's accident. I'm so sorry.' *No stutter?*

'Thank you. We're hoping he'll make a full recovery,' I say. 'But it's awful seeing him in such a way.'

'I can imagine. We lost touch when he moved away – Scotland, wasn't it? But I've been meaning to call round. I haven't seen him in so long.'

'He'd like that.'

'I'll make it a priority.'

'So, how are you?'

He glances back into the house. 'Been busy. You met my wife, Sasha, and little Megan. Ben is at school.' He sounds proud. 'When people say they grow so fast, they really mean it.'

I feel Natalie's eyes on me, willing me to bring her into the conversation.

'Seb, do you remember Natalie?' I say, gesturing towards her.

His eyes move to meet hers. 'Yes, yes of course.' He sticks out his hand for her to shake. She stares down at it. Makes no attempt to take it. He looks puzzled for a moment, then drops his hand to his side. 'I think we met a few times many years ago.' He turns back to me. 'Listen, do you want to come in? We can chat properly. It would be great to hear what you've been up to.'

'Yes.' Natalie stares my way. There's no mistaking the sudden anger in her eyes. 'Good idea.'

24

Natalie and I sit one each end of a sofa in a long lounge. Bingo, who barked non-stop as we entered the house, is now stretched in front of a flickering gas fire.

The room is beautifully decorated, the chimney breast wall in a rich blue with an expensive-looking antique mirror hanging above the fire. The other walls are pale grey, adorned with paintings of Ridgewater: Ridgewater Cove, the river, the High Street, Sycamore Wood, all signed Sasha Blair.

The pale parquet floor is strewn with toys that Seb is presently picking up and throwing into a stunning hand-built wooden toy box with the name Megan on the side.

'I'm heading out, my love.' It's Sasha in a crimson coat and high boots, standing in the hallway with the toddler, who's wearing a woolly hat and a pink, hooded coat, snuggled in a pushchair.

'Don't be long, sweetie,' Seb calls after her as she disappears from view. 'We're visiting Dad later, don't forget.'

As the door closes, I say, for something to say, 'She seems nice.'

'She is. I don't know what I would do without her.' He throws a plastic doll with tangled hair into the box with a clatter and closes the lid. 'Can I get you ladies a drink? Coffee? Tea?'

We shake our heads. 'We've just had some at the cafe,' I say.

He drops down into the armchair. 'It's good to actually stop for a moment,' he says. 'The business has really taken off. I could do with two pairs of hands.' He pauses. 'So, what about you ladies? Married? Kids?'

Natalie tenses beside me. She can't think Seb attacked her, surely? We're here to find out if he saw or heard anything that night.

'I guess I've been married to my job all these years,' I say, my eyes still on Natalie. She's agitated. I can feel it.

'Did you get to fulfil your dream, Annie?' Seb asks.

'Well, I'm a doctor.' *No longer a dream.* I'm aware I sound stilted and feel bad. This man has invited us in, and we're not being completely honest.

'Elliot used to go on and on about how clever you were,' he says.

'Did he?' I wave away the compliment, a surge of sadness following an initial burst of joy that Elliot was proud of me.

'Oh yeah. As you know, he was great with his hands but wished he had a brain like yours, his dyslexia holding him back.' He smiles. 'Are you sure I can't get you ladies anything?'

'Honestly, I'm good, thanks.' A silent pause. 'How's your dad? I noticed the shop's closed,' I say, willing Natalie to join in, but she's withdrawn into herself, arms folded around her like a straitjacket. Has she remembered something?

'Yeah,' Seb says. 'My dad's now in Ridgewater Care Home. He stopped working in the shop years ago. And being vegetarian, I wasn't about to take over. When I met Sasha, she gave me the strength to do what I wanted to do with my life.'

'Your business?'

'That's right.'

Natalie jerks towards the edge of the sofa, as though she's going to spring to her feet and pounce.

Seb glances at Natalie out of the corner of his eye. She's unsettling him. 'Remember how Elliot and I studied woodwork at A Level?'

I nod, although truth is I only recall my brother taking the course.

'Well, I ventured into making bespoke furniture eight years ago, and eventually my business took off. I even hire three staff members – though they only do the basics. Couldn't be happier.' His smile is wide, and I'm pleased for him, can't imagine he had anything to do with Natalie's attack, but she's fidgeting, crossing and uncrossing her arms. She wants me to talk about *that* night.

'Do you remember the night, twelve years ago, that we all met up with Elliot at the Fox,' she says. 'Then went to Sycamore Wood?'

He nods slowly. 'I do, yes. We were all a bit worse for wear, if my memory serves me right.' I pick up on a slight stutter – he hasn't lost it completely. 'Elliot tried to freak us out with his ghost stories.'

Natalie pushes her fingers through her short hair.

'Is everything OK?' Seb asks, furrowing his forehead. 'You don't look too well. Would you like a glass of water?'

'Do you recall going after Natalie when she stormed off?' I say.

'Vaguely.' He shrugs, stares at Natalie. 'But I lost sight of you. Went home.' He pauses for a moment, before returning his eyes to me. 'What's this about? You both seem a bit tense.'

Natalie rises to her feet. 'We should probably go. My head is thumping.'

I rise too, feeling a darkness fall on the room. 'It's just, do you remember anything odd? Anything at all?'

He rubs a hand across his chin. 'God it was so long ago.' He pauses to think. 'Yeah, now I come to think about it. There was something.'

'Go on.'

'A noise. Twigs crunching under heavy feet. I thought it was you, Natalie, so followed the sound. Called your name a couple of times. But...' He rubs a hand across his neck, shakes his head. 'I never saw anyone. Properly freaked me out at the time. Must have been an animal, I guess. I legged it after that.'

Natalie glares at him. 'You left me.'

'No, it wasn't like that. I thought you were long gone.'

There's a silence for several moments before I say, 'Well, thanks for chatting with us, Seb.' I sound breezy – overcompensating. 'Once Elliot is well, we'll have to go out sometime.'

'Sounds good.' He rises too. 'And I'll pop round to see him, if that's OK.'

'He'd like that.'

'It was nice seeing you again, Annie. I know we didn't know each other that well, but I always had a soft spot for you. Like a little sister.' He looks towards Natalie, who is making a beeline for the front door. 'Is she OK?' he whispers, and I nod, though I know she's far from it.

It's as we step out of the front door that Seb hands me his card. 'Keep in touch,' he says. 'My number's on there.'

'Thanks,' I say, looking down at the card:

The Wooden Man – bespoke furniture for all tastes.

25

'Are you OK?' I call, struggling to keep up with Natalie as she dashes down the road towards the town centre. Breathless, I reach for her arm.

She stops, looks down at her feet, shaking her head. 'I'm not going to say that was easy. I kept...' Her voice is full of tears. 'I kept wondering if it was him, you know.'

'Was there something specific about him?' *Please don't let it be Seb.*

She shakes her head. 'Nothing. It's just... it *could* be him – he came after me that night.'

We've come to a halt next to the park, which is still empty. 'Let's sit down for a minute, shall we?' I point towards a bench near a willow tree next to the river, and we make our way past brightly coloured play equipment and sit down, leaving a small distance between us that feels like an ocean.

'Are you sure you still want to do this?' I say, leaning over and placing my hand over hers.

'I have to.' A tear rolls down her cheek, and she wipes it away with her free hand. 'I have to know who wrecked my life.

It's eating me alive. You have to understand I've been haunted by this for twelve years. I need to be brave. Face this head on. Kill my demons.'

'But will putting a face to... well, will it help?'

'Christ knows.' She rams her face into her palms, and I place my hand on her arm, not sure if knowing who violated her is going to make the pain go away. I ask myself if she's being amazingly strong, brave, or is she so damaged by what happened she no longer sees things clearly? I try hard to put myself in her position, but I'm not Natalie. I have no idea how the enormity of what happened to her would affect me – has affected her. All I can do is support her.

'We need to speak to the Turnaround Man.' Her voice is calmer, her tears drying on her cheeks.

'Colin Blair?'

'Mmm. If we visit him, he'll be able to tell us more about Seb, what he was like when he was younger.'

'And that will help?'

'Yes, if we know what he was like as a child we can get a better profile of the man he's become. Colin will be able to help us with that.'

She sounds like someone preparing for a crime podcast. I'm lost for words.

'And we could talk to Sasha too. There was something odd there, don't you think?'

I shrug. 'I thought they seemed a normal happy family.'

'What with all that "sweetie" and "my love"? Nobody behaves like that in the real world.' A beat. 'Listen, are you free tomorrow to visit Ridgewater Care Home?'

'I'm not sure—'

'It will have to be in the afternoon, as I'm doing overtime in the morning. Please.'

'OK. I can pick you up from the vet's if you like. The home is a bit of a way out.'

'Great.' She gets to her feet. 'Thanks, Annie,' she says, walking away, leaving me sitting alone on the bench. And as she disappears into the distance, I feel confused and bewildered. It seems I'm trapped in Natalie's quest for justice, with no way of escaping.

* * *

I spend the afternoon in Ridgewater, feeling guilty that I'm avoiding going back to Fairy Cottage. The sight of my brother so lifeless upsets me each time I see him, but it's not only that. I need space. I don't go in any shops, just stroll along looking in the windows at the designer clothing and expensive art, spotting a painting by Sasha Blair in one of the windows.

I end up on the picturesque walk by the river. There's been another flurry of snow, and the scene looks like a Christmas card. My thoughts carry me along, re-treading my journey since I arrived here: Tom, Mum, Elliot, Natalie, Seb and Sasha, and of course, Margot. And, suddenly, almost as though I've entered a dream, a child skips up and down the whitened verge next to the river. She's six, maybe seven. Laughing. The fading rays of sunshine picking out the gold in her hair. *Giselle.*

'Rebecca, come on, or we'll be late,' a woman calls, and the child – so like my childhood friend at that age – races towards her mother.

The winter sun, low in the sky, drifts behind a heavy grey cloud. It's getting colder, snow-laden branches tower over me, dusk hovers, it will be getting dark soon. It's time to head back.

* * *

The lane leading to Fairy Cottage is lonely this time of day, and my phone torch barely penetrates the darkness. The drop in temperature is shiver-worthy. It's making my bones ache, my toes and fingers numb. It's almost four-thirty, and I'll be glad to get back to the cottage, thoughts of the roaring fire in the grate spurring me on.

I flick my torch across the trees, my footfalls crunching in the silence.

A flicker of light. Quick steps. Someone's approaching, their torch so much brighter than mine, the glare making me squint.

'Annie, you gave me quite a start!' It's Margot, dressed immaculately in a belted beige woollen coat, and heeled boots that look hazardous to wear on icy ground. Apple-red lips shining in the torchlight.

'Hey,' I say. 'How's things?'

'Good, thank you, dear.' She drops the beam of her torch towards the ground, picking out fallen sticks glistening with frost. 'Where have you been all day?'

I'm taken aback that she not only knows I've been out most of the day but that she's demanding a reason. Her steady eyes fix on mine, and a chill snakes down my spine. She has a weird sort of power over me I can't seem to shake free of, even in adulthood.

'I met a friend for coffee,' I say. 'Then went for a walk. Lost track of time.' *You're talking too fast.*

'Well, I'm off to the tiny Tesco to buy a bottle of wine. I fancy treating myself. I don't suppose you'd like to join me?'

'Mum's expecting me, I'm afraid.' It's not a complete lie. Mum texted me earlier asking where I'd got to, and I really need to get back. Not only that, I'm dying for a pee. The cold is playing havoc with my bladder.

Margot smiles. 'Actually, I'm glad I caught you. I wondered if you would like to come round for a meal later in the week.'

'I...'

She touches my cheek with her leather-gloved hand, and I freeze. 'You know, I can't believe my Giselle would be your age now,' she says. 'I wonder what she would be doing, had she lived.' A beat. 'You will come, won't you?'

It's emotional blackmail. But I sense the woman is desperately lonely. I try one more attempt to get out of it, 'It's just, I'm helping Mum with Elliot.'

'Surely if you can find time to go for walks and have coffee with friends...' She removes her hand from my cheek, narrows her eyes. 'I hope you're not making excuses, dear.'

My sympathy dwindles. 'No, no of course not.'

'Then you'll come to dinner?'

I'm silent for a moment, attempting to fumble together another excuse. But then the child in me is curious. The house I was forbidden to go into – had only glimpsed through the window – beckons me in. And, on a more level-headed note, maybe it would be another chance to talk to Margot about my father. I'll never believe she was having an affair with him.

'Annie?'

'OK. Yes, thank you.'

'Good.' She struts onwards, glancing back just once. 'Friday at 7 p.m. OK? I thought I might cook duck à l'orange.'

I haven't eaten duck since Mum kept a couple in the garden when I was a child. 'Lovely,' I call after her, feeling my stomach churn.

I reach the end of the lane and head past Sycamore House, imagining Giselle waving to me from one of the many windows.

26

I push open the front door, and step into the hallway, passing Michael on his way out.

'Bye, lovely,' he says, with a flamboyant wave of his hand. 'Your brother's seemed content this afternoon.'

'That's good.' *Though I'm not sure how you can tell.*

'Annie, is that you?' Mum calls from the lounge, and Michael leaves, closing the door behind him.

'Yes, it's me.' *If you kept the house locked, you wouldn't need to ask.*

I take off my boots and hang up my coat, glancing up the stairs before heading to where Mum is sitting crocheting the tiniest woollen hats. She doesn't look up, her red hair unruly, tendrils escaping her ponytail hanging about her face. She's always made hats and little jackets – leaves them out on the rocks where I'm sure some bird or animal takes them, or perhaps they simply blow away in the wind; they're certainly not taken by her non-existent fairy friends.

I crouch down by the fire, rubbing my hands together to warm them. 'How's Elliot?'

She puts down the wool. 'Silent. Still. The physiotherapist came.' She narrows her eyes, and, after a long beat, tilts her head, 'Where have you been?'

I'm not a child. I don't have to explain my every move. Except something in her eyes tells me I do. 'I met up with Natalie again. We went to see Seb Blair.'

'Elliot's old friend?'

'Yes.' I rise, turn my back on the fire, avoiding Mum's glare by sliding my eyes to the multicoloured wool in the basket at her feet. 'He's married, with a little girl and boy.'

'I know,' she says. 'I've seen him from time to time over the years. He's a carpenter, isn't he?'

I nod. 'Doing well for himself.'

'Well, I'm pleased for him. Always liked the boy. Poor thing suffered a lot at the hands of bullies, especially that awful Aiden Shaw.' She shakes her head. 'Tragic, after what happened to his mother. Makes my stomach turn to think of how she died. You know that's why Colin Blair did that odd thing of turning in the street.'

I feel a sudden pang of guilt that Natalie and I are visiting the man tomorrow. 'I heard.'

'It was the trauma, you see. He never got over it.'

'What happened to Seb's mother?' I ask, curious. 'I know she took her own life, but...'

'Tablets,' she says, sniffing and wiping at her nose. 'So sad. Seb and his dad found her.' She picks up her crocheting and continues twisting the wool into hats. 'Seb seems to have come to terms with it all now.'

'Yes. He seems happy,' I say.

27

Kerry stares at the small plane on the digital screen in front of her, making its way from Singapore to Heathrow. She's on the second leg of her journey to the UK. Her quest to search for her sister. Her stomach churns.

She spent two hours at Singapore Airport thinking of Fi – her sometimes bossy but always caring older sister, who took off travelling alone on a gap year. '*I'll miss you so much,*' she'd said over twelve years ago, planting a kiss on Kerry's cheek, then hugging her close, and she can almost feel those arms around her now. '*I'll phone and message whenever I can.*'

Kerry bats away tears and heaves her travel bag from under the seat in front. She pulls out the card the children had made at the primary school where she works:

Have a lovely time, Miss Brewster.

She'd explained to the principal that she had to go to the UK, that she would have to resign. He'd asked why, and once he knew he told her to go, that he would get a supply teacher to cover. *'Good luck,'* he'd said.

She pushes the card, flaky with over-dry paint, back in her bag and pulls out her Kindle – reading will keep her mind focused. She's about to turn it on when the drinks trolley pulls up level with her. She reaches in her bag for her purse, takes out her debit card. 'White wine, please,' she says, and the air steward hands her a plastic bottle, a cup balancing on top.

She pours the wine and takes a sip, winces, not much of a drinker – her diabetes making her cautious, and seeing her mum lose herself down a bottle most nights after Fi disappeared putting her off alcohol. But it will hopefully settle her bubbling nerves, a feeling she doesn't recognise. She takes another sip, annoyed with herself that this journey is so much harder than she ever imagined. She'd thought she would cope, despite never flying before. But the whole experience of travelling so far, alone, treading in Fi's footsteps... well, being confident and self-assured within your comfort zone is totally different from this.

Pull yourself together.

She thinks about her father, how she's ignored his calls, given blunt replies to his messages over the years. Should she have told him she was coming to the UK? He may have come with her. No, he abandoned her, leaving her to live with a mother who was falling apart.

The woman next to her is snoring as she breathes in and out, a mask, crooked, over her eyes. In fact, fifty percent of the passengers are sleeping. There's another four hours until the plane lands at Heathrow. 10 p.m. UK time. She's booked a room at an airport hotel, will catch the Elizabeth line into central London first thing in the morning to Paddington Station. There she'll begin her journey to Devon.

She yawns, finishes the wine. Drops her Kindle back into her bag, abandoning her idea to read. She doesn't really need Riley Sager's latest thriller freaking her out right now. She needs sleep. She moves her seat back a couple of inches, rests her head and closes her eyes.

She still has a long journey ahead of her, but as soon as the plane lands, she'll channel her confident self once more – she has to, for Fi.

28

Annie

I lie on my bed, propped up against the wooden headboard, attempting to read the book I picked up at the bookshop, but my thoughts keep drifting to Giselle. Could I have made more of an effort to stay friendly with my once best friend all those years ago? I try telling myself that eleven-year-old me is another me, a stranger now who I barely recognise. A child just starting secondary school. A child on the cusp of growing up. A time when it was about fighting for survival in a strange new world full of hormones, boys and acne. And it isn't like I didn't try. Margot wouldn't let me inside the house, so any contact between me and Giselle was strictly through a half-opened door.

I shake away any regret, though thoughts of Giselle still niggle. I want to know more about her skin condition, why she suddenly couldn't come out in sunlight. I key 'xeroderma pigmentosum' into a Google search on my phone, and I'm right that symptoms usually appear by the time a child is two years old. Odd. It doesn't make sense. Perhaps her condition wasn't xeroderma pigmentosum. Maybe it was something rarer and she was misdiagnosed? Or had it all been a lie? No, it couldn't have been, I saw the welts on Giselle's face through the window, they were horrific.

The book I'd forgotten I was holding slips from my hand and clatters to the floor. Sighing, I slide down the headboard and press my head against the pillow, closing my eyes, knowing sleep won't come.

29

After a restless night, and a morning spent helping Mum and sitting with my brother, I head to the veterinary surgery. It's almost one o'clock when I drive into the car park. Natalie flies across the tarmac towards me and, before I can kill the engine, flings open the passenger door and flumps down into the seat. 'Hey!' she says, clicking the seatbelt.

I stare at her profile, her pallid skin, her tense jaw. 'Are you sure you want to go to the care home?'

'Yes. Why?' She turns, glares my way as though I suggested chopping off her head.

'I'm still unsure what you hope to gain from seeing Colin Blair.' My hands clench around the steering wheel. I can't help feeling that disturbing him is unfair. 'It's just... I'm worried about you.'

She clenches her fists. 'Don't be.' She turns to face the windscreen once more. 'This is what I want, Annie. What I need to do.'

'I understand, but should we really be playing detective with something as awful, as devastating, as what happened to you?' I can tell I'm not getting through. She's going to go. And at least if I go with her, I can limit any damage to her, to Colin.

'It's like I said before,' she says. 'The Turnaround Man can tell us about Seb's childhood.'

The stony look on my old friend's face tells me to drive. And despite everything inside me crying out not to go to the care home, I pull onto the road in its direction.

There's a chill in the car as I drive, despite the heater on full.

'Seb's mother took her own life,' Natalie says.

'Yes, I'm aware of that.'

'Seb was bullied as a kid and in his teens.'

'Where is this going?'

'And he worked in his dad's butcher shop. What I'm saying is, he's a criminal psychologist's dream.'

I can't think how to respond – she's building her so-called profile of Seb with absolutely no qualifications or skills to back it up. A thick silence falls, cloaking the rest of the journey.

'Here we are.' I indicate to pull onto the drive leading to the care home. A large Victorian house is the main building, the rest, extensions added in what feels like no particular plan, I'm guessing from the sixties onwards.

Natalie snaps free of her seatbelt and flings the car door open. I kill the engine.

'So, what are we going to ask him?' I say, my thudding heart telling me this is *such* a bad idea.

'We'll ask him if he came looking for Seb that night.'

'What? What has that got to do with anything?'

'He knew where we were going, Annie. Seb called him, remember?'

'You can't think it was Seb's father.'

'He was odd.'

'That doesn't make him—'

'We can't be sure. We need to be meticulous. No stone unturned, that's what they say, isn't it?'

I'm beginning to realise she isn't functioning normally – though it's hardly surprising.

She gets out of the car. Slams the door.

I take a long deep breath, get out too, lock up. She stares at me long and hard, arms folded tight across her body, a black jacket and black trousers making her look thinner than ever.

'Can't you see, Annie,' she says. 'If I can prove Seb or Colin attacked me, that lets Elliot off the hook.'

What? I feel sick and my heartbeat quickens. This is too much. 'Elliot was never *on* the hook. He didn't attack you, and...' I want to say neither did Seb, but I'm suddenly unsure. Does he fit the profile? *Christ! Who the hell do I think I am, judging him? This is getting so out of hand.*

'Then I'll say it again,' she says. 'Help me find out who did.' She shrugs. 'You don't have to come in with me. Wait in the car if you like. But I'm going, with or without you.'

I'm so close to getting back in the car, but I worry about her going in alone. What she might say to Colin. She strides towards the entrance, determination in every step. I have to go with her, if only to protect the man from her possible allegations.

A man in a blue polo shirt helping an elderly man into a wheelchair lets us in and points us towards the reception desk.

'We're here to see Colin Blair,' Natalie says to the woman behind the counter.

'Are you family?'

'Old friends,' Natalie says, tilting her head. 'I went to school with his son, Seb.'

'Well, Colin is in his room at the moment.' She pushes

forward a guest book. 'Please sign in and include your car registration.' She hands Natalie a pen and we fill in the book. 'Abdul,' the woman calls to a young man coming through a door. 'Could you take these ladies up to see Colin Blair?'

'Sure,' he says, approaching.

Abdul is smiley, chatting away about the cold weather, his love of skiing, and the latest Marvel film as we travel to the first floor by lift. We follow him along a corridor. He stops about halfway down, taps on a door with a laminated card Blu-Tacked to it with Colin's name on.

I take a deep breath. I have little memory of the man behind the door. Mum has never eaten meat, so as children we didn't go into his shop, though I do recall the animal carcasses hanging from hooks in the window, the slightly metallic smell of them turning my stomach. As for Colin, he was tall and thin and wore a mac when he was out and about, even on sunny days – and, of course, he always took three steps forward, turned around, took two steps back.

Colin sits in an armchair facing the door, the light of the window behind him giving him an almost angelic glow.

'Visitors,' Abdul says, beaming at the man with thinning grey hair, wearing striped pyjamas.

'Is it my wife?' Colin asks, looking from Natalie to me. And it hits me in seconds: this man has dementia. We need to leave. Now!

'Not this time, mate. This is...' Abdul turns to us, as though waiting for us to speak.

'I'm Elliot's sister, Annie,' I say, directing my words at Colin. 'Elliot went to school with your son Seb.'

'So, my wife's not here yet?'

'Not right now.'

'Come closer. I can't quite see you,' he says.

I look back to see Abdul disappearing through the open door and Natalie frozen next to a cheap teak chest of drawers, her hand placed against the wood as though she's holding herself up. It seems I needn't have worried what she might say. She's clearly not about to speak up any time soon.

The man beckons me with his slim finger, and I approach and sit down.

A photograph in a plastic frame sits next to the bed. In the picture is an attractive woman, a little dark-haired boy I know must be Seb, and a much younger, smiling version of Colin that I barely recognise.

I look again at Natalie, who is fiddling with her phone, her body tense, then back to Colin. 'Do you see much of Seb?' I ask him, for something to say.

He shakes his head. 'He never visits.'

'What about Sasha?'

'His wife? Yes, she came yesterday with my son.'

My heart goes out to the man, and I turn to Natalie and shake my head. Try to tell her we're wasting our time. We'll find out nothing here. That this poor man has lost his way, past and present tangled inside his head.

'Do you know if my wife is coming?' he asks, brown eyes fixed on me, and a surge of tears prod, so close to the surface. Life's an absolute bitch.

'I'm sorry I don't,' I say. I know enough about dementia to be aware that telling him his wife is long dead isn't the answer. 'I'm sure she'll be here soon.' I pat his hand gently before rising to my feet. 'It was nice talking with you, Mr Blair.'

'Colin. Call me Colin. And it was nice talking to you too, dear lady.' He takes my hand as I'm about to walk away. 'Thank you for coming.'

'You're welcome.' My eyes continue to burn. This is one of

the cruellest of diseases, and here we are disturbing him for no reason I can understand. There's no connection between Natalie's attack and this man, I'm certain of it.

'I know you, don't I?' he says suddenly, narrowing his eyes at Natalie. 'My son liked you. He had a picture of you on his wall.'

Natalie's eyes widen.

'Christina,' he says. 'That's it. Christina Aguilera. Nice to meet you, Christina.'

He moves his gaze to me, worries his lower lip. 'He hurt her, you know.'

'Who did, Colin?'

'He hurt her, and she couldn't cope any more. She should have told me.' His eyes glaze over, and I can see I've lost him.

I head for the door, reach for Natalie's arm and yank her with me as I leave the room. 'That was bloody intrusive,' I say, as we head for the lifts. I'm angry with her. Angry with myself. The man is in a poor way. 'What did you think you'd discover?'

I press the lift button with three thumps of my thumb.

'I told you earlier, I thought if we spoke to him, we'd get an insight into what Seb was like as a child, how he's been over the last twelve years. How he's transformed himself, you know.' She shakes her head, seems vulnerable. 'I had no idea he had dementia. I'm so sorry. My thinking is all over the place. Dragging you to see the man was unforgiveable. I'm an idiot.'

'Not an idiot,' I say, calming down as the lift doors slide open and we step inside. 'And I'm sorry for getting so angry. But I seriously don't know what we can do now.'

'I'm not giving up,' she says. 'I need to see Aiden.'

My heart sinks, and as we travel down in the lift, I silently cry. I don't want to be in Ridgewater. Or in London, come to that. I want to be miles away from here. To get on a plane and head for the furthest country I can think of – run away. But I know I can't, because Mum, Elliot and now Natalie need me. All three of them leaning on an already broken reed.

As we leave the lift and make our way to reception to sign out, my phone pings. I pull it from my pocket. Stop to look at the screen. It's Tom:

> Hey, I don't want to be one of 'those' guys and keep pushing, but I enjoyed our evening together and wondered if you fancied a quick drink. No strings, I promise. It's just it would be great to see you again. Tom.

I really should ignore his text. I've got enough to think about right now. But I'm struggling to keep things together and a few hours with Tom could help stabilise me. I stare at the screen, recalling how upbeat he was that night in the One Trick Pony, how he chased away my anxiety, albeit for a short time. On impulse, I tap the screen, answering his message:

> Sounds good x

His reply came through within moments, lighting up my phone screen:

> Great. A drink tonight? X

I shove my phone back in my pocket. I'll reply later.

As I walk towards reception, passing a white-haired woman sitting on a sofa reading, and noticing Natalie exiting through the main door, I hear someone singing in the near distance. It's coming from inside one of the rooms.

'Sugar and spice and all things nice, that's what little girls are made of. Slugs and snails and puppy-dog tails, that's what little boys are made of.'

'Someone sounds happy,' I say to the woman sitting on the sofa.

She leans forward, 'Joan Bancroft,' she says in a gossipy tone. 'She likes to sing.'

Joan Bancroft? Margot's mother?

A crash, and Joan yells, 'Get out! Piss off! I don't want you here.'

'She's in her nineties. Has dementia and can be quite aggressive on occasions.' The woman closes her Stephen King book with a snap. 'Always been a bitch.'

'I'm pretty sure I live next door to her daughter,' I say, almost certain there's a connection.

'Margot?'

'That's right. Do you know Joan well?'

She pats the sofa beside her, and I feel obliged to sit down. 'We were friends at school in the nineteen-thirties,' she says, her voice a little croaky. 'Were friends into our twenties. Then met again in here. Not that I've ever liked her. So, you know Margot? She comes here sometimes. I'm Agnes, by the way.'

'Annie. Nice to meet you.'

She taps my arm with a frail hand. 'When Joan was young, she dreamt of being a ballerina, but she was far too dumpy. Am I allowed to say that?' She shakes her head, her white hair, thick with hair spray, barely moving. 'And those older brothers of hers ridiculed her something chronic. Called her some nasty names. They died, all three of them, in World War Two. Joan told me once she was pleased they were dead. Relieved they wouldn't be back. I think she thought her parents would lavish their affection on her. But it wasn't to be. Her parents went into decline, mourning the loss of their sons. They didn't pay Joan the attention she desperately craved. And boy did she crave it. She was eighteen when her parents died. Pop. Pop. One after the other. Heartbreak, they say. Joan blamed her brothers for their death.'

'So, she ended up alone in that big house?'

'It turned her brain. When Margot was born, it was clear by the time she was two that she was beautiful, willowy, everything Joan wasn't. So, Joan began living vicariously through her daughter. Margot would fulfil all of Joan's dreams. I think she planned that she would, long before the girl was born. I mean she named the girl Margot after the famous ballet dancer.'

'And Margot's father?'

'Some local Joan met when she was in her forties. He stayed around for a couple of years but took off when Joan got pregnant again.' She pauses for a long moment. 'It's Joan's son I felt so sorry for. Young Joel. He came here a few years back.' She flaps her hand. 'What a commotion that was. I was sitting in this exact spot when I overheard two nurses discussing how he told his mother he was glad she's not dead, that dementia was a far more fitting punishment. He was banned from seeing her again.' The woman – Agnes – suddenly rises. 'Anyway, dear,' she says, now leaning against a walking frame. 'I'll love you and leave you as I have my yoga class in five. I can't sit here all day, gossiping.'

30

The train pulls into an old-fashioned station at Ridgewater with a squeal of brakes. Kerry's exhausted.

She steps onto the platform, her eyes swimming over the red brick building, the dark green paintwork, as she struggles to take in how far she's come.

She shivers as the train pulls away. Alone on the platform, imagining Fi standing in this same spot twelve years ago. Had her sister really come here to meet The Wooden Man?

She pulls her jacket around her and winds round her neck the long stripy scarf her mum knitted, the fabric softener she always uses making her feel homesick. It feels bitterly cold after the scorching temperatures in Sydney. She was expecting it, but it seems her body didn't get the memo.

She heaves up her rucksack and straps it to her back, then picks up her holdall before making her way towards a pretty gate, painted in the same shade of dark green as the windows and doors. She hurries down a treelined path, pulling out a map she's drawn herself, copied from an image on the internet. She's booked a week at a B & B on the High

Street. It isn't far from here. Five minutes. But it's getting dark and she just wants to get there, check her sugar levels and crash for a few hours before she starts her search for her sister.

The path opens up onto Railway Street, and a row of Victorian terraces stretch out in front of her. She must have missed a turning in the path; there's no Railway Street on her makeshift map. She spots a man appearing from one of the houses, pushing a little girl in a stroller. He looks friendly.

'Hey,' she calls, raising her hand as he closes the gate at the foot of a black and white tiled path. He waits until she's caught him up, and smiles.

'I think I might be lost,' she says, smiling at the little girl with golden curls and wearing a pink all-in-one, who slides down in the pushchair, shy.

'By about nine thousand miles, I'd say.' The man laughs, but Kerry doesn't get it – too tired to absorb much at all right now.

'Your accent,' he says, clearly seeing her puzzled expression. 'Australia's a long way.'

'Ah, yes.' She smiles. 'I see.'

'So, where are you off to?'

'The High Street. I've booked into a B & B.'

'Well, it's not far,' he says, directing her.

'That's great. Thanks.' She starts to head away.

'If you need any info on Ridgewater, I've lived here man and boy, as my father used to say. I'm Seb. Just give me a knock. Happy to help if you need info.' He turns the stroller in the opposite direction to her and begins pushing it towards the station.

'OK, thanks,' she calls as she hurries away, turning the corner at the end of the road. The man seemed nice – friendly.

But her antennae are up. She won't trust anyone in this town until she finds out what happened to her sister.

Once on the High Street, she passes a cafe, a chalkboard outside welcoming friendly dogs, spots the B & B opposite. A white building three storeys high. She scoots across the road, looking both ways, and heads up three steps and through a double-fronted door.

The entrance is small, a bit dated, but cosy. She passes a bar to her left decked out with dark wooden tables and a dull, patterned carpet. A motherly looking woman stands behind the counter.

'Good afternoon, can I help?'

'I've booked a room.' Kerry says, reaching the woman and dropping her holdall to the floor with a thud. 'My name is Kerry Brewster.'

31

Annie

I'd agreed to meet Tom at seven o'clock, and it's now ten past. I can't see him anywhere. I'm about to go inside the bar – it's freezing out here and I'm stomping from foot to foot – when I hear his voice.

'Hey, Annie!'

I swing round to see him approaching. He looks good, his dark hair poking from a beanie, his hands stuffed in the pockets of a dark jacket. 'Hey,' I say.

'Sorry I'm a bit late.' He smiles. 'How are you?'

'Good. You?'

'Great.' He comes in for a hug, wraps his arms around me, smells good. 'Been looking forward to seeing you.' He opens the door to the bar, allows me to go in first. Not only cute, but a gentleman. OK, so some women aren't into the whole chivalry thing, but call me old-fashioned, it feels nice.

'What can I get you?' he says.

'New Zealand Sauvignon, please.' I leave him at the bar,

head for a little table in an alcove, where a candle burns. It's hard to believe this place was once the Fox. Dark wood, scratched tables and floorboards soaked in beer now replaced with light tiled flooring and pale square tables, the local band once blaring out Eagles classics replaced with Taylor Swift singing her heart out through speakers.

Once sitting down, I look at Tom chatting with the bartender, who lets out a laugh at something Tom says. A flutter in my chest tells me I like Tom. But I know I can't afford to fall for him. Not right now.

'Good choice of table,' he says, putting a glass of wine in front of me. He keeps hold of his beer as he sits down opposite and drags his fingers through his dark hair. 'So, how have you been? Nothing worrying you?'

It's a weird thing to say, but I let it ride, take a sip of my drink. 'I'm OK, thanks.' I want to tell him about my brother, about Natalie. I want to spill everything to this stranger. Would that be so wrong of me? But I know I can't tell anyone about Natalie, it's not my secret to share, and I'm not sure I know Tom well enough yet to talk about my brother. I fumble around for something neutral to say. 'So, you enjoy D and D?'

He furrows his forehead. 'D and D?'

'Dungeons and Dragons?'

'Ah, yes. Though I haven't played since I was in London.' He looks suddenly awkward, knocks back his beer in greedy gulps and rises once more. 'Another?'

'I'm good, thanks.' I look down at my full glass, feeling as though he's shut me down, however pleasantly. It's frustrating to know so little about him.

He strides away, laughing once more with the bartender, who pours him another pint and jokes about Tom coming in on his day off – *can't keep away.* I move my eyes across the old photographs of Ridgewater scattered higgledy-piggledy on the walls, distracted when the door opens and Seb and Sasha appear, Seb handsome in a white shirt open at the neck, black jeans and a dark jacket, an air of sophistication about him. Sasha, a few steps behind, looks stunning in a slinky red dress and heels. They look incredible, as though they've stepped from the pages of *Vogue*. I still can't believe how much Seb's changed in twelve years.

I'm pretty sure they haven't seen me tucked away in the alcove, where I'm ogling them as they approach the bar, Sasha taking Seb's hand and squeezing.

'You OK?'

I look up with a start to see Tom lowering once more into the seat opposite, another beer in his hand, and despite my attraction to this man, I get a shudder of unease that I can't quite explain, though if it's caused by Tom or Seb and his wife, I can't be sure.

'I'm fine,' I say.

Tom looks over his shoulder to where I've returned my gaze, as Seb and Sasha, clasping a bottle of wine and two glasses, sit at a table by the window. 'Someone you know?'

'Mmm… Seb Blair. An old friend of my brother's.'

'Want to go talk to them?'

'No! God no. No.' A beat. 'I'm happy here with you.'

'Is the right answer.' He laughs, and my doubts about him disperse. 'It's good to see you,' he says, leaning forward and curling a straying hair behind my ear. 'I've been thinking about you.'

I fiddle with the stem of my glass. 'I've thought about you too.'

'You have?'

I nod, take a sip of wine. 'It's just, well, I've got a lot going on right now, and not a lot of time for... well, whatever this is.'

'I get that. Happy to be friends. I don't want to harass you.'

'You're certainly not doing that.'

'Good.' He takes a gulp of beer. 'If I can help in any way, you know, with whatever you're going through.'

I shake my head. 'To be honest, there's not much anyone can do. Unless you have a magic wand in your back pocket.'

'Do you want to talk about it?'

I shrug. What harm can it do to at least tell him about Elliot? 'It's my brother. He's been in an accident.'

'I'm sorry to hear that. Is he OK?'

I shake my head. 'He's paralysed, hasn't spoken a word in over six weeks. He fell from a cliff down at Ridgewater Cove.'

'Oh God. That's awful.'

I regret telling him already – more because my emotions are rampaging. 'They hope he'll get better...' I get to my feet, a lump rising in my throat. I'm sharing too much, I know that, and, without a backward glance, I dash between the tables towards the toilets.

I sit on the loo, lid down, dabbing my eyes with screwed-up toilet roll. I'm determined to find out more about Tom and tell him nothing more about myself until I have.

Coming out of the cubicle, the loo flushing behind me, I see Sasha at the mirror refreshing her make-up – combing dark mascara through fair, wispy lashes. I sidle up beside her, aware of how tall she is, and wash my hands. 'Hey,' I say.

She puts away the mascara and pulls out a lipstick. 'Oh, hey,' she says, obviously recognising me. 'We came out in a bit of a rush, hence...' She holds up the lipstick, begins applying it to her full lips, her sea-blue eyes shining, dark hair falling about her face.

I pull a paper towel from a neat pile and begin drying my hands. 'Night out without the children?'

'Yes.' She shoves the lipstick into a make-up bag.

'Your daughter is beautiful.' Hands dry, I throw the paper towel into the bin with the precision of a basketball player.

'Megan? She is, yes.' Her jaw tenses. She doesn't want to talk to me any more, that much is clear.

'It's good to see you and Seb so happy. How did you meet?' The question isn't loaded. Well, perhaps it is a tiny bit. But I'm interested. I liked – like – Seb. I'm pleased for him.

She zips up her bag and turns to face me. 'I'd rather not say, if you don't mind.' She turns to leave. 'Now, is there anything else you want to know about my private life?'

I raise my hands, step backwards. 'God, no, sorry. I didn't mean to pry.'

She looks back, narrows her eyes. 'Didn't you? It seems to me that you and that friend of yours had an ulterior motive for visiting Seb – especially her, whatever her name is.'

'Natalie.'

'I don't care. Seb told me how she wouldn't shake his hand, how angry she was, and I heard you both visited his father. I don't know what this is about, Anne—'

'Annie.'

'But Seb's worked hard to get where he is today. You have no idea what he's been through. He doesn't need a couple of fake old school friends invading his privacy.'

My heart's thumping. 'I'm sorry. I know he's been through a lot.'

'Then, like I say, leave us alone.' She loops her bag over her shoulder and, heels clipping tiles, strides towards the door. Pushing it open, she pauses for a moment and, without looking back, adds softly, 'Please.'

When I come out of the loos, I avoid looking Sasha and Seb's way and head for the table where I was sitting with Tom. But he isn't here, his half-drunk beer on the table abandoned. I look around at the bustling bar – *maybe he's gone to the gents?*

Within seconds my phone buzzes. It's a text from Tom:

Sorry, something came up. Hope to see you again soon. Tom X

I feel odd, not disappointed exactly – more confused. I pull on my coat and drag on my hat and take the long route around the bar to avoid bumping into Seb and Sasha.

'Annie?'

I look towards the window seat where the voice came from and feel myself tense. It's Aiden Shaw, twelve years older but looking much the same, dressed in a black T-shirt with 'Jesus loves you' in gold writing plastered across it.

'Aiden,' I say, but I don't stop. The thought of talking to the creep is too much. I scurry through the door, letting it slam shut behind me, my heart thumping. Out of all the people who could have attacked Natalie, I suspect him the most.

As I wait for an Uber opposite the One Trick Pony, deciding I can't face the walk home, I spot Margot Bancroft walking along the road, clutching a Tesco carrier bag. I step back into the bushes, praying she doesn't see me; I can't face her right now, and certainly don't want to end up sharing the Uber. As she hurries across the road towards the country lane leading to Sycamore House, I see a flicker of movement in the dark alley next to the bar, as though someone is hiding in the shadows, watching her.

32

'Can you understand me?' I've been jabbering away to Elliot all morning. Talking about our childhood and teens – happy memories, hoping to chase away his trauma – and I'm now getting hoarse. He hasn't opened his eyes once.

I'm relieved when the bedroom door swings open.

'You have a visitor, darling,' Mum says, her words aimed at Elliot as she steps into the room in a long purple jumper and jeans.

Behind her, Seb appears in black trousers and a round-necked jumper, smiling. 'Hey, mate,' he says, his tone bright, though I see the shock in his eyes. 'What the devil have you been up to?'

Elliot's eyes ping open at the sound of his friend's voice, and my stomach leaps. I jump to my feet and let Seb sit down next to my brother, glancing at Mum.

Seb places a hand over Elliot's. 'It's good to see you.' He looks over his shoulder at me, and I wonder for a moment whether he saw me last night in the bar, or if Sasha mentioned our conversation in the ladies, but if she did, he doesn't mention it, his eyes returning to Elliot.

'We'll leave you,' Mum says, reaching out her hand for me to take. I don't move. Whatever Seb has to say, I would like to hear it.

'Annie, are you coming?' There's a slight irritation in her voice.

'Don't go on my account,' Seb says. 'It would be good to chat with you.'

'I'd like that.' I perch on the end of the bed.

'Fine.' Mum's jaw clenches. 'I'll put the kettle on, shall I?'

Despite my brother's eyes springing open, he doesn't respond further to his friend, but Seb seems undeterred.

'It must be twelve years since I saw you last, mate,' he says. 'I'm married now, would you believe? Got two little ones.' His eyes glaze over as he glances my way. 'This is awful,' he says. 'He was always so alive. I hate seeing him this way. He was so talented... *is* so talented.' He returns his gaze to Elliot, taps his hand. 'Do you remember that wooden man you made when we were at school? It looked pretty creepy, and you joked that it looked like our teacher, Mr Smith.'

No reaction.

'Well, it always stuck with me. So much so, I named my carpentry business The Wooden Man...' He peters out, struggling.

'Tell him about Sasha,' I say, my intentions not entirely selfless. After seeing her last night, I want to know more about his wife. 'He'll enjoy hearing about her.'

He stares at me for a moment, narrowing his eyes, and I wonder again if he knows I waylaid Sasha, what she said to me.

'OK.' He looks back at Elliot. 'Well, I guess in a roundabout way I met Sasha online. She's great. She has her own business, and she paints too. I don't know what I'd do without her. Much like I don't know what I would have done without you, mate, back in the day. You were a great friend to me. Helped me through some hard times.'

Elliot's eyes flicker. He's happy to see his friend, that much is clear.

Mum returns with mugs of tea on a tray, and I get to my feet, deciding to give them time alone together. 'I'll leave you to it,' I say, taking one of the steaming mugs as I leave the room.

It's later, as I'm showing Seb out, that he says, 'I've been thinking, since you and Natalie came round, about that night we met up in Sycamore Wood.'

I respond too fast. 'Have you remembered something?'

He shakes his head, narrows his eyes. 'What's going on? Did something happen? Did something happen to Natalie?'

'Why would you think that?'

He shrugs. 'There was just something about the way she was when you both visited. I recognise trauma. I've been through it myself.'

I can't tell him what happened to Natalie without her permission, however concerned he seems. 'It's nothing, honestly. Natalie and I just wanted to track down some old friends.'

'My father being one of them?' Another narrow of his eyes. 'The staff told me he had a couple of visitors.'

'We just wanted to see him, is all.' It sounds pathetic, he must know I'm lying.

He runs a hand across his tense jaw, is quiet for a few moments. 'I'm guessing Aiden Shaw won't be on your list of old friends.'

'God, no – we'll avoid him like the plague.' I cringe at another lie.

'He was quite the bastard to me – him and his brother. Made my life a misery. And Natalie's too, if I remember rightly. I never understood why she went out with him in the first place.' He pauses for a moment, his hand resting on the door. 'He's still in Ridgewater.' *I know, I saw him last night.* 'His mother and weird brother are long gone. He lives with his father, last I heard. Same house.'

'I'll make every effort to avoid it.' I wish my words were true.

He leans in for a hug, and I accept it readily. Seb would never have hurt Natalie, I'm certain of it.

'Take care,' he says as he heads down the path towards his car.

33

I've told Mum I'm seeing Natalie this evening and hoping, as I dash through the darkness towards Sycamore House, that she isn't watching me. I risk a glance back. The curtains are pulled tight across the windows of Fairy Cottage, and I let out a sigh of relief.

I confess I feel guilty. Mum would hate the thought of me chatting over dinner with Margot Bancroft. And the truth is I don't even want to go. I'm not sure how Margot persuaded me, or why I can't say no to the woman. But then it's more than that. It's my own nagging curiosity – about Dad, about Giselle – that makes me walk up her path and knock on the front door.

Margot opens up and gestures for me to enter with a flourish. In her defence, the duck smells good. I'm just going to have to push Daisy and Donald (the ducks who came to our garden every spring to lay their eggs and raise their ducklings, seeming more like pets than wild birds) out of my mind. Margot looks glamourous, which is nothing new, dressed in a calf-length cream dress gripped at the waist by a narrow red belt that matches her lips, her nails. Her tights are sheer, her heels high.

'You didn't dress up?' she says as I remove my coat to reveal jeans and a beige sweatshirt.

'To be honest, I haven't got all my clothes with me,' I say. Though in truth, I only own one dress, a plain black thing that I bought from a charity shop for a function at work. I've only worn it once. Dressing up isn't my thing. And even if it was, it wouldn't have crossed my mind to make a huge effort. Though perhaps I should have known better – a simple meal was bound to be an extravagant event at Margot's.

'Never mind,' she says, looking me up and down, 'come through.' She beckons me with one manicured finger, and as I follow her into the lounge, I pick up on voices, quickly realising she's playing videos on the TV once again. Giselle looks to be about five in this one, is skipping up and down the garden, hair shining in the sunlight. A time long before she developed her skin condition.

'I so love my home movies.' Margot's apple-red lips spread into a smile. 'I thought you might like to see more of them. You and Giselle were so close for a while. Drink? I have spirits or wine.'

'Wine would be good,' I say, my body tingling with anxiety at the sound of Giselle's voice. 'Thanks.'

'Red or white?'

'White, please.'

'Do sit down, dear. You're making the place look untidy.' She laughs, leaves the room.

I notice, as I lower myself onto the edge of the sofa, that the coffee table with ornate legs is laden with roasted almonds, olives and fancy crisps in delicate green glass bowls. Far too much for two of us, especially if we're having a big meal shortly.

'Here you are.' Margot's back and handing me a glass of

wine. I take a gulp. 'I hope you've brought your appetite,' she goes on. 'Dinner will be ready in half an hour.'

The video jumps to when Giselle is older. The same piece of footage I saw last time I was here.

'Don't get your clothes ruffled, dear,' a younger version of Margot calls. 'Don't forget Uncle Joel is visiting, he's back from Canada, and I need to do your hair. Make you look beautiful.'

'I didn't realise Giselle had an uncle,' I say, as Margot perches next to me, her floral perfume cloying.

She looks startled. Quickly composes herself. 'Oh, Joel. Yes. My brother. Younger than me by two years.' She looks towards the screen. 'At that time, he'd suggested he might visit. I'd been looking forward to it, though it didn't go particularly well.'

'That's a shame.'

'Perhaps. You get on well with your brother?'

'We were close in our teens, argued sometimes as children. He was jealous I spent so much time with Giselle. He's always been Mum's favourite. I'm not sure she ever really wanted me.' I regret the words as they leave my mouth. I shouldn't be sharing so much.

'Siblings argue when they're young, rivalling for their parents' affection, that kind of thing. But it was different with Joel and me. I was always the favourite, you see. Don't get me wrong, it didn't mean I had a happy childhood. Far from it. My upbringing was strict, Mother wanted me to be a ballerina. I had to practise all of the time. It was gruelling. And then, when I failed, she switched her hopes and dreams to Giselle.'

I recall Giselle practising her steps, like a delicate butterfly. I take another sip of wine, wondering whether to mention Margot's mother Joan singing then yelling when I visited the care home, deciding better of it.

We're silent for some time, the tinny voices from the TV

getting inside my head, and I feel more and more tense the longer the film continues: Giselle doing handstands. Giselle on the swing. Giselle dancing, dancing, dancing, dancing, like a wind-up doll.

'She was so beautiful,' Margot says, breaking our silence and taking one, two, three gulps of wine in quick succession, her voice almost swoony. 'So beautiful. Mother always thought so too.'

I'm relieved when a beeping sound emits from the kitchen.

'Dinner!' She jumps to her feet and smooths her dress. 'If you'd like to come through to the dining room.'

I rise and follow.

The dining room, lit by floor and table lamps, has a heavy oak table, six chairs surrounding it. Candles flicker, casting shadows. The smell of polish fills the air. A photographic portrait of Margot and Giselle hangs on the far wall, velvet curtains are pulled across two sets of windows. Paintings of ballerinas fill the long wall.

I stand in the doorway for some moments. There's something about this setting that gives me a chill. Maybe it's the familiar classical piece playing from an old stereogram – Tchaikovsky's 'Dance of the Swans'. Or maybe it's the sensation of stepping into a dated room, clearly rarely used, or perhaps it's simply Giselle's startling blue eyes staring down at me from the portrait.

'Take a seat.' Margot touches her necklace, and I realise it spells out the name Giselle. She sees me looking. 'It was my daughter's,' she says, but I already know that. I've seen it before – Giselle often wore it. 'She was wearing it when they found her.'

'I'm so sorry.'

She stares at me for a moment, before turning and leaving the room.

'Do you need a hand in the kitchen?' I call after her.

'No, just help yourself to more wine.'

I'm not sure where to sit, but I needn't have worried, only two places are set, one each end of the table, both with a place card. I take the open bottle of wine from an ice-bucket and fill up my glass before taking my seat.

'I really hope you enjoy this.' Margot carries a covered casserole dish in with oven-gloves and places it in the centre of the table. She returns to the kitchen for potatoes and vegetables and, once back, removes all the lids, steam rising.

'It looks good,' I say, as she uses a ladle to fill our plates. Handing me mine.

'Help yourself to vegetables.'

I try to convince myself, as I fork in the duck, that this is not Daisy or Donald. And even if it is, I'm being ridiculous. I'm not even vegetarian. I take another glug of wine.

'Is anything wrong?' Margot asks, lowering her cutlery.

'No. It's lovely,' I say, covering my mouth and swallowing. 'Thank you.'

We eat in silence, the music ramping up, as we both drink at speed, Margot emptying the remains of the bottle of red into her glass.

When we've finished Margot collects our plates. 'Good girl. I'm pleased to see you've eaten it all up.' She smiles. 'I did wonder if I'd chosen unwisely, as you doted on those ducks in your garden as a child. Daisy and Donald – have I got that right?'

'You remember that?'

Her smile is almost sinister. *No, I'm imagining it.* The oppressive atmosphere has got me jittery.

'We have lemon cheesecake for dessert,' she says, leaving the room without looking back.

She returns within moments, putting down a large slice of cheesecake on a porcelain plate in front of me.

I pick up the gleaming spoon, glimpsing my taut reflection in the shiny silver. Thankfully, I love cheesecake, though I'm not sure I've got room for it.

She uncorks another bottle of red, pours herself a glass. 'Would you like some?'

I cover my glass. 'Not for me, thanks. I've had way too much already.' I probably shouldn't be drinking at all while I'm taking antidepressants, yet I've necked three glasses of white wine. *The tension made me do it, m'lord.* Thank goodness for the meal soaking up at least some of the alcohol. 'Have you always lived here at Sycamore House?' I ask.

'I grew up here with Joel and Mother. I was never especially happy – Mother was quite the tyrant – but I never went without. Did you know that Fairy Cottage was once the folly for Sycamore House?'

'Yes, I think Mum told me a long time ago.'

'When I was in my teens, Mother sold the folly to our groundsman and housekeeper – told them she had no more work for them at Sycamore House, and if they wanted to keep their home, they would need to buy it. They died a few years later, and the place was inherited by their son, who let it get pretty run down. Then, when Giselle was five, the son sold it to your parents. Joel had left long before then, of course.' She takes another gulp of her drink. It must be the alcohol that's making her open up.

'When I was eighteen,' she goes on, 'around the time Joel left, I got a place at a London ballet school. I wanted so badly to please my mother.' Her eyes are faraway. 'I was certain life would be wonderful in London, that I would never return to Sycamore House, but life had different plans for me.'

'You had Giselle?'

She nods. 'I became pregnant with my beautiful daughter.'

'What happened to Giselle's father?'

She snaps me a look, arches a plucked eyebrow. 'I think I've shared enough, don't you?'

'Yes, sorry. It's none of my business, ignore me.'

She presses her lips tightly together. 'Let's just say Giselle was the best thing that ever happened to me. But I knew I would never cope bringing her up alone. That my only option was to come back to Ridgewater – to Mother.' She looks down at her cheesecake, pokes it with a fork. 'To be honest,' she continues, 'I'm not hungry. Shall we go back into the lounge? Watch some more videos?' She rises, her napkin fluttering to the floor, picks up her glass and bottle, and, half-staggering, leaves the room.

34

In the lounge, Margot refreshes her apple-red lipstick in a gold-framed concave mirror, and I'm oddly reminded of the wicked queen in *Snow White.* This is nothing new. I've always felt that there was something not quite right about Margot.

Images of Giselle still play on the TV screen. The upbeat 'Dance of the Cygnets' plays in the background as she prances in her ballet shoes, wearing a white tutu. 'Look Mummy,' she cries, standing on one leg and extending her other leg behind her, and my stomach twists with sadness. The little girl who never got to live a life.

I perch once more on the edge of the sofa, wondering if I could leave without offending. But Margot's rummaging in a cupboard, bringing out two photo albums, clasping them close to her chest as she hurries towards me.

One album looks older than the other. She opens that first.

'My mother,' she says. The photo is a full-length image of a stern-looking woman, her hair in a neat, grey bun. She's dressed in a tweed skirt suit, tan tights and low-heeled black shoes. 'She was extremely strict,' Margot goes on. 'Can you see it in her eyes?'

I can. They are demon black.

'Don't get me wrong, she rarely hit me,' she says. 'And if she did, I deserved it. Ballet was everything to her, and if I didn't try, she would get exasperated with me. Just as she did with Giselle.' A beat. 'Don't look so shocked. It was acceptable to smack children back then. Anyway, as I say, she rarely hit me. She didn't have to. One of her looks was enough. Sadly, my brother didn't get off quite so lightly.'

'Has your mother passed away?' I know she's alive, of course I do, but feel I'll break the spell if I tell Margot I heard her in the care home. After her brief suggestion that she's sharing too much, she's opening up once more as though a dam has broken, and I don't want to jinx it.

'Good lord, no. The old bat is still alive and kicking – care staff mainly.' She half smiles. 'I put her in a home twenty years ago. She had breathing problems and was becoming a burden. Madder than a box of frogs – maybe she always had been. She was seventy-five by then. My mother was older when she had me and Joel. She had me when she was forty-two, and Joel when she was forty-four.' She gulps the remainder of her wine. 'I remember coming home with Giselle thirty years ago, Mother was living here alone by then, my father was long gone, my brother had moved out. It was just the three of us.' She yawns and relaxes back into the sofa. 'Gosh, this is nice, isn't it?' she says, kicking off her heels and curling her legs under her. 'Just you and me together for the first time in so long.'

Her eyelids flutter down, covering her eyes, and as soon as I'm sure she's sleeping, I take it as my chance to leave. She's still sitting up, the empty glass in one hand. I take it from her and ease her down onto the sofa, the plastic covering squeaking as she rearranges herself. Thankfully she doesn't wake. I rest her head against a cushion, cover her with a throw.

Without a moment's delay, I switch off the TV and video player, the hefty VHS tape ejecting.

Should I clear away the endless bowls of savoury snacks?

Get out of the house.

I head into the hallway, about to put on my boots, when my eyes are drawn up the stairs. A heavy velvet curtain is pulled across the top and my curiosity rises. What is the rest of the house like? Giselle's old room was on the first floor – are her toys still there? Her dolls? Is the ballet room she told me about still there? And what's in the attic room? I asked Giselle about it once, and she said it was never used – what if Margot's hiding something? I mean, why are all the windows shuttered?

I feel like the child I once was. Alice peering down the rabbit hole. Curiouser and curiouser.

I glance towards the front door. I should leave. Any sane person would. But it's as though the Pied Piper is hiding behind that curtain, playing to me. I creep towards the staircase, make my way up, pausing every few moments to listen. The house is silent but for the creaking stairs.

The curtain across the top is streaked with dust, in extreme contrast to the pristine lower part of the house. I take a deep breath and drag the velvet fabric back, stifling a cough as dust particles catch in my throat.

A dark landing stretches out before me, four doors stand open. Another set of stairs lead upwards to what can only be the attic room.

I flick on my phone torch, taking one, two steps, listening. But it's still. Deathly silent.

I push open the attic room door, the dank, stale smell

immediate. It's dark inside, shutters closed at the window. I shine my torch around, picking out a single metal bed with no mattress, an old-fashioned chamber pot beneath it. Inch-thick dust has settled on a battered chest of drawers, mouse droppings are strewn across the wooden floor, mould climbs the walls. Nobody has been up here in a long time. I step into the room, getting caught in a spider's web. Trying not to freak out, I peel free the web, relieved there's no spider attached. School exercise books are stacked on the bed. I approach, shuffle through them. According to the name on the covers they once belonged to Joel Bancroft: Maths, English, Science, though they have little work inside. I turn to leave, but spot a screwed-up piece of yellowing paper in the corner. I pick it up, flatten it out on the chest of drawers.

To my evil Mother

I hate the sight of you. The smell of you. The very essence of you.

If I never see you again it will be too soon.

I hope you burn in hell.

Joel

A sudden scamper of tiny feet. I turn as a mouse scurries across the floorboards. 'Shit!' I grasp my pounding chest. I'm not scared of mice. It's the adrenaline distorting my thinking. After a moment of attempting to slow my heart rate, I leave the attic room and head back down the stairs.

On the first-floor landing once more, I listen out for Margot before moving along the corridor, my phone torch juddering in my shaking hand. The first room I come to is spacious, empty, walls painted cream, wooden floorboards dark. A floor-to-ceiling mirror fills the entire wall at the far end, and a barre runs across the room, several pairs of dance shoes hanging from it. It's where Giselle practised her ballet.

I move on. An abandoned nursery sits to the right. There's a musty smell in the air similar to the attic, though not as toxic. And the same mould grows up the walls. A rocking horse covered in a film of dust stands in the far corner, a cot in the other. Giselle's Victorian dolls sit along a shelf looking down at me with eyes that look as though they might blink in a moment.

On a small dusty table sits a jewellery box. I bend to open it, and icy fingers tickle my neck as a tiny ballerina in a net tutu pirouettes to 'Swan Theme' from *Swan Lake* – a tinny, unsettling sound. I hastily close the box. It's creepy up here in Sycamore House, yet my curiosity continues to push me on, the little girl with the grubby hands and nails embedded with dirt in control.

A cricket bat is propped against a wall, a red ball nestled against it. There's a heavy oak wardrobe at the far end of the room, partly in shadow, but I can't make myself venture further into the nursery.

I leave the room and make my way to the next. This one is huge, shutters closed, just as they were in the nursery. The torch beam picks out a double bed covered with a red duvet dominating the room. A freestanding bath stands by the window. A large mirror is secured to the ceiling over the bed.

I continue down the hallway, to the final room. The door stands open, but I don't go in. It's smaller than the rest with a double bed, a TV, an abundance of books and DVDs crammed on a bookshelf, and several paintings propped against the wall. Once again, the shutters are closed.

A floorboard creaks behind me. A footstep. I swing round to see a shadowed figure at the far end of the corridor. *Margot.*

'It seems curiosity runs in the family,' she says, and although I have no idea what she's talking about, I hear the fury in her voice.

'I just—'

'Just what?' She sets out towards me with angry strides. 'I told you I no longer use the upstairs of the house. What possessed you to come up here?' She slams the ballet room door, the nursery door, the door of the room with the free-standing bath, startling me each time. 'Curiosity killed the cat,' she yells, reaching me and grabbing my arm, her nails marking my skin.

'Sorry... sorry, I thought I heard something, is all.' I yank away from her, my heart thudding, and run down the corridor and pull back the velvet curtain, before racing down the stairs, snatching up my coat and boots. In socked feet I race down the path, barely feeling the icy ground, and towards Fairy Cottage.

I look back, my breathing ragged. Margot's not following, but I see her silhouette in the window.

Inside the cottage, I slam the front door and lean against it, breathless. I get that she was angry, finding me snooping around her house must have upset her, but it was more than that. She'd become violent. What is she hiding?

Once my heartbeat has returned to a normal pace, I take in the dark silence of the cottage. It's late, but I'm far from tired, and I know I won't be able to sleep tonight. I make my way into the lounge and flick on a lamp. The fire in the grate glows orange, it's almost out. Mum must be in bed already.

I sit on the sofa, sinking my head into my hands, so close to tears, my lack of sleep making it hard to think clearly. Coming back to Ridgewater is more painful than I ever dreamt it would be. I desperately want to pack my holdall and leave. But I can't. Not while Elliot is still lying upstairs unable to move or talk.

I lift my head, noticing a spiral-bound notepad on the coffee table amongst the magazines, a pen threaded through the wire rings. I need to get my head straight, and there's nothing like a list to help do that.

I start writing:

What did Margot mean when she said curiosity runs in my family?
Who assaulted Natalie?
Why did my brother fall?
Was there more to Giselle's death?
Did Dad have an affair with Margot? (No!)

I tear the sheet of paper from the notebook, and, after reading my list over and over, coming up with nothing, my head spinning, I screw up the sheet of paper in frustration and throw it onto the dying embers. Watching it blacken, its edges igniting, is almost therapeutic, but I know the questions are still there in my head, tormenting me.

I rest back against the sofa, my eyes growing heavy, feeling myself slipping away into a chaotic nightmare.

A voice, so clear yet distant. It's a small child and she's calling my name. I'm searching long, dimly lit corridors that stretch into the darkness. The voice echoes around me as I open door after door, finding empty room after empty room.

'Let me out!' The voice grows louder as I approach the final door and throw it open. This room is darker than the rest. No window to let in the light of the moon. But I see her. A small child dressed in white huddled in the corner, cradling her knees, rocking, blonde, straggly hair covering her face.

'Giselle?' I say from the doorway. The girl looks up, but there's no mouth, no nose, just ice-blue eyes set in waxy, pale skin.

The door swings closed in my face.

I wake with a start, my mouth dry, head pounding, the air around me freezing. I need a glass of water, so get to my feet, wrapping a throw around my cold shoulders as I head for the door and step into the hallway, almost falling over Mum's crocheting basket as I go.

The tick, tick, tick of the hall clock tells me it's almost one in the morning. I'm about to go into the kitchen when I have a sudden desperate need to check on Elliot. I climb the stairs on tiptoe, avoiding areas that creak, and head across the landing and into his room.

In the dim lamplight I see that he's sleeping, his chest rising and falling rhythmically, and I get a sense of relief that he's OK, not really knowing why I doubted he would be – perhaps it was the unsettling dream.

The curtains aren't quite closed, so I make my way across the room, about to pull them to, when I notice through the gap that it's snowing. I move closer to the glass. A sheen of white brightens the area, and my eyes take me across the tall, white-topped trees of Sycamore Wood, and down, down, down to the wilderness that is Margot's garden.

Someone is sitting on Giselle's swing. I peer closer to the glass, trying to make out who it is. Whoever it is, they're in shadow, swinging back and forth. Margot? *Giselle's ghost?* Whoever it is jumps from the swing and disappears from view. I drop the curtain, my stomach lurching as the thick fabric thuds against the window.

I rush down the stairs, an icy fear clawing my back. I turn the key in the front door, locking us in. *A ghost? The ghost of Giselle?* I'm being ridiculous. 'Pull yourself together.'

My eyes drift to the small window next to the front door. I

step forward, and something wills me to pull back the curtain and look out.

As I do so, I gulp back my fear.

Someone has etched in the fresh snow in large capital letters:

ELLIOT'S IN DANGER.

35

Annie

'What's this?'

I startle awake, aching everywhere, having spent the rest of the night on the sofa.

Mum is kneeling in front of the fire, staring down at a fragment of paper in her hand. She turns, eyes shimmering, and passes it to me with smoke-blackened fingers:

Did Dad have an affair with Margot? (No!)

'It's nothing,' I say, straightening up, and feeling slightly hungover. *Who was on the swing? Would the message in the snow still be there?*

I go to rise, but Mum's staring at me as though I've massacred her fairy friends.

'Why would you write such a thing? You know what Margot told me.'

I take a deep breath, words I've wanted to say for so long

close to pouring out. I've no time for this. I need to show her the words in the snow.

'Annie?'

'Because I don't think he had an affair with Margot. There. I've said it. I think there's another explanation. I always have done. I think Margot lied.'

'Why would she?' She snatches the sliver of paper from me and throws it back into the grate. 'If you're so sure, tell me why he died in her house.' She gulps back tears. 'Why he went to see that awful woman. Tell me why Margot Bancroft would admit to an affair she never had.' Mum rarely gets angry – snippy yes, angry no – but she's giving it her best shot right now. She wipes away a tear on her cheek with the back of her hand, leaving a black smudge from the burnt paper. 'Go on. Explain why he was there, then. Why he was only half dressed.'

I lower my head. 'OK, I can't. But—'

'There you go.'

'But you were so happy together, and Dad wasn't the kind of person to cheat.' I shake my head. It hurts. 'Can we not talk about it right now? I need painkillers.'

'Why?' She softens slightly. 'Are you OK?'

'Yes, just a rotten headache.' *From drinking too much wine with Margot,* I don't say.

'I'll get you some tablets.' She disappears, and I rise. I need to see if the words are still there in the snow and make my way to the front door.

I hear Mum running water as I turn the key and open up. The words are gone. It's snowed again, and although I can vaguely make out where the words were, the ground just looks uneven.

'Ooh, shut the door,' Mum says, hurrying through the hallway. 'It's freezing out there.'

I close the door and follow her into the lounge. We sit down and she hands me tablets and a glass of water, seeming more composed.

'Thanks.' I rub my temple. 'You didn't hear anything in the night, did you?'

'What sort of thing?'

I swallow back the tablets, unsure what to tell her. She needs to know that Elliot could be in danger, but, on the other hand, I don't want to worry her any more than she already is. I put down the glass.

She furrows her forehead. 'Did you hear something?'

She doesn't need to know about me seeing someone on Giselle's swing – I'm not even sure exactly what I saw – and bringing up Sycamore House again won't go down well, but I must tell her about the message. I have to. 'It's just that in the early hours I saw a message in the snow.'

'What? Where? What did it say?' She looks panicked already, and I haven't even got to the worst part.

'I may have been mistaken,' I say, knowing I wasn't but trying to reduce the stress Mum's clearly feeling. 'It was on the front garden.'

'What did it say?' Her eyes are growing bigger by the moment. 'Annie?'

'It said *Elliot's in danger*.'

'Elliot's in danger?' She jumps to her feet. 'Show me.'

'Well, it's gone—'

'Show me!'

I lead the way into the hallway and open the front door. 'It was there last night,' I say pointing to the area where I saw the message.

'Oh, love,' she says, touching my arm as we stare out at the uneven snow. 'I know how hard this is for you – for both of us.

And you're clearly not sleeping well. I see your light on most nights, and now you've spent the night on the sofa in your clothes. You look pale, darling, and your eyes are dark. You are worried about Elliot, as am I.'

'You think I imagined seeing the words?'

She removes her hand. 'I think you thought you saw them.' She ushers me inside. 'Now, I need to go shopping,' she adds, with an abrupt change of subject. 'Why don't you catch a couple of hours' sleep? Michael will be here shortly.'

I open my mouth to insist I did see the words in the snow, but she's closed off – she doesn't believe me. Or is it that she doesn't want to?

* * *

Michael arrives ten minutes after Mum leaves. Bright and breezy, as always.

'It's chilly willy out there this morning. The weatherwoman said a snowstorm is on its way.' He hangs up his jacket and brushes the cold from his arms. 'I decided to walk, and now wish I hadn't.'

'Do you live close?'

'Half an hour walk, is all.'

'Have you always lived in Ridgewater?'

'God no. My partner has. I'm from Kent. But I adore it here. So quaint. Well, I better scoot off to see our lovely Elliot.' I watch him go, taking the stairs two at a time, wishing his zest for life would rub off on me.

It is midday when there's a knock on the front door. I glance out of the side window to see Margot stepping from one foot to the other.

'I'm sorry to land on your doorstep, dear,' she calls through the letterbox when I don't answer. I honestly can't face her after last night. 'But I feel we need to talk. Can I come in?'

OK, so she must know Mum's out and that I'm here, hovering in the hallway like a disorientated fly. But why she thinks she would be welcome inside Fairy Cottage is beyond me.

'The sooner the better,' she continues. 'Before your mother gets back.'

I put on my coat and boots and open up. 'Won't be long, Michael!' I call up the stairs as I step out. 'To be honest,' I say to Margot. 'I was about to go out for a breath of fresh air. Let's take a walk.'

'If you prefer,' she says, straightening her fur hat, the kind I associate with Russia. It looks to be made of animal fur, as does the mink stole around the shoulders of her coat.

Before I can button my coat, she eyes my sweatshirt and jeans. 'You really would look stunning in a dress, dear,' she says. 'And your hair would pay for a few curls and blonde highlights.'

Seriously? I slam the door.

'About last night,' she says, as I deliberately walk fast in the opposite direction to the one Mum will approach from, snow crunching under my feet like meringue. She hurries to keep up with me. 'I feel bad about the way I reacted. I'd had far too much wine.' She pauses for a moment. 'But what exactly possessed you to go upstairs?'

'I don't know.' I shake my head. 'It was wrong of me, and I apologise. I guess it was a primal thing. I was never allowed in your house as a child.'

She nods, her red lips curving into a smile. 'Apology accepted. I'm glad that's settled. I wouldn't want for us to fall out over something so silly.'

I think about the figure on the swing last night. Wonder whether to mention it but think better of it.

'I thought you might have seen her,' Margot says.

'Sorry?'

'Last night. Giselle. She visits me sometimes.'

'Like a ghost?'

'Exactly like a ghost.' She nods. 'I feel her in the house sometimes, though I've never seen her.' Tears well in her eyes. 'It gives me comfort to believe she comes back to visit.'

Despite a prickly feeling on the back of my neck, I get how seeing a loved one after they've passed away would give comfort. A memory of hearing Dad's voice just after he died fills my head. I'd known it was my imagination but needed desperately to believe there was something else after death. 'Margot, did you really have an affair with my father?'

She stops, rubs her gloved hands together. 'We should probably head back.'

'It's just he wasn't the kind of person who would—'

'I'm sorry. I know it hurts to believe your father wasn't the kind of man you thought he was. But, yes, we were sleeping together. It was all about the sex, nothing more. Well not for me anyway.'

I wish I hadn't asked.

She turns, begins heading back, stepping in the footprints she made. 'Come along, dear. You'll catch your death out here, and we can't have that.'

And as I watch her go, I'm certain she's lying. My father wouldn't have slept with her. I know he wouldn't.

* * *

Mum hasn't returned when I get back to the cottage, so I head straight upstairs to see how Elliot is.

'Hello, love.' It's Michael. He closes the book he's been reading. 'You look chilled to the bone.'

'Why don't you take off?' I say to him. 'I can read to Elliot.'

He looks at his watch. 'What, ten minutes early? You spoil me.'

'I do my best.'

He laughs, taps Elliot's hand, and rises. 'I'll see you tomorrow, darling, for more exciting adventures with Hercule Poirot.' He looks at me, crinkles his pierced nose. 'I brought it from home. Love, love, love Agatha!'

I'm not sure Elliot does, I don't say. Instead, I smile and tell him what a brilliant job he's doing.

Once Michael has gone, I sit down beside Elliot and stroke his face. 'Love you,' I whisper. His eyes flicker open at the sound of my voice, then close again. 'Please get well. I miss you.'

36

Yesterday was a washout, to the point where Kerry wondered what she was doing in England, on the other side of the world, friendless and freezing.

OK, so the room at the B & B is cosy, and last night she spent the evening next to a real flickering fire in the bar – *very British*. But around nine, after her mum called making sure she wasn't going anywhere lonely, that she wasn't talking to strange men, and reminding her to take her insulin, and monitor her sugar levels, Kerry had decided there wasn't anything for her to stay up for and had headed to her room for an early night.

Today will be different, she tells herself as she tucks into bacon and egg in the quaint little dining room with its daisy-print tablecloths and matching curtains. In fact, she's already had some luck. It was about three weeks ago, before she left Australia, that she'd sent a message to the email address on The Wooden Man's blog. She hadn't expected a reply. It hadn't been updated in years, so what were the chances? But first thing this morning a reply popped up in her inbox:

Dear Kerry,

Yes, I remember talking with Fi online. It was twelve years ago now. She said she was heading to Ridgewater, but I never met her. She didn't turn up where we'd agreed to meet up. I'm working up at Willow Farm, just outside of Ridgewater. Happy to chat if you want to pop by?

Best wishes, Sebastian Blair

She replied immediately:

Hi Sebastian,

I'd love to chat. How's 3 p.m. today sound?

Thanks,

Kerry

Now she places her knife and fork across her plate and drains her mug of coffee. This morning she'll trawl the shops and bars in the hope someone recognises the picture of Fi that she carries with her always.

* * *

It's around one o'clock that, enthusiasm drained, she opens the door to the One Trick Pony. It's her final hope that someone might recognise Fi. She's had no luck in the town. It seems that, apart from a sweetshop and a second-hand bookshop, most places have either changed management or changed altogether. And, if she's honest, this crowded bar doesn't look as though it will be any different. The barman, with his trendy beard and man-bun, was probably at junior school when Fi went missing.

Still, Kerry's not about to give up and approaches the bar, squeezing through the throng, reaching the counter as another dark-haired man in his thirties appears from a door behind the bar, wearing a name badge: Tom.

'What can I get you?' he says with a smile.

She doesn't want a drink. Needs to keep alert. 'I just want to ask you a question, if that's OK?'

'Sure. Fire away.'

She pulls out the photo of Fi. 'I wondered if you've seen this woman?'

He takes it from her, stares at it for some time before shaking his head. 'Sorry. Though I've only been in the area for a short while. Is she missing?'

It's the usual response. Though one guy in Fat Face did ask if it was a picture of the actress Amanda Seyfried.

'Yes, she is.' Kerry's having to raise her voice above the chatter and a Kate Bush track playing through the speakers. 'She went missing twelve years ago. Came to Ridgewater as part of her travels on a gap year. I'm trying to find her, but so much has changed in the town.'

'That really sucks,' the man says, sounding sincere. 'What's her name?'

'Fiona... Fi Brewster. I'm Kerry, her sister.'

He moves his fingers across his lips, not meeting her gaze.

'I wondered if you would put up her picture behind the bar. I've got several copies in my bag.' She pulls out an A4 copy and hands it to him.

'Got a contact number?'

Kerry gives him her phone number, and he grabs a pen, scrawls it across the bottom of the photo:

Call this number if you've seen this girl.

'Where are you staying, in case someone needs to find you?'

'The B & B just round the corner.' She thanks the barman as he puts the photo up on the wall behind him next to some other posters – a Dungeons and Dragons evening, a quiz night – before pushing back through the drinkers. She's at the door when she feels a strange tingle on the back of her neck – as though someone is watching her. She swings round, but it's only the barman, Tom, who raises a hand before turning to serve another customer.

37

Annie

We're outside the coffee shop. Natalie's clearly agitated, her hands stuffed deep in her pockets, jaw clenched. I'm not surprised she's strung out. Aiden was an aggressive teenager who'd tried to force himself on her. She should stay away from him.

'So, Aiden definitely lives with his dad?' she says.

'Apparently.'

She shudders, and I wonder if she's thinking about how she flirted with Lance all those years ago.

'I hate who I was back then,' she says, chin crinkling. 'I hate everything about *her*.'

I touch her arm. 'Few of us are the same as we were when we were young. You were rebelling against your parents. Listen, are you sure it's a good idea to visit the house? I mean—'

'We have to. Please. I need to do this. He may remember something. Or, something might come back to me. In fact, last night, I had this weird memory – well I think it was a memory –

that there was more than one person there that night in the woods. I heard a voice in the distance.'

'Would you know it again?'

She shakes her head. 'I doubt it.'

'Was it male?'

'I think so, but I'm not a hundred per cent sure it was a real memory. It could be my mind playing tricks.' She bites down hard on her lower lip. And, with an attempt at brightness, says, 'Anyway, let's go before you change your mind.'

'OK,' I say. 'But if you need to leave at any point—'

'I won't stay any longer than I have to. Thank you. I seriously owe you.' She moves towards the kerb, looks left and right. 'We'll need to cut through the back alleys to get to his estate,' she says, walking briskly across the road and along the High Street, arms swinging back and forth.

Her words rattle round in my head. *A voice in the distance.* Maybe it was one of us? Elliot or Seb? 'Hang on,' I call. 'I'm struggling to keep up. Slow down.'

'I can't. I must face my demons. I have to. Because if I don't, they're going to haunt me forever.'

'But what happens if you find out who did it, Nat? What then?'

She stops dead. Turns to face me. 'Then I'll kill him, of course.'

* * *

I'm still reeling from Natalie's statement as we reach Aiden's house on Branson Drive. The place looks much the same as it did when we were young. Detached. Huge. Built in the sixties.

'Please tell me you were joking,' I say.

'What the hell is there to joke about?'

I feel scolded. 'Natalie, if you mean what you said, I…' I tail off not knowing what to say.

From the pavement, she's looking towards the house, eyes flaming. She turns to face me. Forces a smile. 'Don't panic. Do I seriously look like a killer?'

'Of course not,' I say, shaking my head, but I don't know. *What does a killer look like? They don't all go round with scary masks and axes.*

She moves her eyes back to Aiden's house before making her way down the path towards the front door, but I find I can't move. This is getting too dark. Could Natalie seriously be considering killing the person who attacked her? I mean, in all fairness, if I was the killing type, which I'm not, I'd be right there beside her with the second knife if we were to find the bastard.

With a clenched fist she strikes the door, once, twice, three times.

'Why don't we go back into town, have a coffee, talk for a bit?' I say, my heart thudding so hard I fear I'll have a panic attack.

She swings round, raises her eyebrows. 'Why?'

'Because you just told me you intend to kill—'

The door swings open and there he is: Aiden Shaw, just as I'd seen him in the One Trick Pony – twelve years older but looking much the same, dressed in the black T-shirt with 'Jesus loves you' in gold writing and loose-fitting tracksuit bottoms that he had on in the bar.

'We're Catholic,' he says, looking directly at Natalie. 'Try the neighbours.' He goes to shut the door, but Natalie puts her foot in the frame.

'Aiden,' she says.

He opens the door again, eyes widening. 'Christ, Natalie

Ford! What the hell happened to you?' He peers over her shoulder to where I'm trying to look nonchalant and failing. 'Annie Blake? Twice in a short time.'

Natalie shoots me a look. 'Twice?'

I make my way slowly down the path. 'We saw each other briefly in the One Trick Pony.'

'You never said.'

Aiden smiles. 'I admit I preferred the Fox back in the day.'

Natalie's still staring at me, clearly miffed I didn't tell her I'd seen him. Her eyes flash to Aiden. 'Can we talk?'

'I guess so.' He shrugs, his forehead crinkled. 'You'd better come in.'

The lounge has the same carpet, though more threadbare, the same rocky fireplace. The three-piece suite is black leather, and there's a fifty-inch TV in the corner. I recall his dad sitting at his laptop at the large dining room table last time we were here and wonder briefly where he is.

There's a large wooden cross on the wall, and various religious trinkets dotted across surfaces.

Catching where my eyes have landed, Aiden says, 'Does it surprise you?' He smiles. 'That I've found God?'

I shrug. 'It's not what I would have expected,' I say. 'After knowing you when you were younger.'

'No, well, I'm not proud of who I was back then. But God forgives.' He looks at Natalie. 'What about you? Could you find it in your heart to forgive who I once was?'

Christ, he doesn't waste much time.

'I'm not quite as forgiving as your God.' She perches on the edge of the sofa next to a sleeping ginger cat, and folds her arms.

I stay near the door, can't bring myself to sit, this is all so uncomfortable.

'People often aren't forgiving,' Aiden says. 'But I am truly sorry for who I was in my teens.' He lowers himself into the armchair, the fabric creaking under his weight, his eyes meeting Natalie's. 'I was a kid,' he says.

'You weren't a kid. You were a nineteen-year-old man.' She clenches her fists. 'Anyway, what exactly do you want me to forgive?'

'Ah. A trick question?' He stares at her for a moment, then at me. 'OK. I want forgiveness for the way I treated you and a hundred other girls. I was a dreadful person. I bullied other kids; I stole, took what was never mine to take. Not that you were an angel. You were a flirt, Natalie. A tease. I saw you in the kitchen with my dad.'

Natalie rises. 'So is that why you attacked me?'

'What?' He shoots to his feet. 'Hang on! Fuck's sake, what is this?' But there's something in his eyes. Fear?

Natalie runs a hand across the back of her neck, and I can almost hear her confused thoughts, feel the anxiety exuding from her body. 'I was attacked in Sycamore Wood, Aiden, and I swear to God when I find out who did it, I'm going to kill them.'

'I'm sorry you went through that, but I swear it wasn't me. OK, yes, I was one hell of a shit back then, but that day you said no, when my brother saw us; I would never have pushed it further, you have to believe me.'

I glance at the baby picture of Aiden and his brother still on the wall.

'Where is your brother?' I ask.

'Mouse left Ridgewater a long time ago. Never came back.'

'Did he turn to God too?' Natalie blurts.

'No.' A beat. He raises his eyebrows, looking from me to Natalie. 'He left long ago.'

'So, where is he now?' I repeat.

He shrugs, frowning, and voice tense, says, 'Truth is, I've no idea, and to be honest I don't care. We were never close. He was troubled, but I honestly can't believe he would...' He shakes his head, but his expression is wary.

'Why not? Didn't he go to a special school, chase you round the house with a knife? Flash people in the wood—'

'Yes, but—'

A roll of wheels crosses the ceiling above us. We all look up.

'Dad.' Aiden blinks, runs a hand across his chin. 'He's back from the US, can't work any more. He was assaulted, left immobile from the waist down.'

'That's awful,' I say, but Natalie is silent.

'Yeah, it was,' Aiden agrees. 'He never did find out who hurt him. Anyway, it's up to me to look out for him now. He is my dad, after all.'

38

Natalie's eyes are wide and wild as we leave the Shaws' house. What she's putting herself through is clearly affecting her already fragile mental health, and it's not doing mine a lot of good either. She takes off down the road, not looking back.

'Hang on,' I call after her, trying to come to terms with what just happened. How transformed Aiden seems to be. But my main concern is still Natalie's outburst that she intends to kill whoever ruined her life.

She hurries down the narrow, graffitied alleyway. Me, I'm three steps behind, attempting to avert my eyes from a giant orange penis on the wall, tagged by someone called Dizzo.

'What was that?' Natalie says, swinging round and stopping so I almost run into her. 'Did you hear it?'

'What?'

'Someone's following us. I know they are.' She's flushed, breathless.

I look around but can't see anything suspicious. 'I didn't hear anything.' I want to say again that she should give up her search. Get help. Therapy. But I know she won't listen.

She continues at speed along the path, and I'm trotting to keep up once more.

'This is seriously too much,' I cry. 'It's going to send you crazy.'

'*Going* to send? Pretty sure I've already arrived at Crazy Station.'

I continue to follow. But I've had enough. I can't do this any more. I care about her, I really do, but I need to spend my time with Elliot – keep him safe. *He's in danger.*

She stops again as we reach the end of the path. 'I know I'm not coping too well,' she says, her head down. 'And I shouldn't put all this on you. I'm so sorry. But I can't do this without you, Annie. I need you.' A tear snakes down her face as she darts a look around her. And then her eyes widen. 'Ah, jeez!' she yells, pulling her hand from her pocket, blood dripping from her finger onto her coat.

I rush towards her, struggling to take in what's happening. It's as though the inside of her pocket attacked her. 'Oh my God.'

'I've bloody cut myself.' She spins on the spot. Squealing, 'Shit, shit, shit.' Bending over. Gripping her injured finger.

I shake my head in disbelief and yank a handful of tissues from my pocket. Shove them towards her. 'Press these against the wound and lift your arm above your head.'

'OK, OK, Doctor Blake.' She stops spinning, pushes the tissues against the wound and lifts her arm, the flow of blood slowing, though her face is drained of colour.

'How the hell did you cut yourself?' I say, waiting for an explanation, my heart thumping.

After a few moments she brings a sharp knife from her pocket. The blade is shiny, about three inches long. The handle small.

'What the—!'

'It's precautionary, is all.'

I cover my mouth with my palm, my eyes feeling as though they're about to spring out on coils. 'My God, Nat.'

She shoves the knife back into her pocket and inspects her injury. 'Well, it looks as if it's only a small cut despite the blood and the fucking pain.'

'So… when you say precautionary… what does that mean exactly?'

'It means, if one of these men is the bastard who attacked me twelve years ago, I need to be prepared. He could come after us.'

My stomach churns. Despite everything, and I know it sounds absurd, I hadn't really absorbed the fact we could be stirring up a rapist – a man who left Natalie for dead. I shudder, even more certain this has to end. Now.

Suddenly she falls against the wall. 'Oh God, I feel a bit wobbly.'

'I'm not surprised.'

'You wouldn't walk me back to my place, would you? I'm not sure I'll make it.'

All I want to do is go home. Attempt to get my thoughts in order. But I can't abandon her. 'Of course,' I say, taking hold of her arm.

* * *

Natalie's apartment is on the ground floor of a three-storey building in the middle of a new-build estate. She keys a number into the keypad, and we enter into a carpeted corridor with fake flowers in vases on windowsills and generic seascapes on the walls.

We're halfway along when a door swings open and a man appears.

'Hey, Nat. You OK?' he says. He's tall and big built, around forty, with a flaming head of ginger hair and an equally ginger beard.

'I'm good, Duncan, thanks,' she says, as he slips his jacket on over tattooed arms.

He furrows his forehead. 'Honestly?'

'I'm guessing I screamed out in the night again, huh?'

He nods. 'These walls are paper-thin.'

'I'm so sorry.'

'No, don't be. I just wanted to check, you know.'

'I'm fine.'

The man turns to her and smiles, raises his hand. 'If you need me, you know where I am.'

'Thanks,' Natalie says.

'He seems nice,' I say, glancing over my shoulder, watching him leave the building. 'One of the good guys?'

'Is there such a thing?'

Once inside Natalie's flat, we pass through the lounge on our way to the kitchen. I take in the creams and hints of beige, the tall vase full of dusty fake flowers and a large table lamp sitting on a modern three-drawer sideboard. A small sofa faces a TV. But there's nothing in the way of ornaments, pictures, no photos of her family, no books. In fact, nothing that speaks of Natalie's personality. But then I guess she doesn't know who she is. She's lost her way.

In the kitchen, Natalie holds her wound under the cold tap, blood dripping onto a plate, mug and cutlery in the sink. Thankfully, she was right, the cut is not too bad. Nothing a large plaster and a blob of antiseptic won't cure.

'Can I make you a coffee?'

'Thanks,' she says. 'But I need something stronger.' She opens a cupboard, brings out a half-full bottle of gin and a glass, sits down.

'I should probably make a move,' I say. I'm really not coping at all well and feel desperate to flee to Fairy Cottage.

'Well, thanks for getting me home.' She pours the gin and takes a gulp. 'I appreciate it.'

I realise I need the loo before I trek back to the cottage, perhaps it's my nerves. 'Could I use your—?'

'Second door on the left.'

I leave the kitchen and make my way along the hallway, opening the door second on the left. It's not the bathroom. It's a box room, empty apart from a white laminated chest of drawers, a cork memo board on top, propped against the wall. I step in, spotting four photos pinned to the board: Seb, Aiden, and a frail-looking Colin. Elliot's there too, looking much younger – a red circle around his face. It's a photo I remember getting for Natalie from one of Mum's albums when we were in our teens, when she had an enormous crush on him.

'What the hell are you doing?' Natalie's right behind me. Seconds later she's yanking me from the room and slamming the door behind us. 'I meant second door on the right.'

'You've got a suspects' board?'

'Yes. Yes, I have. What of it?' She's really pissed. 'You know who I suspect anyway.'

'Where did you get the photos of Seb and Aiden?'

'You can find almost anyone online.'

'And the one of Colin? Please tell me you didn't take it when we were at the care home?' I know already that she must have.

'It's not a crime.'

'Pretty sure it might be. And why the circle around Elliot?'

'Think about it. Seb, Aiden and Colin have lived in Ridgewater since the attacks. Attacks that stopped when Elliot left.'

'So, you *do* suspect my brother?' I'm angry now.

'I don't know.' She tugs at her hair. 'I don't know anything any more. But seriously, you're telling me that if it was him, you would protect him?'

'Yes, I mean no. God, Nat, can't you see this is getting out of hand?'

'Well piss off then! I couldn't give a shit.' She flings her hand in the air. Slings herself down the hallway towards the kitchen. 'Go! Get out of my apartment. I'll do this alone – find my attacker, with or without you.'

'Fine.' My jaw tenses. 'But could I use your loo first?' I sound stupid, as though I'm quoting a line from a sit-com – cue canned laughter – but I desperately need to go. It's the cold weather.

'Whatever.' She turns, points to the loo door, folding her arms as she watches me scuttle away. If I was a dog, I would have my tail between my legs.

As I'm washing my hands, I hear Natalie cry out. I race from the bathroom, down the hallway and into the kitchen. She has her back to me, sobbing.

I edge towards her. 'Are you OK?'

She turns, eyes wide, body trembling, a note held in shaky hands. 'It was on the mat.'

I move closer and she gives me the handwritten note:

Stop searching, if you whant to live.

Natalie doesn't speak for several minutes, her head buried in her hands, her sobs slowly depleting, until she's finally silent.

'I'm here for you,' I say then. What else can I say? I know we rowed, and I meant everything I said, but she's distraught, and has no one but me.

She lifts her head, her face so pale, and stares into my eyes. 'Thank you,' she says.

'But let's be honest, Nat. We can't go on like this. *You* can't go on like this.' I glance down at the letter. 'We've rattled whoever attacked you, all those years ago. You need to call the police. You could be in danger.'

'I will,' she whispers, but I'm not sure she means it. They'll want to know what the letter refers to. Will she have the courage to share that information with them?

She takes the letter from me. 'The misspelling?'

I shrug. 'Someone who struggles with the English language?'

'Aiden? He's dyslexic. I remember from school.'

So is Elliot, I don't say. There's no way he could have sent it, in his current state. Though I'm not sure I would volunteer the information anyway. The thought sends a chill down my back. If I discovered he was guilty, would I really protect him?

I stare at Natalie. A completely different person than the one I knew at school. But she's still my friend and I care about her, and I know, despite wanting this all to be over, I will continue to help her find whoever attacked her, because, I realise now, I need to know too.

39

The taxi driver comes to a stop outside Willow Farm after bumping along an uneven, snowy track. It doesn't look like a working farm. In fact, it looks deserted.

'Thanks,' Kerry says, getting out of the car and handing the driver a ten-pound note, her stomach churning at the thought of meeting Sebastian: The Wooden Man.

Before she's barely got her bearings, the taxi pulls away, and soon the sound of the engine fades to nothing. She's alone, her confidence slipping. It's quiet here. As though a huge blanket has been thrown over the area, suffocating it. She straightens her shoulders, needs to be strong. He might be able to tell her something that will lead to her sister. But what if he abducted Fi? The thought has jabbed her mind several times since she got his email. But honestly, would he have answered her message if he had?

She looks about her, then up at the thick grey sky. It's only just gone three o'clock, yet the night is already closing in. She looks again at the farmhouse in front of her. There's no car on the drive. No sign of life. She takes a deep breath and continues towards the front door.

She goes to knock, but the door's ajar. 'Hello,' she calls, poking her head inside as she taps the door, a feeling of unease washing over her as the hinges creak. There's no sign of Sebastian Blair, or anyone else for that matter. Despite the cold, heat spreads across her neck. Whatever made her come? This man encouraged her sister to come to Ridgewater, and now she too is in the middle of nowhere, at an isolated farmhouse. She can hear her mum's voice in her head telling her to stay safe. Hands trembling, she pulls out her phone and calls the taxi company. She's made a mistake. She knows that now. It rings, and rings and rings. 'Pick up. Pick up.'

She turns on the spot, her gaze sweeping across the snowy area. A figure's approaching through a copse of trees. She can't see their face, but they're dressed in a long, dark coat. Oh God, should she run? But the farm is a fair way out of Ridgewater. She's not even sure she would know which way to go. She tries the taxi company once more, pinning her phone to her ear. Still no reply.

'Kerry Brewster?' The man approaching calls. He's almost upon her, carrying a log and an axe. 'Seb Blair. We spoke over email.'

Should she run?

'Martin's Taxis.'

'Yes. Hi,' she says into the phone, ignoring the man. 'You just dropped me off at Willow Farm. I'm Kerry Brewster. Can the driver come back please?'

'He can be there in ten minutes.'

'Ten minutes?'

'Best I can do at short notice.'

'But he just dropped me off.'

'Take it or leave it.'

'I'll take it.'

'You're leaving already?' Seb says as she ends the call, dropping the log at his feet, but keeping hold of the axe.

Kerry's frozen to the spot, unable to move. Did this man chop her sister up into tiny bits with an axe? Her stomach churns.

He smiles, holds out his free hand for her to shake.

She doesn't offer her hand because she can't move. She feels sick. *This is ridiculous.*

'You look familiar,' he says, something cautious in his expression.

OK, she knows she needs to say something. 'Some say I look like my sister.'

'I never met your sister. I told you that.' A freak gust of wind bangs the front door closed, and the branches of an old sycamore creak, spilling a scattering of seeds. The promised storm is approaching. He raises his eyes towards the dark grey sky, then snaps his fingers. 'The other day, on Railway Street. You were lost. I had my daughter with me.'

Recalling him with his little girl gives him a whole different vibe. She needs to calm down. Fight the fear.

'So, are you coming in?' He looks towards the house. 'I'm doing the kitchen at the moment. I promise the place looks better inside, well at least the kitchen does.' He smiles once more. 'I can put the kettle on?'

'I can't, the taxi will be here soon. Sorry.'

He narrows his eyes. 'It's you who wanted to see me, remember?'

'Yes, but I've only got ten minutes.' She glances over her shoulder, there's no sign of the taxi. 'Perhaps we could talk here until the car arrives. You could tell me what you know about my sister.' Another gust of wind almost knocks them off their feet.

'The storm is getting closer,' Seb says, finally putting down the axe and running a hand across his neat beard.

She perseveres. 'So, you met my sister online?'

'That's right, via blogging, and we'd been talking for a while over email. She told me all about her travels, and I suggested she might like to come to Ridgewater. We'd planned to meet in the Fox one evening and, like I said in my email, she never turned up. To be honest, I wasn't much of a catch. Hadn't had any girlfriends. I stammered, something I thankfully rarely do any more.'

'And you never thought to look for her?'

He shakes his head. 'If I'm honest, when she didn't turn up, I simply thought she'd taken one look at me and bolted; it wouldn't have been the first time. I tried calling her a couple of times. She didn't pick up. Ignored my messages. So that was that. In fact, I've not given her much thought since.' He pauses. 'Sorry if that sounds a bit harsh in the circumstances, but I hope you understand. I was used to rejection. I'd come to expect it.'

'So, you never heard from her again?'

'Never. I'm sorry she disappeared. She seemed really nice in her messages.'

'She was.' Kerry feels a surge of emotion and is relieved when she hears a car approaching. Apart from anything else the wind is getting stronger, and snow is falling once more.

'This must be your taxi,' Seb says. 'Call me if you need anything. It can't be easy being alone in a strange country.'

40

Elliot

Nights are the worst.

In the day, people are in and out, breaking up the monotony. Mum disinfecting the seats, the mat, talking to me like I'm a kid again. Annie. Nurses. Doctors. Michael and his songs. It was Tina Turner today. The bloke clearly means well, I know that. But really? 'I Don't Wanna Lose You'? Please. Shut the fuck up!

But now in the darkness I wish he was back here to kill the quiet swirling inside the house, leaving room for outside noises to penetrate the walls, creep inside: the creak of branches, the raging wind, the scuffle of an animal hiding from the storm.

I have no concept of time, but it must be gone midnight when I hear a creak on the staircase, then another. It can't be Mum or Annie; they went to bed long ago. A surge of panic rises inside me. I'm not safe here, I know that, and nor are they. We need to leave.

Another creak follows soft footfalls.

Mum never locks the door, and that scares me. She would if she knew.

The bedroom door eases open. I can't see anything, but I feel the sensation of someone in the room with me, moving closer. I beg my arms to move, my legs, but they refuse. Helpless.

My visitor stops moving, as though deliberating. Deliberating how to kill me? How to finish the job they started? They can't leave me alive, not with everything I know. They pick up a pillow from the chest beside me, step closer.

'Annie!' I scream inside, no words leaving my lips. 'Mum! Please! For God's sake, help me!'

* * *

Annie

Wind whips around the cottage, tree branches hammering against the window. The howling sounds angry, alive, the banging and crashing of objects caught up in its path unsettling. The snowstorm that's been promised for days has arrived.

The clock tells me it's 1 a.m., and as I lie here unable to sleep, my thoughts far too loud, I can feel the sorrowful silence of Fairy Cottage in my bones. I drag myself out of bed and head towards the window. The swirling, blustering snow claims the view. I can barely see past the feathery whiteness.

I squint, can just make out the trees in Sycamore Wood swaying and thrashing. I wonder if they will all survive the night.

I need the loo, so make my way onto the landing in my PJs and a pair of slippers that Mum's lent me. It's as I pass Elliot's room that I notice the door is open. My heart kicks off, thudding against my chest. Someone is in there, leaning over Elliot.

'Mum?' I whisper, but I know already that it isn't my mother.

Whoever it is looks around, their face covered with a black balaclava.

I hurtle into the room. 'What the hell—?'

But they're shoving past me, racing down the stairs. I'm about to go after them, when I realise a pillow has been placed across Elliot's face. 'Oh my God.' I race to pull it away. 'Elliot!' I cry, moving close to his face, thanking God I can feel his breath on my skin.

Mum appears, buttoning her tapestry gown and flicking on the light.

'Someone was here, Mum!' I cry. 'In the house. They tried to kill Elliot!'

She dashes across the room. 'Oh God!' She sits on the edge of his bed, takes hold of his hand in a tight grip. 'Elliot.'

'I'll call the police, an ambulance,' I cry, leaving to get my phone from my room. Once I've called the emergency services I make to return to Elliot's room. And then I hear it. Outside. A thunderous crash as one of the older trees in Sycamore Wood falls to the ground.

By 3 a.m., police and paramedics have been and gone. They'd arrived quickly and I'd hoped they might be able to follow footprints to find whoever had been in Elliot's room, but with the snow falling so heavily, any tracks were long gone by the time they arrived. I told an officer about the warning in the snow, and, when Mum was out of the room making tea, I suggested that Elliot's fall might not have been accidental. 'What if he was pushed?'

The detective sergeant didn't reject my idea and said they would look into it.

The ambulance crew checked Elliot over, happy with his condition, considering the circumstances. Although I'd already made sure he was OK. *What are doctor sisters for, if they can't check your vitals?*

'You got there just in time, Miss Blake,' one said. I didn't correct him. To be honest, 'Doctor Blake' doesn't seem to fit any more.

Now I stare from my bedroom window into the darkness, trying to come to terms with what happened. I'm about to return to my bed, to at least attempt some sleep, when I spot someone out there, at the foot of the garden. A black shape in the shadows. A flicker of movement. Could it be whoever tried to kill Elliot?

I shoot down the stairs and into the kitchen, instinctively grabbing a knife from the rack, opening the door and stepping onto the patio. A light illuminates the area, but I still can't see who's down there. 'Hello?'

'Annie?'

It's only Mum, and I sigh with relief as she appears, an old blanket wrapped around her.

'What are you doing out here?' I say, guiding her into the kitchen, returning the knife to the rack. She suddenly looks much older. 'It's freezing out there.'

We head into the lounge and sit down. 'Do you need anything?' I ask. 'A warm drink?'

She shakes her head. 'I saw him.'

'Who? The intruder?'

She shrugs. 'It was the man with the grey hair. He was in

the garden. I saw him from my bedroom window and hurried down, but he'd gone by the time I got out there.'

'We'll tell the police in the morning. Give them a description of him.' I'm trying to sound calm, but my heart is thumping. I take hold of her hand. 'You're so cold.'

'I've been out there talking to the fairies.' She stares deep into my eyes. 'Listen to me, Annie. Please. The fairies say a darkness is coming. An all-consuming darkness. We're not safe here. None of us are. We have to keep the door locked and bolted. And until the police find who tried to kill Elliot, we shouldn't go out alone!'

The following morning, Mum called the police about the man who's been hanging about, and an officer called in and took a description. Since then, we've spent some time going over and over what happened.

When Michael arrives around eleven, we go through everything once again with him, and he makes all the right horrified noises. 'So, you didn't see who it was?' he says, shaking his head, a hand cupped over his mouth.

I shake my head too. 'If you want to rethink your position here, we will understand. We'd be devastated, but—'

'Good God, I wouldn't desert you or Elliot. I just thank baby Jesus our boy's OK.' He points towards the ceiling. 'Is it OK to go up?'

'Sure,' I say, and Mum nods.

I receive a message from Natalie at midday:

There's a couple of things you need to see.

I want to ignore her, but I know I can't.

What are they?

Three flashing dots appear on the screen. 'Hurry up,' I whisper.

Meet me in One Trick Pony. I'm here now.

I desperately want to say I can't make it. That someone tried to kill my brother. That I've been up half the night with police and paramedics. But I don't. I agree to meet her. To be honest, I think I may have lost my mind.

Mum watches as I slip on my coat. 'You're going out after everything the fairies said, after what happened to Elliot?'

'I won't be long.' I'm out of the door before she can argue. 'Lock up behind me.'

The storm has moved on, only its calling card remains: branches scattered across snow, lost limbs from battered trees. Margot's bin is overturned, several wine bottles, half covered with debris, lie cracked in her front garden. I take in a breath as I look around me, deciding to walk into Ridgewater; it's much safer than driving.

* * *

'Annie!'

I turn, almost at the door to the One Trick Pony, to see Tom heading my way in jeans, black boots and a thick jacket with a fur collar. 'I was going to call you,' he goes on. 'I'm so sorry again about the other night.'

'No worries.' It had stung at the time, having him disappear while I was in the loo, and certainly snapped me out of any thoughts of romance. I'm not bitter about it – he's far too cute for that. Though he has got a bit of making up to do.

'It's great to see you again,' he says. 'Good to see you're OK. How's your brother?'

'We're both OK, thanks.' He's not someone I want to discuss what happened to Elliot with. 'And it's good to see you too.' I mean it. Despite my instincts telling me there's nothing there between us, I still like him. I can't help myself.

We're barely through the door of the bar when Natalie flies at me, eyes wide, pupils dilated.

'Have you seen it? There's got to be a connection.' She's slurring her words, and I notice that, on the table she just sprung from, an extra-large wine glass stands empty.

'What can I get you?' Tom says, aiming his question at me.

'Another of these wouldn't go amiss,' Natalie says, turning to pick up the glass and thrusting it towards him, barely looking his way. 'It's the cheapest Sauvignon, if you would be so kind.'

He looks at me, widens his eyes. He seems to have taken a bit of a dislike to Natalie. 'What about you, Annie?'

'I'll have the same, but better make it a small one. Thanks.'

As he heads for the bar, Natalie grabs my arm and whisks me to the table, where we sit down. I stare into her eyes. 'What's this about?'

'Listen, before I go there.' She reaches into her pocket and brings out a necklace. Drops it onto the table. I recognise the pendant – a silver butterfly.

'You used to wear it—'

'Until it was taken, the night I was attacked.'

I cover my mouth with my hand. 'Where did you get it?'

'It was posted through the door of the vet's. The envelope had my name on.'

'Oh my God.'

'Whoever sent it... They must have taken it that night.' Her eyes shimmer. 'They know where I work.' She pulls out the envelope. 'And there's this.' She hands me a piece of paper. 'It was with the necklace.'

I take it from her and read the typed words.

Stop searching, or I'll finish what I started.

My stomach churns. 'Oh God, do you think it's from the same person?'

She shrugs. 'The other letter was handwritten, misspelt.'

I continue to study the note before looking into her eyes. 'You must tell the police.'

She snatches it from me, shoves the necklace into the envelope with the letter, and I take her silence, the sullen look on her face, to mean she still won't be talking to them. 'And now there's another girl.' She points at a photo on the wall behind the counter and, dropping her voice to a whisper, says, 'She went missing around the same time Giselle was killed, the same time I was attacked. There's got to be a connection.' She reaches across and squeezes my arm so tightly it hurts. 'Three women, all young, all blonde.'

I pull away, my eyes homing in on the picture. I get up, move closer to the photo. She's beautiful. Just like Giselle. Just like Natalie looked when she was younger.

I feel a shiver of unease. *Yes, there's got to be a connection.*

'I called the number on the flyer,' Natalie says, as I return to the table. She picks up a serviette, begins shredding it.

'Really? What did they say?'

'Well, that's how I know she went missing around the same time. The person looking for the woman in the photo is Australian, she's called Kerry Brewster.' She's talking fast, rip, rip, ripping the serviette, her knees bobbing against the wooden table. 'And the photo is of her older sister who disappeared from Ridgewater twelve years ago. I'm meeting her this afternoon at two o'clock. You must come.'

'Right. OK.'

'This has to be connected,' she repeats, abandoning the serviette and picking at the plaster on her hand. 'It won't be long before we get some answers. I can feel it.' She's hyper, overexcited.

Tom appears and plonks a tray of drinks on the table. He nods towards the photo. 'Do you recognise her?' he says to me. 'I saw you looking.'

'No!' Natalie's on her feet, knocking back the wine he just bought her in greedy gulps. 'But it could all be connected—'

He furrows his forehead. 'Connected?'

'The woman in the picture disappeared twelve years ago,' I explain. 'We think there could be a connection with a couple of other happenings around that time.' I glance at Natalie, who finishes her drink and slams the glass on the table.

'I've got to go,' she says. 'But I'll see you later, Annie. Two o'clock at the B & B on the High Street, yeah?' She's looking at me for an answer, her eyes glassy, her cheeks pink.

'I'll be there.'

'Great.' She turns to Tom, looking his way for the first time. 'Cheers for the wine…'

'Tom,' he says.

She stares at him for a long moment. 'You look kind of

familiar. Like a tall Tom Cruise.' She laughs. 'In his younger days, of course.'

And then she's gone, flying out through the door, and I wonder for a moment if she's still carrying a knife.

'Natalie's a bit of a—'

'Whirlwind?' I finish, as she disappears from view. 'She's troubled. Has some issues.'

He nods, as though he completely understands. But he can't do. He can't know what she's been through.

'So how are things with you?' he says after a few moments, leaning forward. 'How's your brother?'

'I already said he's fine. We're fine. What is your obsession with our well-being?'

He raises his hand. 'Sorry.'

'No, I'm sorry.' I feel awful. I take a swig of wine, but I'm not enjoying it. Not in the mood to drink, especially at lunchtime. 'Actually, I should probably make a move.' I push the glass away from me. 'I've got a few things I should do before meeting Natalie later.'

He doesn't put up an argument. Simply says, 'Take care of yourself,' as I leave the bar.

41

I arrive at the B & B at 1.50 p.m. Natalie is sitting in the bar, halfway down another glass of wine.

'My lovely friend.' She rises, gives me a long hug, patting my back as though I'm a baby. She's hammered. 'There's something I need to tell you,' she goes on, placing a finger to her lips. 'Shh, it's very important.' She looks from side to side as we sit down. 'I remember a smell.'

'A smell? What, when you were—'

'Aftershave. I remember it. The brand. No, that's not right.' She wiggles her index finger. 'I don't know the brand. But I know the smell. He was wearing it that night, and it was familiar.' She nods three times. 'That's good, right?'

I feel her excitement. 'Yes, yes, it is.'

'All we need to do is go into Boots and sniff all the colognes, and once we know what it is, we'll see who out of all our suspects wears it, right? Simple!'

'I guess so. Though it's not foolproof. They may no longer wear the same aftershave after all these years, or maybe someone else might wear it.'

She frowns, opens her mouth, but before she can form any words, a young woman approaches the table. 'Natalie?' the woman says, looking at me.

'That would be me.' Natalie raises her hand in a flamboyant gesture.

'I'm Kerry.' Her eyes are now on Natalie slumped in a tub chair, long, lean legs sprawled out in front of her. 'We spoke on the phone.' She tightens her blonde ponytail as she sits down in the remaining chair.

'I'm Annie,' I say. 'Natalie's friend.'

'Hey, Annie. Thanks both of you for coming.' She's Australian, about five foot two, curvy, and dressed in beige combats, trainers and a black hoodie. Her smile is bright, the kind that lights up a room, though her blue eyes look tired.

'I'm so sorry about your sister.' Natalie pulls herself up straight.

'Thanks. You said on the phone you might know something about her disappearance?'

I look at Natalie, waiting for her reply. She flicks me a look, then moves her eyes back to Kerry. 'Maybe. It's just when you said that you haven't seen her for twelve years, that she came here to Ridgewater—'

'On a gap year to travel round Europe.' Kerry's looking down at her hands, picking at her fingernails, her cheeks flushed. She's finding this difficult.

'Yes, well, I thought you should know that around the same time I was attacked, here in Ridgewater.'

'Oh… I'm so sorry. That's awful.'

'Yeah. Yeah, it fucking was.'

I'm shocked Natalie is being so open, but I see the desperation on her face. She leans forward, takes a gulp of her wine, then another, and then in a voice so small I hardly recognise it as my friend's, she adds, 'I was raped.'

I take hold of her hand, knowing how much it took for her to say those three horrific words out loud once more. 'You didn't have to put yourself through that—'

'But I did, didn't I? If we're going to find this bastard, we need all the facts – all the terrible, evil facts.'

'I'm sorry,' Kerry says again, and I notice she's trembling.

'The thing is, your sister and I looked similar back then.' Natalie touches her short hair. 'And I feel there could be a connection.'

Kerry's eyes fill with tears. Natalie's suggestion has implications for Kerry's sister, there's no doubting that.

'And the thing is, another young blonde woman from Ridgewater died around the same time. Her death was ruled accidental, but what are the chances?'

Tears run down Kerry's cheeks. 'But Fi can't be dead,' she cries.

We sit in silence for a few moments, and I try to take in properly that these three incidents could be connected. The possibility that Giselle didn't fall from the cliff. That someone pushed her. And could Fi Brewster be buried somewhere yet to be discovered?

'We thought, up until recently,' Kerry begins eventually, wiping away her tears, 'that Fi disappeared in France, but a little while ago I discovered she came to England, to Ridgewater, to meet a man. And since I've been here, I've met him. He insists that the night he agreed to meet Fi, she didn't turn up.' She takes a breath, a sip of water. 'I don't know whether to believe him, and I need to find out more about him, though I'm not sure I can do that alone.'

'We're in this together,' Natalie says with a slur. She gets to her feet. 'We have a monster lurking in Ridgewater. A man who is capable of awful things.' She rams her hands deep into her pockets, and I think for a moment she's about to bring out the knife. 'We have suspects—'

'Nat,' I cut in. 'We need to go to the police. We don't want an innocent man—'

'Aiden Shaw, Seb Blair—'

'Seb Blair?' Kerry says. 'Sebastian Blair? He's the man who arranged to meet my sister the night she disappeared.'

'Well, if that doesn't prove he's guilty...' Natalie goes quiet, clenches and unclenches her fists.

'We still can't be sure,' I say, almost in a whisper. She's volatile, like a flickering flame close to a curtain, making me anxious.

She widens her eyes. 'So, Seb Blair follows me the night I was attacked,' she says. 'And arranged to meet Kerry's sister just before she disappeared. And you don't think he's guilty?'

'It sounds suspicious, yes, but—'

'But nothing.' She tugs at her hair with both hands, her voice rising. 'We need to pay that bastard another visit.'

42

'I'm not sure we should take this into our own hands,' I say, but Natalie's now stomping up and down the room, muttering under her breath, 'Fucking Seb.'

'You're angry,' I go on. 'We don't know anything for sure, and this all feels a bit... vigilante.'

Kerry looks at me with concerned eyes. 'You're right. Maybe we should go to the police. Tell them what we know.'

'Kerry's right, Nat,' I say, trying to keep up as she frantically paces, eyes wild, as though she might self-combust in a moment. 'We need to tell them what happened to you.'

'No! Shit! No!' She stops pacing, clenches her fists. 'I told you both in confidence.' Her usually pale cheeks are flushed red. 'I'll simply deny it. You've got nothing if I deny it.'

'Well, we could still tell them how Seb arranged to meet my sister,' Kerry says.

Natalie shoves her hand in her jacket pocket. Can she feel the knife? Is she capable of using it? 'I'm going to confront him. Even if I have to do it alone.'

'I just don't think Seb would hurt anyone.' My voice is tense. Truth is, how well do I really know him?

Kerry gets to her feet. 'Let's all calm down, take this one step at a time.'

But it's clear Natalie's had enough. She strops out of the bar, letting the door slam behind her. I rise, tempted to go after her, worried she's on her way to confront Seb, but Kerry touches my arm.

'You seem like someone I can trust,' she says, her voice small.

'Sorry?' I'm torn between Kerry's words and running after Natalie.

'It's just, I have no one here in the UK.' Her eyes fill with tears once more. 'This is so much harder than I thought it would be,' she goes on, moving in closer.

I place my arm around her shoulder. She suddenly seems so young.

'I'm so sorry,' I say. 'This can't be easy.'

'It's knowing I'm treading in Fi's footsteps. That I'm walking towards whatever fate took her from me.' She pulls a tissue from her pocket, dabs her eyes. 'I should have known it wouldn't be easy. I've never travelled alone before, and only ever ventured across Australia.' She looks down at her hands, fiddles with her fingers, and I let my arm slide away from her shoulders, feeling awkward. 'I just want to find her.'

'You're so brave coming all this way,' I say, not sure I could have at her age, even when I felt at the top of my game. Though it's amazing what we can do if we are determined enough.

Kerry stares deep into my eyes, wraps her hoodie round her. 'This was one of Fi's.' She sniffs the sleeve fabric. 'I'm sure I can smell her perfume.' She smiles through tears. 'She wore hoodies all the time. Never one for dressing up. She was beautiful but always more bothered about how she came across as a person. It's who you are inside that's important, she would say.'

'I'm so sorry, Kerry,' I say again. 'I desperately hope you find her.'

She shakes her head, sniffs. 'I thought, before I came here today, that I would, but I feel less positive. It's as though my sister is telling me to stop searching. That I won't want to discover the truth. That I'm putting myself in danger. And I admit I'm worried that digging around will stir someone up. I know you don't think Seb would hurt her, but what if he did? What if—'

'My brother was friends with Seb back then, and all I ever saw was a gentle, sweet young man.'

'What about the other man Natalie mentioned? Aiden...?'

'Aiden Shaw.' I lower my head. 'He was... well, a jerk. I wouldn't rule him out, but again, we have to tread carefully. I get what we're doing and why. But we don't want to ruin an innocent man's life by wrongfully accusing him.' My thoughts return to Natalie, and I pray she's not planning to visit Seb.

Kerry and I talk for a while longer before I make to leave. 'We should exchange numbers,' I say, pulling out my phone. 'Keep in touch. And let me give you my address too, so you know where to find me if you need me.'

43

I say goodbye to Kerry and dash out of the B & B, spotting Natalie in the cafe opposite, sitting near the window, a large mug of what I assume is coffee in front of her. I'm relieved that at least she's not gone after Seb. Yet.

My phone buzzes and I pull it from my pocket. It's a message from the mental health and well-being team from my old hospital, and I feel a surge of anxiety. It's not the first time they've tried to get hold of me – I spotted another message a couple of days ago, suggesting I give them a call to arrange a chat.

'Go away,' I mutter to myself, though I know I'll have to talk to them eventually. But the hard truth is it will mean admitting to myself and everyone around me that I've failed. That the long hours, the pressure and the heartbreaking scenarios I've had to deal with have invaded my dream to be a doctor, turning it into a nightmare.

Natalie's face is pressed into her hands. She's clearly distraught, but I can't face her right now. I will my legs to move. I need headspace – time out to be alone, to process everything that's happened since I arrived. I make my way through the park gates towards the sparse, snow-covered gardens. With gloved hands I scrape away the snow from a bench overlooking the children's playground, the slide, swings and climbing frame all cushioned with snow. The place is deserted yet again. Too cold for even the most wrapped-up-warm little ones.

Tree debris from last night's storm scatters the area. It feels odd, after such ravaging weather, that everything's now so still. The events of the last few days, in contrast, buzz about my head like angry wasps about to sting:

Who attempted to take my brother's life last night?

Who left the warning in the snow?

Was Elliot's fall really an accident?

Who was out there the other night on Giselle's swing?

Who attacked Natalie? And did Aiden Shaw send the note to warn her off? The necklace?

Was Giselle pushed from the cliff that night twelve years ago?

And where is Kerry's sister Fi?

I thrust my head into my hands, wishing I could run away from all of this but knowing I can't. I pull a tissue from my pocket to dab my leaking eyes. A piece of folded paper flutters to the ground. I reach to pick it up, unsure what it is, unfold it.

Thank you for everything. G x

I'm staring down at it, no idea where it came from, when I catch movement from the corner of my eye. A grey-haired man in a long coat, hands pushed deep into the pockets, approaches. My stomach tips as he dusts away the remaining snow and sits down beside me. Is this the man Mum and I have been seeing? The man who was at Fairy Cottage the night of Elliot's attack?

'Cold, isn't it?' he says, rubbing his hands together. He's in his late forties, perhaps early fifties. I feel instantly uneasy, despite his smile, his friendly brown eyes. There are plenty of other benches, why has he chosen mine? I'm aware my toes and fingers are numb, that, in the brief time I've sat here, dusk has settled around me like a shroud, creeping shadows now casting an eerie vibe.

'Annie?' the man says. He's still smiling. 'Don't look so worried. I'm not here to hurt you.' Just the fact he's said it's not what he's here for causes my heart to thud. I rise quickly, glancing at the gate. It's not far if I run. 'But what if you slip, stumble?' I say to myself out loud, and he furrows his forehead.

'I just want to talk but can tell I'm unnerving you,' he says. With that he gets to his feet and strides away. Tall and slim, his stripey scarf flapping in the breeze. He glances back. 'I'll meet you at the gate, where it's busier.'

I follow, keeping my distance. Once on the street there are plenty of people milling around, and I feel less vulnerable.

'Shall we walk and talk?' he asks, and I nod. He has an accent – American or Canadian – and seems pleasant enough, but I'm on my guard. If he's the man Mum and I have seen near Fairy Cottage, he may be trying to kill Elliot. The thought sends a shiver down my spine.

'Who are you? What do you want from me?' I shove a hand in my pocket, feeling for the security of my phone. Should I call the police? 'How do you know my name?'

'Can I buy you a coffee?' he says. 'I'll explain everything.'

Deciding nothing could happen to me in a crowded cafe, I nod, determined to find out what's going on.

We reach the cafe, and I'm relieved, as I follow him inside, that Natalie has gone, though I pray she hasn't gone after Seb. Once we're sipping our drinks, he begins.

'I heard about your brother's accident at Ridgewater Cove.'

He wipes the back of his hand across his mouth. 'He fell from the same place as Giselle.'

'You know Giselle?'

'There are things I can't tell you. But what I can say is your brother's in danger, and you are too.'

My neck prickles. Does he know about the latest attempt on my brother's life? Was he involved? Mum had seen him lurking about. 'From you?'

He shakes his head. 'No, not from me. I swear.' He pauses, elbows on the table, palms together, tapping his fingers against his lips. 'Get away from Ridgewater, Annie,' he says eventually. 'Go now, take your mum and Elliot, and get far away from here.'

I lean back in the chair, putting more distance between us, and shove my hands deep into my pockets. 'You must be able to tell me more.'

He shakes his head. 'I can't, I'm sorry. But I'm certain Elliot was pushed from the cliff. That someone tried to kill him. I saw the police the other night—'

'Mum saw you hanging about.'

'It's not what it looks like. I would never hurt your brother.'

'Then who?' My heartbeat quickens. 'You must know. Who would want to kill him? Hurt us?'

He shakes his head once more. Looks down at the table, silent.

'The message in the snow? It was you?'

His gaze returns to me. 'Not my finest hour.'

'And you've been following me and my mum.' I fidget, glancing towards the door, needing to reassure myself of the exit, as there's a large part of me that is desperate to run. 'Why?'

'I needed to warn you,' he says, making strong eye contact. 'Was trying to find the right moment.'

'And the swing?'

'Swing?'

'Giselle's old swing. Were you sitting on it in the middle of the night?'

He nods. 'Please. Just get away from here.'

'If you think we're in danger, then come with me to the police.'

'I can't do that. It's complicated. Just heed my advice. Leave Ridgewater! Please.'

I pull my phone from my pocket with shaky hands. 'I'm calling the police,' I say, completely overwhelmed, my heart now thundering against my chest so hard I fear it might break through my ribs, my skin cold, yet clammy.

He rises as I fumble with my phone. 'Get as far away as you can,' he says.

I flash a look around the cafe at the chattering customers, their words muffled whispers. As I try to dial 999, my phone slips through my fingers and clatters onto the Formica table. Before I can say another word, he turns and leaves, out through the door and into the snowy darkness. He doesn't look back.

I pick up my phone and shove it into my pocket. There was something about the man, despite my runaway anxiety, that makes me believe that, whoever he is, he's trying to help us.

* * *

By the time I'm on the lane leading to Fairy Cottage, darkness has crowded in on me, swirling shadows leaving my imagination raw and my stomach churning. I feel watched from every angle, see crouching figures hiding behind every tree.

It's as I round a bend that I see police cars near Fairy Cottage and my heart starts to pound again. Has something happened to Elliot?

As I run, feet crunching into deep snow, my phone rings out. I fumble with it and answer the call. 'Natalie?'

'Oh God, Annie!' Her voice is high, panicked. 'Someone's in my apartment. I've just got back, and the front door's been broken into, it's standing open.'

'Don't go in.'

'No, no I won't. I've called the police.'

'Just get away from there.'

'I'm totally freaked out. I think someone's inside.'

I'm not sure my nerves can take this added onslaught of adrenalin. 'Just get away from there!' I scream into the phone.

The connection goes dead. 'Natalie?' My heart thuds. 'Natalie?'

I try calling her back, but her phone goes to voicemail. I don't leave a message.

I run on, my breathing ragged, my eyes darting across the police cars then towards Sycamore House. Margot's standing like a statue in the window.

Mum is up ahead talking to a police officer. I pick up speed – thoughts darting back to Elliot. *'Your brother's in danger.'*

'Annie!' Mum cries when she sees me, and my heart leaps.

'What's happened?' I cry. 'Is Elliot OK?'

She runs towards me, hugs me close. 'It's the tree that came down in the night... They've found human remains in the exposed ground, Annie. In Sycamore Wood.'

PART III

44

TWELVE YEARS AGO

Anon

I stare at the fresh grave. Will anyone find it here in the deepest part of Sycamore Wood? Will a fox dig up the body? A dog sniff it out? But it's too late now. What's done is done. No regrets.

I throw branches over the area, picking up on an unpleasant cheesy aroma – it's me. I'm soaked through. Sweating. Thighs, armpits, forehead. I desperately need a shower. I pick up the shovel and wearily trudge through the wood, finally reaching the gate into the garden of Sycamore House. It's here I'd found the small tool-shed, the shovel.

As I emerge once more from the tool-shed, after returning the shovel, I hear a twig snap. Catch movement out of the corner of my eye. An animal, I decide.

A surge of nausea rises in my throat. I thought I knew myself. Never dreamt I could take the life of another human being. Maybe we all have our pressure point. A trigger. Something that takes us over the edge. Most learn to defuse it before it explodes. They rant or thump an inanimate object. A lingering dent in a fridge or a car door reminding them how far their anger took them.

I'm no psychopath. I found no joy in killing, no joy on hearing the crack of a skull, but I have to accept I'm a murderer all the same – a fact I'll keep hidden, whatever it takes.

45

NOW

Annie

'They don't know yet how long the body has been there.' Mum's leaning in close, talks in a conspiratorial whisper, as we stand, shivering in the cold night. 'They've erected a tent in Sycamore Wood where the tree came down in the storm last night.'

I stare towards Fairy Cottage. 'Is Elliot OK?' I need to tell her about the grey-haired man, explain why I'm on hyperalert, but it can wait until we're inside.

'Don't worry, he's not alone. Michael's hanging on for a bit, while I find out what's going on out here.'

I stare at the cottage. 'What do we know about him?'

She glances back at the house. 'Michael?'

'Yes. What do we *really* know about him?' I'm not sure where I'm going with this, but my nerves are wrecked, like live wires buzzing and fizzing, and I don't trust anyone any more.

'Well, he's from a reputable care company, has been through checks.' She flutters her fingers across her slim neck. 'You don't think...?'

'No. No I don't, I'm sorry. I'm anxious, is all. Worried about Elliot.'

She touches my cheek. 'And you're right, I should be with him after everything that's happened. I'll go inside.' She turns and jogs back to the cottage, and I'm relieved.

I stay outside for some time. The area is buzzing with officers, which is reassuring, despite a body being found. Whoever is targeting Elliot is surely less likely to do so with a police presence.

I'm about to head inside when car headlights dazzle my eyes, and a Fiat 500 comes to a stop near me. The door is flung open, and Natalie steps out. She spots me and hurries my way, almost slipping on the slick snow.

'Oh, Annie!' she cries, reaching me. 'I'm sorry we got cut off. My phone died.'

'Are you OK?' I tentatively put an arm around her shoulder. 'What happened?'

'I was terrified, especially after the notes, the necklace. But as it turned out there was nobody inside my flat.'

'You went inside? Alone? God—'

'No…' She looks about her, as though only just seeing the police cars. 'What's going on?'

'They've found a body.'

Her hand goes to her mouth. 'Jesus! Where?'

'In Sycamore Wood.'

She stares through the dense trees for some moments, looking cold, her arms wrapped round her thin body. She's only wearing a sweatshirt and jeans. 'Do you think it's Kerry's sister?'

'Oh God,' I say. The thought hadn't reached my over-full mind. 'Should we call her?'

She shrugs, eyes shimmering. 'Let's see what the police come up with.'

I touch her arm, my thoughts returning to her. 'So, there was nobody in your apartment?'

'No, but someone had definitely broken in. Duncan, my neighbour, went in first. Nobody would dare mess with him.'

A saloon pulls up. A man and woman climb out. Plain-clothed detectives, I suspect. A different pair to those who visited us after Elliot's attack.

I bring my eyes back to Natalie.

She takes a deep breath. 'Someone had been in there. They must have blagged their way into the building, then broke in. They scrawled across my kitchen cupboards in permanent marker.' She closes her eyes, and a tear squeezes through her lashes, rolls down her cheek. 'Someone had written "If you don't stop talking about the attack, you will pay". And there were spelling mistakes too. Just like the first note.'

'Oh God, Nat, that's awful. Have you told the police?'

She rubs a hand across the back of her neck, her face far too white. 'I don't want to talk to them about the attack, you know that. There's nothing they can do.'

'But this is happening in the here and now. I get that you don't want to talk to them about what happened—'

'There's no point—'

'But they may be able to catch whoever's been threatening you. And it's likely it's the same person who attacked you twelve years ago.'

'Two birds. One stone.' She's shivering all over now, her teeth chattering. 'It's got to be someone we've spoken to, hasn't it?' she says. 'Seb, Aiden and Colin Blair are the only people who know I'm asking questions.'

'There will be others who know by now, you can bank on it. Seb will have told his wife; Aiden may have told his father—'

'Lance.' She shudders, and my mind springs to how she flirted with him in her teens. 'And Kerry knows – she may have told someone.'

And I told Elliot. And Michael arrived just after that. Had he heard?

'What if the person threatening me is protecting someone?' Natalie bites down on her bottom lip. 'I'm scared. My apartment has been broken into. I've been threatened three times.'

'What will you do?'

'Duncan said he'll call in a favour to get my locks replaced, but I don't want to go back there tonight. I couldn't stay over, could I?'

'But there are only three bedrooms—'

'I can crash on the sofa.'

'What about the B & B?' I don't want her staying at Fairy Cottage. Not after what happened to Elliot, not while he's so ill, so vulnerable. Not while she carries a knife. *Am I an awful friend?*

'Please.' She grips my wrist for a moment. 'I need you right now. You're my only friend.'

I feel a pang of guilt. 'OK, I'll check with Mum.' I put my arm around her, attempting to be a better friend. 'Let's go ask her.'

46

I could tell Mum wasn't happy when I asked if Natalie could crash on the sofa, but with my pale, shivering friend standing right beside me, she had no choice but to agree.

'Just the one night,' she said – a statement not a question.

'Hopefully,' Natalie replied.

Once Mum and I were alone, I told her I'd seen the grey-haired man again, that he'd spoken to me, said we're in danger. She called the police, who sent round an officer to take down the information. 'Nobody scares me away from Fairy Cottage,' she told him.

Now I'm upstairs, hiding under the duvet, my head so full I can barely think coherently.

At just after ten Mum knocks and comes into my bedroom. 'Are you awake?' she whispers.

'I'm always awake,' I say, pulling myself up to a sitting position and flicking on my lamp.

She stands for a moment before moving across the room in her fuzzy slippers and tapestry dressing gown, lowering herself onto the edge of the bed with a sigh.

'Am I wrong to be worried with Natalie in the house after everything that's happened?' she whispers. 'The fairies don't dislike her, but they see a lot of anger in her.'

I want to say Natalie is fine, that she's my friend and she's been through hell, that we must be kind, but I can't help thinking how Elliot was attacked and what the grey-haired man said about us being in danger. And then there's the photo of Elliot pinned to the cork memo board in Natalie's flat. The fact she carries a knife. 'I could sleep in Elliot's room if you like?' I say, climbing out of bed and grabbing my pillow and duvet.

Mum doesn't argue. She simply nods, and with an almost inaudible 'Thank you,' rises and leaves the room.

Once I'm crashed on the floor of my brother's bedroom, listening to him breathe, watching his chest rise and fall in the lamplight, I become aware that the TV downstairs is on, booming through the floorboards. I grit my teeth, angry that Natalie's being so inconsiderate. I'm about to get up when everything goes quiet.

I squeeze my eyes closed. But it's no good, sleep isn't on the menu – it rarely is. It could be partly down to the fact I've rolled off the pillow and am now lying nose pressed against the sterile rug, or maybe it's the strange buzzing in my ears, or the peculiar feeling that my eyes feel wide open despite being tightly closed. Or could it be that I've missed taking my sertraline tablets for a couple of days in a row? I'm a doctor, for goodness' sake. I know how side effects of withdrawal might affect me. I need to take one in the morning. It's not good to mess with the dosage, though deep down I wonder if my weird feelings are down to my long list of worries. My worries about my career have been pushed behind Elliot's, Natalie's and Kerry's awful situations, but it's still there, raising its hand for attention. What does life hold for me when I return to London? Do I even want to be a doctor any more?

After some moments, I pluck something randomly from my tangled brain. The note I found in my pocket:

Thank you for everything. G x

How had I ended up with it? Had I picked it up from somewhere? It certainly wasn't meant for me. And then it hits me. The day I strolled down to Ridgewater Cove with Mum. She dropped it. She was wearing Elliot's coat.

Still not able to make sense of it I toss and turn, the floorboards creaking under my weight, cramp in my calves, legs jittery. Mum said Elliot wasn't wearing his coat when he was found unconscious. That his coat appeared on the doorstep the following day.

I'm getting more and more restless, and the last thing I want to do is disturb Elliot. I need to stretch my legs, so rise and pad towards the window. There's still a police presence outside. Could Fi be the body in the wood? Could Seb have met up with her that night twelve years ago? Killed her?

My eyes drift to Margot's house, the garden, the swing. But there's nobody out there, only creeping shadows making my neck tingle.

'Giselle!' Elliot cries out.

I swing round. Stumble across the room towards him, hardly believing what I've just heard. Elliot spoke.

Heart pounding, I touch his shoulder, noting his eyes are still closed.

'Elliot,' I say, too loudly, but he doesn't stir. *Why did he call for Giselle?* 'Elliot!' I try again, but there's no response. Should I get Mum?

When he doesn't stir, I finally move back to my quilt and slump to the floor, propping myself up against the wall, trying to force down my fears, stamp them out before they ignite and cause a wildfire in my head. Why would my brother cry out for Giselle? Does he know more about the day she died? He would never have hurt her. *I know him. He'd never hurt anyone.* But that spark of worry won't go out. The fire burns. Where was he the night she died? Why did the police question him about her death? 'It was an accident,' I whisper. 'Wasn't it?'

The flames inside my head claim Natalie in their rampage. I left Elliot in the wood the night she was attacked. Were the two events connected?

I hate myself.

Hate where my mind is going.

Hate that I'm pulling out my phone and doing a Google search of attacks on women over the last twelve years in the area of Scotland where my brother lived.

Hate is a strong word, Annie.

But there are no attacks, and I'm ashamed. Ashamed I thought there could be. What the hell was I thinking? *I know him. He would never hurt anyone.*

I lie down and curl up like a foetus, my head on the pillow, pulling the duvet over me, making myself invisible to the world. And then... I cry.

* * *

It's 8 a.m., and I make my way downstairs and into the kitchen. The kettle is warm. The blind is up.

Mum is sitting at the bottom of the garden, her gloved fingers woven around a mug. She's talking to the fairies. I know she is.

I make coffee for Natalie and me, swallow down an antidepressant and make my way into the lounge. Natalie stirs as I enter, lifts her head from the sofa, blinks her shadowed eyes.

'I'm so sorry, Annie,' she whispers. 'I'm such a burden.'

'Don't be silly.' I put the mugs on the low table, pull back the curtains and, removing Mum's crocheting from the armchair, I sit down.

'You're the only true friend I've ever had.'

I smile, wondering if that is true, whether, if it is, I feel the same way about her. For a moment I consider telling her about Elliot calling out, but then I think of her suspects board, my brother's face looking out from it, and think better of it.

She throws off the duvet I'd found for her last night and sits up, leaving a dent in the pillow. As she pulls her sweatshirt over her bra, I can't help but notice how her shoulder blades protrude, how visible her ribs and collarbone are, and a wave of guilt and regret hits me that my first instinct last night wasn't to give her a safe roof – wasn't to protect her.

'I'm so grateful that you're letting me stay,' she says, adding to my anguish. 'I'm going half crazy, I know that. I probably belong in a psychiatric ward, will probably end up in one. But I won't give up searching. Especially as I'm sure now that whoever attacked me is still here in Ridgewater.'

'You need to be careful. Whoever they are, they know you're digging around. Talk to the police. Today.'

She nods. 'I will. I was thinking about it in the night, realised I have no choice.'

'Do you want me to come with you?' I pick up my drink, take a sip.

She shakes her head. 'Thanks, but I need to do this alone.' She rises. Picks up her coffee, and unplugs her phone from where it's been charging. 'Is it OK to take a shower?'

'Sure. And Nat?' I say, as she heads for the door. 'I'm here for you. You know that, right?'

Once she's left the room, I pick up the duvet and fold it over my arm. As I pick up the pillow, something clatters to the floor. I bend to see the knife she was carrying the other day, still tinged with her blood. She'd hidden it under her pillow.

Water pipes clank as Natalie showers, and I tell myself she still has the knife because she's understandably scared. That she needs to protect herself. But I admit I'm relieved when, ten minutes later, she hurries down the stairs and into the lounge, her cropped dark hair damp against her skull and says, 'I'm going to head off. I need to face my flat. Duncan's just messaged to say the locks have been changed, so I need to be strong.'

'OK.' I rise from the sofa, the knife now tucked behind a cushion. 'And you'll talk to the police?'

'I will, yes.' She leans in for a hug. It seems she's forgotten about the knife.

'Do you want to borrow a coat? It's freezing out there.'

She shakes her head, and I follow her into the hallway. 'I've got the car,' she says, opening the front door. 'I'll ramp up the heating.' She tilts her head, leans in and kisses my cheek. 'Thanks, Annie. I appreciate you putting me up. I'll call you later, OK?' And with that, she dashes down the path and away.

Not long after Natalie's departure, Michael arrives. He looks more subdued than usual, his fizz flat.

'Are you OK?' I ask, as he makes his way up the stairs.

'All good,' he says. 'Just didn't sleep too well.'

I dither for the next half an hour: folding washing, wandering from room to room trying to make myself useful and failing miserably. I'm about to go into the garden to chat with Mum when the doctor arrives. She's a bright young woman, full of energy. I envy her enthusiasm for the job – recalling the passion I once felt, the ambition I once had.

'You must be Elliot's sister.' She scoops her shiny black bob behind her ears. 'Your mum told me you're a doctor.'

I nod, watching from the hallway as she takes the stairs towards Elliot's room.

'It's good to have you on the premises,' she adds, glancing back just once. I wish I could believe her words.

Once she's disappeared from view, I head into the lounge. The murmur of her and Michael's voices, the whir of the electric bed – audible through the ceiling – remind me once more that my brother isn't getting any better, despite him calling out Giselle's name, and my eyes sting with tears.

I plonk down on the sofa and pick up my phone, scroll for Kerry's number and press call. She needs to know that the police have found a body.

'Hey, Annie,' she says, her upbeat tone making me wonder if I'm doing the right thing.

'Kerry, there's something you need to know.'

'OK... should I be concerned?'

'I don't know, quite honestly. It's just that a body was found in Sycamore Wood last night. A tree came down in the storm, and that's where they found it.'

'Is it Fi?' Her voice trembles.

'I've no idea. I pray it isn't but thought you should be aware. I don't know any details, but I think you have every right to make enquiries with the police.'

'Yes, thanks. I will.' I can tell I've sapped her energy. Her voice suddenly lifeless.

'Are you OK?'

'What do you think?' she snaps. There's a beat before she

adds, 'Sorry. Listen, thanks for letting me know, it couldn't have been easy. I better go.'

She ends the call, and I'm unable to suppress a surge of tears. And it's as I let out a sob that Mum puts her head round the lounge door. 'Oh, love,' she says.

'I'm broken, Mum,' I say, which sounds a bit dramatic. But I am. I bury my head in my hands and through my fingers see Mum making her way towards me, arms open wide.

'It's hard.' She lowers herself onto the sofa next to me, takes me in her arms. 'So bloody hard.'

You don't know the half of it, I don't say.

She releases me. 'Has Natalie gone?'

'Yeah, she left a couple of hours ago.'

'If I'm honest, I don't really want her here for another night.'

'It's OK, she's gone back to her apartment.' I sniff, pull a tissue from a box on the coffee table and dab my eyes. 'But she's going through a hard time,' I say.

She taps my knee. 'Fancy a hot chocolate?'

I don't, not especially. But it's Mum's go-to in a crisis. Originally, she made them for Elliot when he came home cold after a fishing trip with Dad, but one day I came home from school crying – Natalie had pushed me over because I 'went off' with another girl – and Mum made me one. 'Sounds lovely,' I say.

As she potters in the kitchen, I notice through the open lounge door the doctor making her way down the stairs. 'He seems well today, Mrs Blake,' she calls through to Mum. 'Has a sparkle in his eyes.'

Mum hurries out of the kitchen to show the GP out, grateful for good news of any kind, and I wonder if Elliot really does have a sparkle in his eyes and, if so, is it connected to him talking – albeit just one word. I get to my feet, I need to mention it to the doctor, to Mum, but by the time I reach the door, the doctor has gone.

Five minutes later, Mum and I sit on the sofa, fingers wrapped around mugs overflowing with hot chocolate and whipped cream.

'Mum,' I say, knowing I can't keep it to myself any longer, 'Elliot said something in the night.'

Her mouth drops open, her eyes widening. 'Why didn't you tell me sooner? This is brilliant news. What did he say?'

'That's just it. He called out Giselle's name.'

'Giselle's?'

'Mmm. And there's something else. There was a note in his coat pocket. It said "Thank you for everything. G."'

'That's very odd.'

'Could *G* be Giselle? Is there any chance Giselle and Elliot... well—'

'What? Before she died?'

Well, hardly after. 'Yes. In their teens. Something we didn't know about.'

She shakes her head. 'No. No, definitely not. I would have known. And the note, it must have been something more recent, surely. Someone who he'd done a favour for. He wouldn't be carrying a note in his pocket from someone who died twelve years ago.'

'No, you're right.' I rub my eyes.

'You look so tired,' she says.

'I'm not sleeping too great.'

'That's my fault. I shouldn't have agreed to you sleeping on the floor.' She dips a finger into the cream, licks it off. 'I don't know what I was thinking.'

There's a sudden creak on the stairs, and we turn towards the door.

'Michael, is that you?' Mum calls.

Silence. 'Hello?' I call, and sensing something is wrong, I get to my feet and make my way into the hallway.

And there he is. Grabbing onto the handrail. Slumped against the wall near the top of the staircase. My brother.

'His symptoms could disappear as quickly as they came.'

'Elliot!' I cry.

'Annie,' he says, a trickle of blood rolling down his arm where he must have pulled out the drip. He tries to pull himself up. But despite the physio he's been having, there's clearly little strength in his arms. 'There's something I need to tell you.'

'No, don't move,' Mum cries, now by my side. 'Stay where you are.'

And then he loses his balance. Stumbles.

I scream, my heart bashing against my ribs as, as though in slow motion, Elliot crashes down the staircase towards us.

47

Kerry stands outside Ridgewater Police Station, the scarf her mother knitted wrapped around her neck twice, her yellow woolly hat pulled low over blonde hair. The building is one storey, pale brickwork, flat roof, rectangular windows, with steps leading to a double, glass panelled door. A couple of young police officers get into a car in the small car park and set the sirens blaring.

Kerry moves from foot to foot, the cold seeping into her boots. When she first saw the snow, it felt magical – something she'd only seen in pictures – but the novelty has worn off, along with the hope she once had. When she boarded the plane from Sydney, she refused to let her mother quell her dream that she would find her sister alive, but with every step she makes, hope is dying a slow and painful death. Since Annie's call, she can no longer feel her sister here in Ridgewater. Her lights have gone out, and she wishes for the thousandth time that Fi had told their parents that she'd had a change of plan. That she'd decided to come to the UK to meet up with The Wooden Man.

She takes a deep breath and heads up the steps and through the double doors into a small reception area.

Half an hour later, she is sitting in front of DS Templeman, who is part of the team working on the discovery of the body in Sycamore Wood.

'So, Miss Brewster, what is your interest in the case?' He leans back in his chair, scratches his head. He's around forty, slim, not bad looking, but a little too sure of himself.

'It's like I explained to the officer on reception. My sister, Fiona Brewster, came to Ridgewater twelve years ago and disappeared, and I wondered...' The words stick in her throat. She's close to tears.

He leans forward. 'Did we investigate your sister's disappearance?'

She shakes her head. 'We had no idea, until recently, that she came to Ridgewater.'

'I see.' He taps his pen against his super-white teeth. 'OK, so do you want to report your sister's disappearance now?'

'I guess so.' She looks about her at the plain walls, the oblong table between her and the detective. She feels as though she's in a scene from one of those crime shows she sometimes watches. She takes a deep breath. 'But mainly, I want to know if the body you found in Sycamore Wood is her.'

The sergeant shakes his head. 'The body was male, Miss Brewster. We have yet to identify him.'

'Thank God,' Kerry says with a surge of relief. But deep down she still can't shake the feeling that she's already lost her sister.

'Let's get some information down about Fiona, shall we?' the officer says.

* * *

It's just after two o'clock when Kerry heads through the front door of the B & B where she's staying. She hasn't eaten since breakfast, but she's far from hungry.

'Oh, Miss Brewster, this was left on the counter for you,' the woman on reception says, handing Kerry a letter.

'Who left it?' Kerry doesn't recognise the handwriting, just her name scrawled across the envelope.

The woman shrugs. 'No idea, I'm afraid. It was on the counter when I came back from a ciggie break.' Her laser eyes are pinned on the letter, as though she can see through the envelope. 'Aren't you going to open it?'

Kerry freezes for a moment, considering who she's met since she's been in Ridgewater. Who knows she's staying at the B & B? Who knows her name? She looks up, meeting the woman's curious gaze. 'Thanks,' she says, stepping backwards, before making her way up the stairs to her room.

Once inside she rips the letter open.

Hi Kerry,

I've been thinking a lot about what might have happened to Fi, and there's something you need to know. Any chance we could meet up at the farm? It's important. I will be there at four o'clock.

Seb

Why a letter? They've been in contact through email up until now. She pushes away the thought that there's something about this that doesn't feel right, desperately needing to believe the words he's written. Believe he had nothing to do with her sister's disappearance – but might have information, know where she is.

But what if he tells her something she doesn't want to hear?

What if he suspects Fi's dead? Does she really want to know that? Is the torture of not knowing what's happened to her sister worse?

She picks up her phone from her bedside table – she should call Annie. But the mobile's dead. She fumbles in her bag for her charger and plugs it in before heading into the shower.

Once dressed, she shuffles into her coat and boots and grabs her phone from the charger needing to call a taxi.

Five minutes tick by before she hears the toot of a horn. She makes her way down the stairs, and out into the cold air, to where a taxi is parked a few yards down the road.

* * *

It's gone four when the taxi drops Kerry off, leaving her standing alone on Willow Farm's cobbled driveway as it pulls away. The sky is dark, heavy with more snow. The air bitter. She'd forgotten how it gets dark so early. She shouldn't be here.

A green Mini is parked in front of a double garage some distance away, and snow-covered fields stretch for miles. She takes a deep breath, pushing down a similar fear to last time she was here. As though her sister is whispering in her ear, *Leave.*

Lights are on in every window of the farmhouse, giving out an amber, warm glow, and her apprehension lifts a little. The place doesn't look as deserted as before. It looks almost welcoming. *A gingerbread house.*

She fumbles in her pocket for her phone. She needs to tell Annie where she is before she heads inside. She likes Annie. In fact, she wishes now that she'd asked her to come with her. She finds Annie's number and calls. It goes straight to voicemail.

'Hi, Annie, it's Kerry.' She explains where she is and why she's here. 'I wanted someone to know where I am. Also, just to let you know, I talked to the police about the body they found. It's male, so not Fi.' She pauses for a moment. 'Which is good, I guess – though I can't help feeling... Well, anyway, give me a call when you get this.'

She straightens her shoulders, takes a deep breath and approaches the farmhouse, all the time pushing against the panic rearing inside her. She's here in the UK to find out what happened to her sister, and this could be it, the clue that leads to the truth – however unbearable that might be.

She knocks on the door with a clenched fist, then steps back looking up at the row of windows on the first floor, feeling sure she catches a flicker of movement. 'Seb,' she calls.

She pushes the door, and it eases open with a creak. Peeking her head inside, she takes in the smell of sawdust and coffee. 'Hi! Seb! it's Kerry. I got your letter.'

She steps into a square, quarry-tiled hallway, the walls painted a deep shade of green. Three closed doors and a staircase lead from the entrance. It's warmer inside and she slowly unravels her scarf. 'Seb?' she calls once more. 'Are you here?'

She makes her way through the first door to find a kitchen being renovated. She flicks a switch and spotlights illuminate the room. It's clear the finished product will be stunning, modern, yet keeping a farmhouse charm. A huge coffee machine is on, making low puffing sounds into the silence. There's a pile of brightly coloured Duplo scattered on the floor. Kerry's eyes take her to a large, washed-out pine table. A closed laptop sits at one end with a pile of papers and old diaries. Kerry approaches. There's a couple of photo albums, and, on top, a photograph of a naturally beautiful blonde woman. Kerry flips the picture over.

Caroline Blair

She drops the photo and looks at the pile of diaries, the same name scrawled across the front of each one. Kerry looks about her, then picks up the top diary. She flicks through the pages. The entries are disturbing, random.

He won't leave me alone.
I'm afraid of him.
I can't live like this.

Kerry hears a noise. Someone's upstairs.

She puts down the diary and leaves the kitchen, returning to the hallway. Heart thudding, she looks up the stairs. 'Seb?'

And then she hears a small child's voice breaking into the chilling silence.

'Let me out.'

48

Natalie looks up at the message scrawled across her kitchen cupboards. It must be the tenth time today. She needs to google something that will remove permanent marker; there must be something that will get rid of the cruel words.

Despite the locks being replaced, she feels uneasy. Duncan gave her the new key when she arrived back from Annie's this morning, asked her if she was OK. He was heading off to visit his parents overnight. 'Promise me you'll call the police if anything weird happens,' he'd said, staring into her eyes, and for a moment she'd wished she was a normal functioning human being. Someone who would dare to go on a date, someone who might get married and have children, because, like Annie had said, Duncan was one of the good guys. He ran a hand across his wayward beard then. Not handsome, yet somehow his gentle kindness made him appear so. 'I'll be in Newquay but can be back in no time if you need me.'

Now she takes a bottle of wine from the cupboard, splashes the red liquid into a fishbowl-sized glass. She'll drink the bottle, she knows she will – one glass is never enough. Alcohol numbs the pain. Makes her feel less soiled.

However much she'd wanted to, had meant it when she told Annie this morning, she still hasn't called the police. The thought of reliving what happened twelve years ago, explaining it in detail: the bag being thrust over her head, the way... No, she couldn't face explaining it to a stranger. Instead, she will recharge and carry on searching for the attacker herself. He's got to be close. And when she finds him... She pulls a six-inch blade from the knife-rack and plunges it into the wooden work-top. *She'll kill him.*

She'd left the knife she'd been carrying since her return to Ridgewater at Fairy Cottage. Suspects Annie will have found it by now. She'd sensed both Annie and Florence didn't want her there. Afraid for Elliot.

She looks once more at the words splashed across her cupboard, takes a gulp of wine before gripping the stem of the glass and heading into the spare room. Elliot, Seb, Colin and Aiden stare at her from the cork memo board. She feels slightly guilty about the photo of Colin, but he didn't have dementia twelve years ago – he still could have attacked her. She needs to get photos of Aiden's twin brother, Mouse, and his father, Lance. Then she'll have all six suspects. Together. A collection of suspects. A murder of suspects. A haunting of suspects. A laugh, her laugh, sends a jolt through her body. She puts her glass on the table, rubs a hand around the back of her neck. 'One of you is rattled,' she whispers, pointing the knife at each picture in turn. 'One of you is afraid I'm on to you. But which one?'

She still needs to go into Boots and smell the aftershave samples. Try to find the brand her attacker wore. She'll do that as soon as possible, with or without Annie. And maybe she'll remember where she smelt it before that awful night. Who wore it? And she's become convinced now that there was someone else there that night – that it's a real memory. She heard another voice. She knows she did.

It's as though a thousand skinny arms reach into her brain, trying to drag the past to the future.

Someone had shouted something in the near distance as someone else tugged the hessian bag over her head.

Was it a name?

Yes, it was a name. She feels the pulse of blood in her ears, the realisation fizzing in her chest. Oh God, it was a name. Whoever cried out before she lapsed into unconsciousness was calling a name.

She closes her eyes, a hot tear squeezing through her lashes. And then it hits her.

'Tommy!'

Someone was yelling the name Tommy.

She grabs her phone. Calls Annie. But her phone goes straight to voicemail. She won't leave a message. This is too important. She throws on her coat and opens her front door. And then she freezes.

Someone is standing at the far end of the corridor in the darkness. She can't see their face, but she knows whoever it is, they are here for her.

49

Annie

It's been five hours since an ambulance took Elliot away, yet it feels like a year since Mum, sitting in the back holding her precious son's hand, her face red and blotchy, eyes puffy with tears, told me to hold the fort until they get back.

The house felt quiet then. Mum had sent Michael home, *'No point in you staying, love.'* He'd explained that he'd been reading to Elliot when my brother climbed off the bed, pulled out his tubes and staggered towards the stairs. Michael said he was so shocked he couldn't move – that he was 'profusely sorry' for not helping him. To be honest, his story doesn't make a lot of sense to me. I'm still struggling to understand why Michael couldn't move, why he didn't react. I'm determined to ask him next time I see him. OK, so he's a great bloke, flamboyant, funny, a tonic, but... I trust no one.

Elliot had stirred briefly at the foot of the stairs after his fall, crying out in pain, bleeding from his nose, his head. He tried to say something – a jumble of words – spoken like a toddler trying to form a sentence. I could only pick out 'my coat' before he drifted unconscious.

I had a call from Mum when they'd been at the hospital for about an hour. 'They've sedated him, for now,' she said. 'They want to do some tests, X-rays.'

'Has he said anything else?'

'No. Oh, love, I can't believe the fairies are letting this happen.'

'Keep me updated,' I said through a lump in my throat, knowing he would be safer in the hospital than at Fairy Cottage. 'I'll go into town and get some shopping later.'

I found myself pacing after that, even tried talking to the fairies myself for a while, and, if nothing else, it was therapeutic getting everything out there, even if the invisible beings didn't come up with any answers.

About an hour ago, Mum called again with nothing much else to report. 'I'm going to go down to the hospital foyer to get a magazine or a book,' she said. 'Perhaps pick up a sandwich. Not that I'm hungry.'

'Why don't you come home?' I said. 'I can cook you something. You can have a rest, and I'll go to the hospital, sit with Elliot.'

'No, I need to be here, Annie. Though I'm sure they'll throw me out soon.'

'OK, well I'll go into town and get some shopping.' I needed air. 'We're low on a few things.'

'Yes, good idea, and could you check on the hedgehogs later too?'

* * *

It's dark now, as I trudge back down the lane towards the cottage, carrying two heaving bags-for-life, though the moon is full and the brightness of the snowy ground helps guide my way. It's a good thing, as I left my phone at home – which was stupid of me. I'm seriously not thinking straight right now.

Earlier, I saw Seb coming out of a menswear store. He waved from the other side of the road. His smile wide. Am I wrong to disregard him as Natalie's attacker? He did go after her that awful night and the trauma of finding his mother dead, together with his father's breakdown, must have had a terrible effect on him. And what about Fi? He'd been talking to her online. No. I still refuse to believe he's capable of Natalie's attack, or Fi's disappearance.

Leafless trees are laden with snow, branches, like witches' hands, reach across the unmade road. Shadows swirl sending a chill down my back, making me twitchy. I pick up speed. Almost home, when I see someone approaching from the other direction, their head down. I feel suddenly vulnerable, but before fear freezes me, whoever it is dashes into the bushes and out of sight. I shudder. A dog walker, perhaps?

It's as I pass Sycamore House moments later that I hear fast footsteps approaching from behind, the sound of quick breaths, closer, closer, closer.

I go to turn but the strike on the back of my head is excruciating. I topple forward, shades of grey rushing up towards me, my shopping clattering to the ground as I hit the road with a thud. My world turning black.

50

Kerry can't move. Her body's fight or flight response hasn't kicked in, leaving her frozen at the foot of the stairs, listening. The farmhouse has fallen silent. Perhaps she imagined the small voice that had sent a chill down her spine.

Kerry finally moves towards the stairs, her stomach churning. She picks up an umbrella that was propped against the wall and stealthily takes the first step. It creaks. *Crap!*

'Mummy, let me out.'

It's seconds later that a figure appears at the top of the stairs. 'Kerry?'

Kerry stares hard at the woman. She's beautiful. Stunning, in fact, a scarf tied around long dark hair, paint-splattered denim dungarees and a checked shirt hanging on her slim body, the sleeves rolled up to her elbows. A little girl is in her arms, blonde and cute.

'I'm Sasha,' the woman says, heading down the stairs towards Kerry, her face serious, though there's nothing threatening about her.

‘'Ello,’ the little girl says, her blue eyes wide. ‘Green,’ she says, pointing at the paint speckled in her mother’s dark hair.

‘I’m glad you came,’ Sasha says, leading the way into the kitchen.

‘*You* sent me the letter?’ Kerry edges towards the kitchen doorway. ‘Who are you?’

‘I’m Seb’s wife.’ Sasha puts the child down, and on chubby legs the little girl runs towards the pile of Duplo and plonks herself down.

‘I heard her cry out,’ Kerry says.

‘Yes. I’m painting a mural for her soon-to-be bedroom. A forest scene with wildlife. I thought Megan would be OK in her playpen, but she was getting rather restless.’

‘This is your house?’ Kerry says. ‘Seb said he was doing it up—’

‘He is. For us. He lived here from around the age of twelve. It was his grandparents’ house. When they died it went to his mother, Caroline. Now it’s ours.’

Kerry’s eyes fall onto the diaries and photo.

‘Yes, that’s Caroline in the picture,’ Sasha says, picking it up and studying it for several moments, a sadness in her eyes. ‘I never met her, but her loss was tragic, took its toll on Seb. I found quite a lot of her stuff tucked away in the loft when I was clearing it out, even her suicide note. I can recall it word for word: “I’m sorry. I can’t live with myself.” That was it. No hint of why she couldn’t go on.’ A beat. ‘Seb and his father found her, you know.’ Her eyes shimmer, and she flaps her hand across her face. Sniffs. ‘Sorry, I’m getting sidetracked.’ She grabs two mugs from the cupboard. ‘Coffee? I’ve only got oat milk, I’m afraid.’

However normal this situation now seems, Sasha lured Kerry here pretending to be Seb, and it’s left her feeling uneasy. 'No. No thanks. How did you know I was staying at the B & B?'

'Seb told me. Said he gave you directions.'

'That's right.'

'He told me you're looking for your sister.'

Kerry nods. 'Fi.'

'The thing is, I need to talk to you without Seb being about. I'm sorry I lied, but it's important. Please.'

'But why pretend? Why not sign the letter yourself?'

'I wasn't sure you'd come if I did. You don't even know me.'

Kerry shrugs. 'OK. But I don't want any coffee.'

She sits down at the kitchen table, and Sasha abandons making the coffee and sits down opposite her, folding her fingers together, her elbows on the table.

'Seb told me he spoke to your sister online over twelve years ago.'

'Yes, that's right.'

Sasha furrows her forehead. 'Do you think Seb had something to do with her disappearance?' She frees her fingers and rubs circles into her temples. 'It's just I'm getting sick of people snooping into Seb's life, thinking he's a bad person.'

'Natalie?'

'Seb is a good man.' Her voice has risen, and her little girl looks up from playing with her bricks. 'He's gentle and kind. You have to stop this, this... witch hunt.'

'Maybe I should go.' Kerry gets to her feet, unsettled by the flash of anger in Sasha's eyes.

'No, please stay.' She lowers her voice. 'I'm sorry. I just need you to know that Seb couldn't have done anything to harm your sister. You have to believe that.'

'How can you be so certain? I mean he was in contact with Fi just before she vanished. He'd planned to meet her.'

'I know. But—'

'I'm happy to listen.' Kerry lowers herself back onto the chair, 'But, as it is, it's possible that he lured her here to Ridgewater.'

'No! He didn't lure her here. She came because they'd become friendly online, and he was looking forward to meeting her.'

You can't be sure of that. You only have his word. 'You need to know I've spoken to the police.'

'You have?'

'I had no choice, I had to tell them about Seb.'

'Oh God, this will undo everything.' She buries her head in her hands and lets out a cry. 'Why? Why would you do that?'

'Undo everything?'

She's silent for a moment. 'OK... I met Seb years ago when he was at rock bottom.' She takes a deep breath. 'I was his counsellor. He worked so hard at pulling himself out of deep depression. I—'

'Mummy, why are you crying?' The little girl's eyes are wide. 'Mummy?'

Sasha looks up, wipes a tear from her cheek. 'Mummy's OK, darling. This lady has just told her something to make her a little bit sad.'

Kerry studies mother then daughter. Was she right to tell the police about Seb? But he was Fi's only connection to Ridgewater. Her sister wouldn't have come here if it wasn't for him.

'Seb's been through so much,' Sasha says, her blue eyes shimmering as she gets up and crouches on the floor near her little one and snaps two bricks together. 'He saw his mother...' She glances at her daughter. 'And his father had a breakdown. Yet he pulled himself up, and we have a good life – a brilliant life. But this ridiculous quest of yours and Natalie's is going to bring him down. He's a good person. The best.'

Kerry rises once more, unable to cope with the sight of mother and child. 'If Seb's innocent, then there's nothing to worry about,' she says.

Sasha rises too. 'But that's not true, is it? Mud sticks. No smoke without fire. That's what people will say.'

'I'm sorry.' Kerry dashes for the door. 'I have to know what happened to my sister. The not knowing is torturous.'

'Mummy why are you crying?' the child repeats.

'I'm fine, sweetheart.' Sasha lifts the little girl up, cuddling her close. 'Mummy's fine.'

'I understand what you have to do,' Sasha says to Kerry's departing back, clearly defeated. 'But when you discover you're wrong, I hope you can live with yourself.'

Natalie stares at Aiden. He's dressed in black and now sitting in the armchair as she paces the room. The sight of him makes her feel sick.

'Bastard!' she yells. Her spitting anger is keeping her buoyant, though she sounds more fearless than she actually is. Has she found her attacker? Is he really here, sitting in her lounge? The man who ruined her life.

He's holding a knife. He threatened her with it five minutes ago, his aim to get into the apartment. But now it hangs loose in his gloved hands.

She drops down onto the sofa, pulls up her knees and wraps her arms around them, trying to still her shaking body. She stares at his hands. Are they the hands that almost ended her life? Her heart bangs against her chest. She can't let him know she's afraid.

I will turn the tables on you, Aiden. I will kill you.

Her eyes move to his, they look oddly sad.

'I never attacked you, Natalie,' he says, his voice breaking. 'You have to believe that. It wasn't me.' This is the third time he's said those words. Twice she's ignored him. You don't come to someone's apartment with a knife if you're not guilty of something.

'So, you just fancied sending me an anonymous letter. Just decided to break into my apartment and scrawl intimidating words across my kitchen... what, for a laugh?'

'It's not funny.'

'You think I don't fucking know that?' she yells, spittle flying from her mouth.

'I had to warn you. I needed you to stop.'

'Stop?'

'With your pick, pick, picking away at what happened that night. There's nothing you can do to change anything. I had to make you stop.' He looks down at the knife in his hands. Turns it over. 'I had a visit from the police today,' he says.

'Wasn't my doing. I haven't got that far—'

'I know. This was about my brother—'

'Mouse?'

'The body in Sycamore Wood. They've found a wallet with ID. They think it's my brother Tommy... Mouse. They... they think he was murdered.'

Natalie covers her mouth. None of the words bouncing around her head make it to her lips, ranging from *Fuck!* to *Mouse's real name is Tommy?*

'They think he was killed twelve years ago. Do you understand what I'm saying? What I'm telling you?'

'Tommy,' she whispers. 'The voice I heard that night was calling his name.' She looks up, stares into Aiden's eyes. 'Oh God. It was you. Your voice.'

He nods, his body tense. 'It was the day you and I argued in the Fox—'

'You were a complete jerk.'

He nods. 'I know, and I've spent so long trying to be different.'

'God forgives?'

'He does, yes. And I'm grateful for that.'

'Yeah, well your God is a fool.'

He looks down once more at the knife in his hands. 'Maybe.'

'So, what happened? What are you saying?' Tears burn behind her eyes. Has she got this wrong? 'That your brother—'

'Mouse followed you all into Sycamore Wood that night. I was worried. He always had problems. Serious problems. I hung about for hours, waiting. I guess, perhaps, on some level, I was worried what he might do. I saw Seb head for home, then Annie, then Elliot.

'The thing is, Natalie, when you didn't come out of the wood, and I knew Tommy was still in there, I began to panic. I went looking for you. First, I heard footsteps. It was that girl who later died, dressed in white.'

'Giselle?'

'Yeah, she took off when she saw me.'

'Giselle was outside?'

'Yeah, and then I saw my brother.' He runs a hand around his neck. 'Saw what the bastard was doing to you.' He breaks off for a moment, takes a deep breath.

The reality stabs her repeatedly. She can't keep a limb still.

'And you killed him?' Her eyes fill with tears. 'He was attacking me, and you killed him?'

'I couldn't believe what was happening. I cried out to him, hoping I was wrong, that... but you had a bag over your head. I thought you were dead, that he'd killed you. Anger took over. This monster who I'd shared a womb with. My twin. I had to get rid of him. He made my skin crawl and my stomach heave. I hated that we shared the same DNA. So yes, I killed my own brother, and I've been asking for forgiveness ever since.'

51

Annie

I stir, my head throbbing, feeling sure I will throw up.

I'm lying on what feels like a bed, but it's so dark here I can't be sure. I've no idea where I am. A memory flashes in. Being helped to my feet, guided up some stairs. A voice. '*You poor dear. Let me help you.*'

A tap, tap, tap, like a drumbeat. Someone's sitting in the corner shrouded in shadows. I can't see their face. I go to move. Realise I'm strapped to the bed. Thick ropes bite into my wrists and ankles. A light breeze comes from somewhere. A flash of metallic silver bobs above my head, a strong smell of bleach makes me gag.

And then I hear it, the musical box playing the theme from *Swan Lake*.

'Let me go!' I cry out. 'Please. Just let me go.' A tear rolls sideways down my cheek. I hadn't realised I was crying.

So this is what fear feels like.

Real fear.

I stare at the figure in the corner. Tap. Tap. Tap. 'What the hell do you want from me?' I cry. 'What did I do to you?'

The moon creeps from behind a cloud and filters through the window – the shutters are open. The metallic silver I noticed above me is a helium balloon bobbing across the ceiling. There's a full-length mirror on the ceiling too. At first, I don't recognise my reflection. My hair is damp, tied in rag curls, and I'm wearing a long white dress.

As I attempt to move once more, a lamp springs to life, giving off a dim light, and my heart thuds so hard I think it might break through my ribs.

52

Natalie's emotions skitter. She remembers coming round twelve years ago, the bag no longer over her head, Sycamore Wood dark and silent. She'd pulled herself up with the aid of a tree. And after throwing up by the tree, her arm pressed against its bark, she'd run for her life, not looking back.

Now her fists are clenched, nails pushing into her palms. It's a while before she speaks. 'Why the knife, Aiden? The letter? Everything?'

'I just wanted you to stop searching, is all. Selfish, I know. But if you found out the truth, you'd find out I killed my brother.'

'Pretty sure God isn't too impressed with you.' She unclenches her fists, pushes fingers through her short hair, nails scraping skin.

'It's all going to come out now,' he says. 'Once forensics go to work on my brother's body, they'll know you and I were the last to see him alive. They'll know I killed him.' A beat. 'Unless—?'

'Jesus, you've got to be kidding me.'

'He attacked you. You had every right to kill him in self-defence. You said yourself if you found out who attacked you, you would kill him – I simply did it for you. You'll get off lightly after what he did to you.'

She presses her palms to the top of her head, looks up, for what? Guidance? 'Fuck's sake. Not a chance in hell.'

He lowers his head, throws the knife onto the table, where it skids across the wood and drops to the floor, then he buries his head in his hands. 'Worth a try.'

'You killed a rapist who was trying to kill me,' she says. 'The judge will take that into account.'

'Yeah, and then I covered it up.'

'Admit what you did and why, before they find out; it will go in your favour. I'll come with you, tell them what happened to me.'

'You'd do that?'

'Sure. You have no idea the relief I feel knowing who did it, and that he's dead. That's what I'll tell them and the jury.' She stares at him for a moment, and despite the fact he never came forward at the time, she's grateful. She would probably be dead now if he hadn't stepped in. 'Let's hope they're not too hard on you,' she says. 'I mean that.'

* * *

Elliot

I stare at Mum from where I'm lying in a hospital bed. There's so much I want to say.

'Take it slow, darling.' She leans forward in the chair and takes my hand. 'We've got all day.'

But we haven't got all day, and if I don't get my words out something terrible could happen. 'Giselle—'

A nurse approaches pushing a trolley. She checks my vitals. 'Looks like you're on the mend, love.' She smiles as she wheels the trolley onwards towards the man in the next bed.

Mum rises, pulls the curtain around the bed as though the flimsy fabric will keep our conversation private, before returning to the chair, taking hold of my hand once more.

'Mum,' I say, my voice croaky from lack of use. 'Listen to me, it's important.' I breathe in, close my eyes, breathe out. 'It's about Giselle Bancroft.'

53

SEVEN WEEKS AGO

'Leave that bit, dear.' Margot stood on the crazy-paved patio at the rear of Sycamore House, looking much the same as she always had, like an ageing nineteen-fifties movie star in her wide-bottomed, high-waisted trousers, sharp-collared silk blouse and dark sunglasses shaped like cat's eyes. 'I want that area to grow wild. But the rest of the garden needs cutting right back and digging over. I'm hoping to lay a new lawn.'

Elliot ran a hand across his stubbled chin, glancing to where she was pointing. To where nettles grew at their tallest, tangling with rampant golden dandelions. This once immaculately manicured garden had become a wilderness. Giselle's old swing-set was covered in bird droppings, ivy suffocating red plastic. Paint peeled from the wrought-iron table that once displayed napkins and cut-glass. Elliot felt a sudden surge of despair. *I shouldn't be here. Here in Margot's garden. Mum would hate the thought, would be disappointed in me.* But he needed money to get his life back on track. The five hundred pounds in cash Margot had given him upfront would help.

He'd seen the advert for a gardener in the *Ridgewater*

Gazette. Was taken aback when he called the number and a posh woman's voice said, 'Margot Bancroft speaking.'

'Mick Anderson,' he'd said, the lie catching, making him cough. He went to school with a Mick Anderson – or was it Rick? It really didn't matter. He just needed a fake name. If he'd said he was Elliot Blake, she would have surely hung up the phone.

'Homemade lemonade?' Margot said. *Her speciality*. His sister Annie had told him how delicious it was, and he'd often longed to try it. To be allowed over the fence. To play on the swing.

He pulled his cap low over dark hair. There was no reason why Margot would recognise him. Despite being neighbours, she'd barely been aware of his existence as a child and teen, and he looked different now, in his early thirties.

'Lemonade will be great,' he said, *though a lager would go down better*.

With a click of heels, the woman disappeared through French doors into the gloom of Sycamore House.

Elliot took a deep breath, removed his coat and slung it across the table, the money she gave him tucked safely in an inside pocket. He picked up a pair of shears. He knew how to tackle the garden. Enjoyed the outdoors. But it was going to be a long day. Warm for October. He began chopping at the wildness. Sycamore seeds in their hundreds had flown in from the trees in the nearby wood like tiny planes, crash landing into the tangle of weeds, never to escape.

Five minutes later, Margot returned and placed a jug of lemonade and a crystal glass on the mossy table. With a red lipstick smile, she said, 'I've got to pop out, dear. I won't be long.'

'No worries.' He watched her go. This woman who never

allowed him to enter this garden as a child. This woman who he had seen from afar, fussing over her frill-clad, princess-like daughter. This woman who encouraged the police to question him the day that daughter, by then a teenager, had died.

An hour later he'd made some impression on the garden, but it was going to take forever. He rubbed the back of his hand across his sweaty brow, threw down the shears and headed for the lemonade. He took a greedy gulp, but it was warm, tasted bitter on his tongue. Had Annie really liked it as much as she claimed?

He approached the French doors, made a bridge with his hand and looked through the glass into the lounge. It was the first time he'd seen inside. Would Margot mind if he got himself a glass of water? He would be in and out in seconds. He kicked off his trainers and headed inside, dashed across the lounge, followed by the many eyes of Giselle. He shuddered. There were so many photographs of Margot's daughter, staring at him from every angle.

In the hallway there was a full-length picture of the girl in a pink tutu, her hands curved above her head as she posed on tiptoe. She was about five or six in the portrait. It seemed Margot had never got over her daughter's loss. This place was a shrine to Giselle.

He glanced up the stairs, where a faded velvet curtain was pulled across the top. Curiosity surged through him. This house had always been such a mystery to both him and his sister Annie – though at least Annie had the chance to play in the garden.

He turned away from the stairs, needing to find the kitchen. It was the first door he opened. The dark wooden units were oppressive, every surface gleaming, a whiff of citrus in the air.

He took a glass from a cabinet and streamed water into it. Gulped it back.

It was as he returned to the hallway, refreshed, that he heard a tapping sound coming from the first floor. *Margot?* No, he'd seen her leave.

'Hello?' he called, taking one step, then another, unsure what was driving him, other than an uncanny feeling that he wasn't alone in the house.

At the top of the stairs, he pulled back the velvet curtain and flicked on his phone torch. He passed another set of stairs leading upwards and made his way along a dark landing stretching out before him. Four doors. *Tap, tap, tap.*

His heart pounded as he made his way along the landing, floorboards creaking under his socked feet. He reached for the handle of the first door and opened it, poking his head round to see a large, empty room. The walls were cream, wooden floorboards dark. A floor-to-ceiling mirror filled the wall at the far end, and a pole like the ones ballet dancers used to practise ran across the room, several pairs of ballet shoes hanging from it. He closed the door quickly. Took a few more steps to find the next door ajar.

A chill hit as he entered the room. Wooden shutters, closed at the window, blocked out the daylight. This room had clearly once been a nursery – a rocking horse in the far corner, a cot in the other, porcelain dolls with freakishly pale faces looking down at him from a shelf. A cricket bat was propped against a wall, a red ball nestled against it. He'd seen enough scary movies to feel a creep of unease. What the hell would he do if the ball rolled across the room towards him? *Grow up. There's no such thing as ghosts.* But it really was freaky up there on the first floor of Sycamore House.

He stepped out towards a wardrobe, opening the door to

find twenty or more frilly white dresses with silk ribbons that would fit a child. *Giselle's?*

He left the room, closing the door behind him, and started to make his way back towards the curtain when the tapping started again, frantic, irregular. It was coming from the room at the far end of the landing. He wasn't alone up here.

He moved slowly towards the door in socked feet. 'Hello?'

'Let me out.' The voice was a faint whisper. He waited. Listening. He must have been mistaken. *There's nobody up here. Calm down!*

Stomach churning, heart thudding, he made his way further along the corridor, the air getting warmer as he went. A beam of light glowed from under the furthest door.

'Hello?' he called once more. But the silence was thick and heavy, the sort of hush you got at funerals before the coffin's brought in. His body tingled as he saw the final door was bolted on the outside. He looked behind him at the dark stretch of landing, then back.

'Hello? Is anyone in there?' he called, leaning his ear against the wood. Nothing. He took a deep breath and dragged back the bolt, placing his hand on the handle.

A sudden tip tap of heels behind him, approaching quickly. He swung round, pulled back his hand.

'What are you doing up here, Elliot?' She – Margot – was almost upon him. *She knows who I am. How long has she known? What gave me away?*

Elliot froze. Someone was behind the door. He could hear them breathing.

The handle lowered. The door flew open.

Margot grabbed Elliot's arm, dug her nails into his flesh. 'Oh God!' she yelled. 'What the hell have you done?'

54

NOW

Kerry's taxi pulls up outside Fairy Cottage. She needs to speak to Annie. If Seb isn't responsible for her sister's disappearance, like Sasha insists, then who the hell is? She's been playing over the woman's words since leaving the farmhouse. Sasha had sounded so sure her husband was innocent, and Kerry supposes she would be the same in her position. If there was a chance the person you loved, your soulmate, was... what? An abductor? A killer? You would never believe it. You would fight it with everything you had.

There's no reply when she knocks on the door. Fairy Cottage is deserted, no lights on in the windows. She should have called first. She'll now have to walk back to the B & B. But first she pulls out her phone. Tries calling Annie. The call goes straight to voicemail. Next she tries Natalie's number. She's not drawn to Natalie in the same way she's drawn to Annie, but she needs to offload.

'Hey, Kerry,' Natalie says on answering. 'How's things?'

There's something in Natalie's tone that's different. Lighter perhaps. Yet there's emotion there too.

'OK,' Kerry says. 'Do you have any idea where Annie is?'

'I haven't seen her since this morning. Is everything OK?'

'Yes, I just wanted to catch up with her. I've been talking with Sasha Blair. She insists Seb had nothing to do with my sister's disappearance and—'

'He didn't attack me,' Natalie says.

'You sound so sure.'

'The thing is, I've found out who did.'

Kerry's heart gallops. 'God, who?'

'Aiden Shaw's twin brother. Most people called him Mouse.'

'That's huge, Natalie. Are you OK?'

'I'm getting there. But I'm no longer sure my attack had any connection to Fi, other than it happened twelve years ago in Ridgewater.'

Kerry's heart continues to thud. 'So Seb's not off the hook completely.'

'No, I suppose he isn't.' A beat. 'Tread carefully, Kerry. I didn't and, well—'

'Are you sure you're OK?'

'I am. Just about to head to the cop shop.'

'Good luck. I'm here if you need me.'

Kerry ends the call and makes her way down the unmade lane, past Sycamore House and towards Ridgewater. She feels a string of twisting emotions – the loss of her sister, loneliness, helplessness and, at the pit of her stomach, a rising fear she can't quite explain.

55

Annie

I struggle against the ropes, hearing the tinkling sound of the musical box. My back, legs and arms prickle, the stinging sensation familiar. A childhood pain from running through the woods, bare limbed. Nettles! Christ, there are nettles in the bed.

'Don't waste your energy, Giselle, darling.' I recognise her slippery, smooth vowels, and my stomach heaves.

She rises, shoulders back as she comes into view. So proper, so pristine. She moves closer, runs a hand over my cheek. 'You hurt my feelings,' she says, tilting her head to one side. 'Leaving me the way you did. Why would you do that, Giselle?'

'I'm not Giselle,' I cry, my throat dry. 'Giselle's dead.'

Margot drops down onto a chair next to me, the movement jarring the balloon into action. It bounces once, twice, three times – bop, bop, bop – across the ceiling, the words 'Welcome Home' coming into view.

'I so wanted you to be blonde before we go,' she says,

touching my hair. 'But the bleach is taking forever to work on such dark hair. Still,' she adds, pulling free one of the rag cloths, then another. 'At least you'll have curls.'

I lie still as she removes all the rags, feeling curls falling against my skull. 'What do you want from me?' I whimper, avoiding looking in the mirror on the ceiling.

'I'm going to tell you a story, Giselle,' she says. 'Do you recall how much you loved my stories? I'll start at the very beginning, shall I?' She lets out a childlike giggle, before snapping the musical box shut. The music stops.

'I'm not your daughter, Margot.' A pulse thuds in my ears. 'I'm Annie. Annie Blake. Please. Let me go.'

'Calm yourself. I'll take good care of you. I'll keep you safe, my precious girl.'

Her words twist in my brain. This can't be happening.

'Once upon a time, very long ago, there was a wicked, wicked woman called Joan Bancroft.' Margot's eyes drift towards the window. 'She was my mother. Your grandmother, Giselle. A nasty piece of work.' She looks about her and, lowering her voice, says, 'And this was her bedroom, before it became mine.'

'Let me go!' I cry, continuing to struggle against the ropes. But it's no good. My wrists and ankles are trapped so tightly any movement makes my flesh raw. 'I'm not Giselle. Giselle's dead,' I repeat, the stinging in my back unbearable.

She sweeps her gaze back to me, shakes her head. 'I've come to realise that the only way we can be together, Giselle, is in the next world. You always were my little angel.'

It hits me what she's saying – what she's planning – and I ramp up my attempts to get away, but the more I struggle the more the nettles sting, the more the ropes cut into my skin.

'Your grandmother was an evil woman.'

'Please stop!' My life hasn't been easy of late, but I don't want to die. 'I don't even know your mother.' But I remember the old woman's voice echoing from her room at the care home: *'Sugar and spice and all things nice, that's what little girls are made of. Slugs and snails and puppy-dog tails, that's what little boys are made of.'*

'Goodness knows why the woman was so cruel,' Margot goes on. 'Perhaps it was something deep-rooted from her childhood.' She continues to stare into my eyes as though she can see my thoughts. I look for a flicker of emotion – anything, but there's nothing there. 'It often is, isn't it?' she goes on. 'The unresolved traumas we carry into adulthood.'

'You can't blame your mother for everything,' I say. 'You have to take responsibility, Margot.' I've no idea where the sudden surge of strength came from, but the wobble in my voice gives away my fear.

She takes a deep breath. Smiles. 'Joan Bancroft owned this place and the land. Inherited it from her parents – her three brothers long dead by then. She had a daughter, me, and later a son, Joel. She didn't want him. Little boys made her skin crawl. Poor Joel. Apparently, Mother told me in later years, her brothers had all teased her – poor little Joan – and then, much later, my father ran out on her. This was her excuse for abusing Joel. She hated men. I witnessed her pushing him under the bath water once; I was outside the door, could have only been five or six. She heard me and let him go. He came up gasping, spluttering, crying. I don't know to this day what would have happened if I hadn't been there.' She gulps, closing her eyes for a moment. 'How's that for a childhood trauma? I couldn't sleep for a week or more, and little Joel withdrew into himself more and more over the years, taking off as soon as he could. Sixteen he was when he ran away.' She shakes her head. 'He should never have come back to Ridgewater. I should never have let him visit the house. Visit you, Giselle. That was a terrible mistake.'

56

Kerry dashes towards the end of the lane, a strange prickly panic she's felt several times since leaving Australia rising in her chest. She fears, perhaps irrationally, that she won't make it through the darkness and her heart hammers against her ribs. The unmade road she's just raced along was so dark, her phone torch barely enough to guide her way. She'd seen a couple of bags of shopping near a creepy old house, but there was nobody about, and she wasn't about to hang around to find the owner.

She's relieved when she sees the bright light of the High Street up ahead, and scoots towards it, her B & B within touching distance, shoppers and dog walkers in sight.

Footsteps. Someone's right behind her. A creeping fear crawls across the back of her neck once more.

'Kerry?' She turns, relieved to see the bloke from behind the bar at the One Trick Pony. Tom – that was his name. He'd kindly put up the poster of Fi. 'Any luck tracking down your sister?' he says, joining her as she walks.

She shakes her head, amazed he remembers. 'I'm going

round in circles, to be honest, starting to feel I should give up and head back to Australia.'

'Listen, I don't suppose you fancy a drink?' His smile is wide, his blue eyes kind.

She shrugs. 'Why not?' she says – one drink won't hurt. 'They've got a bar at the B & B where I'm staying.'

'Perfect,' he says.

* * *

Florence is still wobbly from Elliot's revelation, her heart pounding. *'It's about Giselle Bancroft,'* he'd said, throwing her into shock.

She looks towards Sycamore House as the taxi disappears into the darkness.

The porch light casts a shadow across the building, giving it an eerie glow, and there are a couple of bags of groceries lying on their sides at the foot of the path, tins and fruit spilling out. She wonders for a moment what's happened but pushes the thought away; she needs to find Annie.

She turns, hurries up the path towards the front door of Fairy Cottage; she needs to speak to her daughter urgently.

Elliot, his voice cracking under the strain, his hand gripping hers as he lay in the hospital bed, had told her how, needing money, he'd taken a job as a gardener at Sycamore House without telling her, fearing she would be upset. That he'd found Giselle alive, locked in an upstairs room. He'd let her out, then he ran from Sycamore House. As he ran across the overgrown garden, he'd glanced back to see Giselle race through the French doors. She'd veered off towards Sycamore Wood, so he'd doubled back, concerned for her. Unable to comprehend that she was still alive. He caught up with her on the cliff edge, to find her sobbing. Terrified.

He'd given her his coat and some money and told her to run and never stop running. And as he watched her disappear through the trees, Margot had appeared, yelling at him that he had no idea what damage he'd done. With one swift movement, she'd lunged at him, pushing him from the cliff to the sand below.

Florence, shocked and confused by her son's revelation, had tried to find out more, but Elliot closed his eyes then. '*Annie needs to be careful. Margot is dangerous,*' he'd whispered, before lapsing into sleep.

Florence has been trying to call Annie ever since, but her daughter's phone keeps going to voicemail. But she's home now, determined to make sure her daughter is safe from the woman she's always hated.

'Annie?' she cries, opening the front door and flicking on the light. 'Annie?'

She dashes up the stairs, taking them two at a time. But the house is cold and silent. There's nobody here.

She tries calling Annie's phone for the umpteenth time. Hears it ring out from her daughter's bedroom. Tries to think who else to call. The police? Yes, she needs to call the police.

She heads into the old study then, where Richard used to do his birdwatching, a swell of tears rising. She never stopped loving him, whatever her son and daughter might think.

She looks out towards Sycamore House. An amber glow seeps from an upstairs window. It's been a long while since she's seen a light on the first floor. Who's up there now? She thinks of the shopping bags on the step, the fact that Annie was going into town to get supplies, and hurtles down the stairs and into the lounge.

She stares at the phone that she hasn't used since before Richard died. The thought of him talking to Margot on it leaving her cold. But now she snatches up the receiver and dials 999.

* * *

Kerry sits down opposite Tom. There's no doubting he's good looking, with the most piercing blue eyes she's ever seen. He's too old for her, probably. Not that she's ever had much of an interest in men, the thought of a relationship too restricting. There'd been a couple of blokes at university she'd dated – quite liked, in fact. But her missing sister has always consumed her – dominated her life.

Tom collects their drinks from the tiny bar. He knocks back his beer fast, and Kerry matches his pace with her Bud Light. It's almost like a drinking competition. Though she's normally not much of a drinker – her mother's addiction and her own diabetes putting paid to any desire to explore her rite of passage and get wasted. But she needs alcohol right now. The rising panic from earlier hasn't fully dissipated. Truth is, she should probably eat something. Her mother would be nagging her by now. But she's far from hungry.

'What was Fi like?' Tom asks, seeming genuinely interested, though she can't help but notice the past tense in his question.

'She *is* the best older sister anyone could wish for,' she says, slipping off her cardigan.

'Strong, intelligent, would save the world if she could?'

'You got all that from a photo?'

He laughs. 'Just the vibe I get,' he says. 'My aunt always says you can get a lot from a photo.'

'Well, yeah, Fi was strong and intelligent and beautiful. She had no idea how she shone. How her presence lit up a room.' Kerry feels shaky, a weird jumpy feeling in her chest. 'Fi cared about everyone. Would do anything to help if someone needed her.'

'Another beer?' Tom rises to his feet, as though he wasn't listening, as though he wasn't aware of the grief rising inside her.

She shakes her head. 'I'm good, thanks.' It's still relatively early, but she's suddenly tired. She should go to her room – book a flight. Call her mum to say she's coming home. OK, so she hasn't got the answers she came for but she's beginning to accept that. That and the fact she'll never find Fi.

Tom is back within moments, holding another beer and taking a gulp before sitting down once more. He puts the glass on the table and takes a deep breath. 'I've been wrestling with myself for a while,' he says, taking hold of both her hands.

She wants to tug free, conscious that her skin is sweaty, but the earnest look in his eyes turns her to stone.

'Ever since you came into the bar and I put up the poster, I... well, the thing is... the thing is, there's something I need to tell you.'

'You know something about Fi?'

He nods. 'Yes. I met her... your sister. Twelve years ago, when she came to Ridgewater.'

57

Annie

'I've told you very little about my life before you were born, Giselle. But I feel now, before we go on our way, it's important that you know. Everything.'

'I'm not your daughter. Giselle is dead,' I cry yet again, my whole body trembling. 'You have to let me go.'

'You know already that your grandmother Joan – I'll call her Joan, as the word 'mother' catches in my throat – wanted me to be a ballerina. She named me after her favourite dancer, Margot Fonteyn, famous long before your time. Joan once dreamt of being a ballerina herself, though she never fulfilled her dream, perhaps because of her teasing older brothers, perhaps because she wasn't the right shape or build, perhaps she wasn't pretty enough. Whatever the reason, she decided if she couldn't be a ballerina, I would be. I spent hours and hours in the dance studio, Joan watching my every move, living her life through me. I was only allowed to break when I'd mastered the next perfect pirouette, arabesque or tendu. And I went along with it. I had no choice. But it was more than that, I wanted to be a perfect ballerina, wanted to make my mother happy. I worked hard. So hard.'

I struggle, the ropes burning my skin. 'Untie me, Margot. Please.'

'And now I come to the part you know nothing of, darling Giselle.'

It's as though I haven't spoken, as though my tears are invisible.

'Nobody was more excited than me when Joan got me a place in a select ballet school in London. And I went there a naïve eighteen-year-old virgin, immediately charmed by the handsome forty-three-year-old owner.' She pauses for a moment. 'He seduced me, Giselle. I fell pregnant with you. My dream – *Joan's dream* – for me to become a prima ballerina turned sour because of one stupid mistake. Of course, the man – your father – didn't want to know. Told me to pack my bags and leave the academy. Told me to get an abortion. But it was far too late for that – perhaps I'd been in denial.'

'I'm sorry,' I say, a part of me, despite being strapped, spreadeagled to this bed by this deranged woman, feeling for her. I'm not quite sure why. She doesn't deserve it.

'Oh, darling,' she says, stroking my cheek. 'Please don't be sorry.' I cringe at her touch. Turn my head away. 'You wouldn't be here if I hadn't gone through that awful year.' She shakes her head. 'This is why I've never told you this before. I didn't want to upset you. I didn't want you to know where you came from. That your father didn't want you. Besides,' she adds with a twisted smile, 'he died shortly after you were born.'

'I'm Annie, not Giselle.'

'I've told you before why I named you Giselle. That it was after the famous ballet. A peasant girl ruined by a nobleman.

Now you know the full reason.' She stands up, reaches for my hair, fiddles with the damp curls. 'It's lightening slightly,' she says. 'Good. Good.'

I catch my reflection in the mirror above. I look nothing like me. It's almost as though Giselle has taken me over and I'm lost forever.

'Suffice to say,' Margot goes on, sitting down once more, 'I only had one option. To return to Sycamore House. To my mother.' She picks up a clear plastic bag from the bedside table, and I notice a reel of thick parcel tape. 'I hate that it's come to this, darling. But we have to be on our way, to a far better place than here.'

'Please,' I beg, not hiding my fear, bile rising in my throat, making me choke, tears soaking my cheeks. 'I'm Annie, not Giselle. Please. Untie me. Let me out. I promise I won't tell anyone.'

'It's OK. I'm going to drug you first. You won't feel a thing. And then I will take my own life, and we'll be together through eternity.' She taps my hand. 'Just how it should be.'

She leans closer to my face, so close I catch a whiff of stale coffee and red wine, feel the warmth of her breath crawl across my skin. 'I've missed you so much, my beautiful baby girl.'

My body shakes. I want to gag, fear wrapping itself round me. She's going to kill me. She's going to put the bag over my head and seal it closed.

But she puts the bag down and picks up a mug I hadn't noticed, the words *Best Daughter* printed on the side. 'This is for you,' she says. 'You'll feel no pain, darling girl, I promise.'

58

Kerry rubs her sweaty forehead with shaky hands, her heart thumping so hard it makes her chest ache.

Tom met her sister.

'Where?' Her anxiety continues to build. It's as though an army of angry ants has crawled into her chest cavity. 'Where did you see her?'

'Here in Ridgewater.' Is he smiling? She can't quite see through sudden blurs on her eyes. 'Are you OK? You look really pale.'

'No. Yes. I don't know,' she says. 'Tell them you saw her.'

'Who? Kerry, is everything OK?'

'The police, you need to tell them you saw her.' The words slip and slide as they leave her mouth. 'We should go right now. You can explain everything to me on the way.' She rises but her legs feel weak, and the room spins as though she's spent an hour on a roundabout. She wants to ask Tom more questions, but she can't seem to form the words. She drops a hand onto the table for support, feels herself rocking to and fro.

'Kerry?' Tom's voice sounds far away, echoes, as though they're in a tunnel. He's rising too, taking hold of her arm as she fumbles for her room key, dropping it to the floor.

Tom scoops it up. 'Here, let me help.'

Should she? Should she let this man, who just announced he knew Fi, help her? But he's moving her towards the door, and she hasn't the strength to argue.

'I need... lie down.' She looks towards the door, can barely see through the blurs on her eyes. 'I...' She needs to get to her room, but it feels so far away, and there's nobody about but Tom, whose teeth look far too big for his face, dazzling white, and she starts to laugh, but doesn't really know why.

'I'll help you up the stairs,' he says, and she's not sure if there's concern in his voice or something more sinister. 'Then I'll call an ambulance.' He helps her through the door, her legs barely moving, then swiftly takes her in his arms and carries her up the stairs.

'Almost there,' he says. 'Not far now.'

And then they're in her room and he's lying her on the bed, and just before she lapses into unconsciousness, his fingers move towards her neck.

* * *

Natalie has been sitting in the police reception area for twenty minutes, perhaps longer, when the automatic door springs open, and a man in a wheelchair comes in. It's a face she recognises, but it takes her a moment to place him.

His eyes snap to her, as though sensing her stare. Lance Shaw, Aiden's father. He doesn't seem to recognise her, his eyes only fixing on her for a split-second, before he wheels his chair towards the officer behind the counter.

Why should he remember her, anyway? It's been twelve years, and she's fully aware she's changed out of all recognition since the last time he saw her at his sprawling detached house. Shame dances on her skin as she recalls how she flirted with him in the kitchen, just to get a bottle of wine. She draws her legs up onto the plastic chair and cradles her knees, disgust at her former self rearing its head. The teen she once was knocks, hoping to invade the present with her darkness.

Lance has changed too. He was good looking in his forties. A successful actor, spending a lot of time in America, becoming well-known out there, but he must be in his mid-fifties now, has gained weight, hair greying.

She recalls how Aiden told her his father can no longer walk following an attack in America.

'You called about my son, Aiden Shaw,' he says to the officer behind the counter.

'If you'd like to take a seat, Mr Shaw. The sergeant will be with you shortly.'

Lance looks around, reverses into a space in the corner, his overuse of aftershave hanging in the air. He pulls out his phone, begins tapping the screen, chewing his bottom lip.

The man must already know that his son Mouse is dead – if Aiden was told by the police, he would have been too. He continues to stare at his phone screen – scrolling. She can't help staring. *You kissed him. What the hell were you thinking?*

He looks up as though sensing her watching. Furrows his forehead. Looks back at his screen. If he recognises her, he's not about to acknowledge the fact.

A side door opens. It's a woman officer with warm brown eyes. 'Natalie Ford,' she says, her tone caring. 'If you'd like to come this way.'

Natalie rises and as she follows the officer, she glances back just once to see Lance staring at her, his eyes narrowed, his phone abandoned in his lap.

* * *

Kerry rubs her eyes to see two paramedics.

'Can you hear us?' one says.

'Yes.' She spots Tom near the window, his back to her.

'You had a hypo, love, and your friend here found your emergency necklace. Gave you sugar water until we arrived. How do you feel?'

'I'm OK,' she says, sensing moisture on her chin. 'I didn't eat after taking my insulin, it's my own fault. I'm sorry—'

'Don't be. These things happen. We'll just check you over and be on our way. The B & B owner is preparing you a meal as we speak. Just keep sipping the sugar water.'

Once the paramedics have left, and Kerry is tucking into sausages and mash, she looks over at Tom now sitting on a chair in the corner. 'You can go. I'm OK.'

'Don't you want to know about Fi?'

She stops eating, fork suspended in the air. She's not afraid of him. If he wanted to hurt her, he would have by now. 'You're going to tell me she's dead, aren't you?' A beat. 'She is dead, isn't she? I can feel it.'

He nods. 'I'm so sorry,' he says, and her heart splinters into so many pieces she knows they will never go back together – not in the same way, at least. She buries her head into her hands. 'How do you know? How come you're so certain?' *Did you kill her?*

'Because...' He lowers his head, pauses for a moment. 'I saw her die.'

'You killed her?' Her words are quiet, resigned, but blood thuds, pounding in her head so loud she thinks he might hear it. 'You killed my sister?'

'No! God no.' He shakes his head. 'But I should have been honest with you. Because I know who did.'

59

Annie

I snap my head to one side, my chin bashing against the mug, the liquid spilling, splashing over the white dress and seeping through the flimsy fabric, cold against my skin.

'If you won't drink up,' Margot says, 'you leave me no alternative.'

She puts down the mug and picks up the clear plastic bag. 'This is as hard for me as it is for you,' she says, climbing on top of me, straddling my body, holding the plastic bag open near the top of my head. 'I'm sorry it's come to this, Giselle, but it's the only way.'

I'm sobbing now, nerve endings jangling as I feel the plastic skim my slowly bleaching, curled hair. 'Stop! Please!'

'Don't cry, dear.' Margot kisses my cheek. And I feel the imprint of her red lips on my skin. I want to scrub it off, taking my flesh away with it. 'This is meant to be, my darling girl,' she continues, manoeuvring the bag over the top of my head. 'This won't take long, I promise.'

The sound of the bedroom door swinging open reaches my ears. My body jerks, but Margot doesn't seem to hear or feel, too busy with her sinister job in hand.

'Stop!' My mother yells from the doorway, a cricket bat in her hand like she's some sort of vigilante, her knuckles bleached white. I sense Margot freeze.

'Florence,' she says, her eyes now on the doorway. 'Well, this is nice. I'd offer you tea and cake, but as you can see, I'm rather busy.' She shoves the bag down further. It covers my eyes, distorting my vision.

'Mum! Get help. She's crazy!'

Mum's footsteps are loud as she races across the room, getting closer. 'Yes, but I'm the one with the bat.'

'Stay away!' Margot screeches, and I feel the cold steel of a knife against my neck. 'This is between me and my daughter. What is it with your family, always poking your noses in?'

'If you mean Elliot—'

'Yes. And Richard.'

Mum is still, three feet from the bed. 'What the hell are you talking about?'

Margot removes the knife from my neck, abandons pulling the bag over my face, and climbs off my shaking body. How has this woman become so deranged?

'He was birdwatching from his study when he saw a rare bird in my garden,' Margot begins. Through the plastic I see their shapes. Both strong. Upright. It's a stand-off and neither is backing down.

'A red-backed shrike, if my memory serves me correctly,' Margot goes on. 'He was practically wetting himself with excitement, wanted to see if he could take a photograph, desperate to get into the garden. But the gate was locked so he pushed his way into my house, invading my home, my privacy – leaping into the lounge. Quite rude, I thought. Giselle was sitting on the sofa reading. "Go to your room," I ordered, and my daughter snapped closed her book and shot up the stairs. But it was too late. He'd seen her.'

'What are you talking about?' Mum says.

'The next thing I know, that stupid husband of yours started asking questions. Said he wanted to try to understand. Asked if it was Giselle's choice? Did her doctor know? I laughed inside at that.' She strokes a hand down my cheek, and I cringe. 'Giselle hasn't seen a doctor once in her whole life, have you, darling? But Richard wouldn't stop there. Kept banging on and on, so much so my head felt as though it would explode. And then, he died! I couldn't believe my luck. The man dropped down dead right in front of me. Well not dead per se, there was rather a lot of rolling around on the floor in agony to begin with.'

'You killed Richard?'

'No, Florence, but I have to be honest and tell you I didn't attempt to save him. Didn't give him CPR, delayed calling an ambulance.'

'You let him die.' There are tears in my mother's voice.

'I let him die. I removed some of his clothes and pretended we were having an affair.' She laughs. 'It entertained me to do so.'

'You are one evil sack of shit!' Mum yells. Years of thinking he was having an affair – something Margot had led her to believe – but he was there at her house wanting to photograph a rare bird.

'You do know I wouldn't have touched him with the drippings of my nose.'

'Mum, please!' I scream. 'Get help!'

'There's no way I'm leaving you, Annie.'

'Stay away, Florence. I *will* kill Giselle.'

'That's Annie, for fuck's sake! My daughter!'

'At least I love my daughter, which is more than you can say. You didn't even want yours. That's what she told me.'

'What? Annie? You can't believe that.' I hear the shock in her voice before she turns on Margot. 'Whatever I felt when I gave birth to my daughter,' she cries, 'the disappointment as they told me it was a baby girl, it passed, passed quickly – and I realised how lucky I was to have such a precious, healthy baby. A tiny bundle of happiness.'

'Oh, how twee. Hold on a second while I vomit.'

'Not twee, Margot. That's what Annie gave me – happiness. I'm not saying I didn't struggle with postnatal depression. I never really understood the workings of a little girl, despite being one once myself. I had two brothers, and my mum died when I was five, so I'd always been surrounded by men. All my friends were boys. The thought of having a girl scared me. I was worried I'd get things wrong.' I hear Mum step closer as she speaks, and my heart thuds. 'Sometimes, even now, I know I veer towards Elliot, but it's not because I love him more – it's because I understand him and his needs better. But I love my daughter with all my heart. I will do anything for her.'

Margot clambers on top of me again, like a wild animal about to devour their prey. She begins tugging the bag further down my face, over my nose, blocking my airways.

Through the plastic I see Mum raise the cricket bat. 'Including going to jail for killing you, Margot Bancroft.'

Margot's scream is deafening. I feel her agony as she slumps heavy against me, pressing me down against the nettles. Her body lifeless, blood dripping onto my plastic-covered cheeks. My stomach surges as I let out a terrified cry.

And then her body is being pulled off me, sliding away like

something slimy, as she thumps to the floor. The plastic bag is pulled from my head and Mum's there, looking like a zombie, all colour drained from her cheeks, eyes wide. The bat slips from her hand, crashing to the ground. 'Nobody messes with my girl,' she says, trying to loosen the ropes that still hold my wrists. I've never felt so horrified, yet loved unconditionally, in my whole life.

'How did you know?' I whisper, as she struggles with the ropes.

'Elliot.'

'Elliot? Is he OK?'

She nods, pulling one of the ropes free, flashing looks at Margot as though she fears the woman might rise from her crumpled position on the floor. 'He told me Margot was dangerous. That she'd tried to kill him twice. She'd pushed him from the cliff, and she'd tried to smother him. He said I had to get back to Fairy Cottage. Make sure you were safe. So, when I saw a light on the first floor of Sycamore House, the groceries spilled across the road, and you weren't at the cottage, I just knew.' She's onto the next rope now, it's almost free. 'And there's something else. Elliot told me that Giselle's still alive.'

'*What?*'

'Margot had her trapped in an upstairs bedroom for years. The poor thing must have been there since we thought she died.'

'That doesn't make any sense. Where is she?'

'Elliot let her out just before his accident, gave her his coat and some money.' She releases the final tie, and I climb from the bed.

Everything moves at warp speed then. The thud of fast footfalls against floorboards outside in the hallway, the appearance of the grey-haired man like a phantom in the half-light. I scream out as the man heads towards my mother.

But he stops before he reaches her. 'What the hell's going on?' he cries, looking down at Margot's lifeless body on the floor. He drops to his knees and takes her pulse.

'She's dead.' He looks up at us, wide eyes shimmering. 'You killed my sister.'

I realise now who he is. Joel Bancroft. Giselle's uncle. 'She would have killed me,' I cry.

'I know,' he says, and after a moment he lies down beside her and takes hold of her hand entwining his fingers with hers. 'Everything is going to be OK now, Margot,' he whispers, as the sound of sirens fills the room. 'Everything will be just fine.'

60

'I met your sister twelve years ago,' Tom says. 'She was sitting on a bench at the far end of Sycamore Wood, looking out over Ridgewater Cove and the sea. She told me how she'd just arrived in the UK, and about a friend she'd met online, who she was meeting up with the following day, though she never told me his name.'

Kerry and Tom are back in the bar, sipping mineral water. Kerry has taken a couple of tablets for a headache, and they are beginning to kick in.

'I approached her,' Tom goes on. 'My bag was packed. I was running away. Had come to realise the life I was leading was far from normal. Fi asked if I was OK. I think she thought I was suicidal. Perhaps I was. I didn't know who I was any more, perhaps I never did.'

Kerry is silent. She has so many questions but needs to hear his every word. Know everything about her sister's last hours.

'Fi said she hadn't found anywhere to stay yet, but when she did, I could stay with her if I wanted. Though my plan even back then was to find Joel. Fi didn't even know me, yet she was so kind. She spent a long time talking to me, making things clear.' He takes a sip of water, licks his dry lips. 'That everything I had ever known was a lie.' He pauses, stares into Kerry's eyes, his own glistening. 'That I was born male, raised as a girl.'

Confusion burns, Kerry covers her mouth with her hand, but still she is silent.

'Fi was so good to me. You have to understand that. She was the first person I'd spoken to in the real world since Uncle Joel – since Annie. Your sister could have ridiculed me, but instead she gave me hope. Was prepared to take me in. Be a friend.'

'So, what happened?'

'My mother happened. Margot happened. She was raging when she found us together, but Fi gave her everything back, told her she was deranged, warped. Truth is, Mother was and still is convinced I'm a girl – her daughter, Giselle – and she saw your sister as the enemy.'

'Oh my God.'

'Fi explained everything – why hair grew on my face. Why my voice was lower than my mother's. I guess in some ways I already knew something was different about me than other girls. I'd seen films, read books. I'd met Uncle Joel. Fi felt sure I'd been brainwashed by my mother. Even my grandmother believed I was a girl.

'Once I showed signs of puberty, Mother shipped my grandmother off to a care home so she would never know she'd lied. Because that's where the lie began. Mother was so worried my grandmother would hurt me if I was a boy. Just as she'd hurt my uncle.' His eyes shimmer with tears, making them a vivid blue. 'She killed her, Kerry. My mother killed Fi.' He lowers his head, stares down at his hands. 'I'm so sorry.'

Kerry bursts into tears, despite the news being almost a relief. She'd known, or perhaps sensed, for a while now that Fi was dead. But to hear that the last night her sister spent on this planet she was trying to do good, trying to help Tom, meant a lot.

'You're Giselle,' she says through her tears, piecing the man's words together. 'But I thought she – you – were dead. I'm sorry, I'm so confused.'

He shakes his head. 'I'll explain from the beginning. If you're OK with that.'

She nods. Takes a sip of her drink. 'I'm OK with that,' she says.

'My uncle is sure my mother would have been happy when she gave birth to a boy. That she only said I was a girl fearing my grandmother would hurt me like she hurt him.

'Eventually, Mother began to believe her own lies, believe that I was a girl, and, of course, I thought I was too. Grandmother was obsessed with how pretty I was, how I mastered the ballet steps she taught me better than my mother had.

'I didn't know anything about the human body, had never had anyone to compare notes with.' He smiles, but it doesn't reach those bright blue eyes. 'Mother became quite... well, peculiar, I suppose. Even when Grandmother went into the care home, things didn't change. I was a girl, and that was that. And I didn't mind when I was small. As I say, I knew nothing of anatomy. I was told I was a little girl as soon as I could understand. I knew no different. Mother home-schooled me. My only friend was Annie, and our playing together was limited to the garden. Mother never let Annie's brother Elliot visit. So, with no TV at that time – only endless videos chosen carefully by Mother – and nobody to compare myself to, I thought I was female. A Disney princess – a prima ballerina, if my grandmother had her way. I thought I was just like you.

'As I grew older, I started to change. It wouldn't have been quite as easy to hide from others that I had been born male, so Mother invented a skin condition.

'During puberty I tried to cope with the changes to my body, which my mother insisted were part of my unexplained condition. Having been isolated for most of my life, I didn't question it. But, by the time I was eighteen, I was becoming more and more restless. I'd had no symptoms for years, so I took myself into the garden for the first time in a very long time, wanting to feel the sun on my skin, wanting to prove I no longer had the condition my mother insisted I had.

'She saw me and dragged me inside, screaming at me, her body shaking.'

'Oh God. I'm so sorry.'

He shakes his head, tears in his eyes. 'I woke up the following day with welts on my skin, itchy and sore – something I hadn't experienced for years. Mother said I should never go out again, that this is what would happen if I did. That's when I found it. A nettle leaf clinging to my skin. I'd discovered her secret. She would cut fresh nettles and put them in my bed while I slept, removing them before morning. I'd never had a skin condition. It had simply been her way of keeping me inside.'

Kerry covers her mouth, holding in her shock.

'I knew right away what she'd done the night before, what she'd done when I was eleven. That's when I started to go out at night, just to feel the freedom, trying to work out what to do – how to get away. Then I met Fi, knew for sure my mother was a monster.'

Kerry's mind spins. 'I'm so sorry, Tom.' She lays a hand on his arm. 'But I don't understand. Giselle – *you* – were found dead at the bottom of a cliff. Margot – your mother—'

'Identified the body as mine – *Giselle's*.' He nods. 'The body was Fi's, Kerry. The day I met your sister was the day she died. I'm so sorry.'

A hand flies to Kerry's mouth. 'How is that even possible?'

'You really want to know?'

A tear rolls down her cheek. 'No, but I need to.'

'Mother forced me to help her put my dress on Fi. Mother said if I didn't help her, if I didn't keep quiet, she would tell the police it was me who murdered Fi. That my life would be hell in prison. I'll spare you what she said the other men would do to me.

'The police accepted the body was mine... Giselle's; why wouldn't they? Fi was wearing my dress, my necklace, which Mother had fastened around her neck. And what mother would pretend her child was dead? Plus, despite initial thoughts that it could be murder or suicide, it was declared accidental. Margot played the grieving mother perfectly. And then she locked me up.'

Another tear pushes through Kerry's lashes, trickles down her cheek. 'How did she think she would get away with it?'

'But she did. For twelve years. Until Elliot let me out.'

'Elliot let you out?'

Tom nods, closes his eyes for a moment. 'I'm sorry I didn't tell you everything sooner.'

'We should go to the police,' Kerry says, a wave of guilt about wrongly accusing Seb of being involved in Fi's disappearance making her shudder, Sasha's angry words ringing in her ears. 'We must set things straight. Sooner rather than later.'

61

Annie

Natalie is singing, out of tune I might add, to 'Natural' by Imagine Dragons, who are trying to make themselves heard from the speakers of her Fiat. Despite it only being two weeks since she found her attacker, she seems happy as she drives. I like this version of my friend. It's as though discovering who attacked her has transformed her life.

Kerry and I are in the back of the car, me wearing a woolly hat to hide my orange hair. I've an appointment later to have it dyed back brown – thankfully my hair is pretty strong and thick, so the bleach didn't do any real damage.

We're almost at Heathrow Airport, and Kerry's hoping, once she's back in Australia, that she will feel like her old, strong self once more. It's been a three-hour journey, made longer by a stop for lunch at a pretty pub in Andover.

I'm glad to get out of Ridgewater for a short while. There's been a lot of media attention, which makes me want to disappear, but I will return. Will stay with Mum and Elliot until things are more settled. I've tried reducing my antidepressants but, with everything that's happened, it wasn't a good time. I certainly picked the wrong week to quit sertraline. But I will come off the drug as soon as I start to feel more normal.

It's too early to tell what I will do next, where my future lies. But what I do know is if I go back to my old career as a doctor, I'll need some more time out first. That's why I've resigned. I want to stay in Ridgewater, get to know Tom, keep an eye on Mum and Elliot, and be there for Natalie. Mum's even agreed I can get another cat. And the old bookshop still needs a full-time assistant, so I've applied for that, with my fingers crossed.

'Sasha Blair came to the B & B yesterday,' Kerry says, bringing me out of my thoughts. 'Basically to say "I told you so" in the most pleasant of ways.'

'I'm pleased Seb had nothing to do with any of it,' I say. 'I've always liked him. And imagine how awful life would have been for Sasha and the children if it had been him.'

'I agree, the poor man has been through enough in his life,' Natalie says. 'I feel guilty for suspecting him.'

'I saw a photo of his mother when I visited Sasha,' Kerry says, as Natalie pulls up at a red light. 'There was a diary, too, from the year she took her own life. She'd written "I'm afraid of him. He won't leave me alone" as an entry a couple of months before the Blairs moved to the farmhouse, before she took her own life. She said in her suicide note that she couldn't live with herself. It's awful to think she was so hounded by someone that she took her own life.'

'Who could she have meant?' I say. 'Could it have been Mouse? Could he have made her life a misery?'

'Surely not,' Kerry says. 'I know he turned into a monster, but he could have only been about eleven at the time of the diary entry.'

'Kids of eleven have done some awful things,' Natalie says. 'And apparently he did. He was a strange child by all accounts.'

'Well, whoever it was, it seems they may have driven her to take her own life.'

My mind drifts to Seb's father Colin, to seeing him in the care home. He couldn't have driven his wife to suicide, surely? I push the thought from my mind. Whoever was wrecking Caroline Blair's life all those years ago, I guess there's no way of finding out now.

'How did your parents take the news about Fi?' I ask, changing the subject.

Kerry sighs, shrugs. 'I'm not sure. I guess I won't be until I see my mum face to face. She talked in clichés when I called her, saying things like "We can finally move on", "Put our best foot forward", that kind of thing, but she has a drink problem, which I worry will always trip her up if she doesn't get help.'

'I'm sorry.'

'Don't be. I'm going to try to persuade her to join a support group.' She pauses for a moment. 'I spoke to my dad for the first time in years. I was shocked how pleased he was to hear from me. He sobbed when he heard about Fi. I'm going to Adelaide after I've spent some time with Mum. Be with him and my little half-brother for a while. It's time I got to know him.'

'That's good,' Natalie says, indicating at a sign for Heathrow, 'but do give yourself time to heal. You've been through a lot.'

'We all have,' Kerry says. 'But I will. Thank you. And you take care, Natalie. I can see you're doing great, but—'

'I'm fine. Honestly,' Natalie says, steering the car towards the drop-off area.

'Never been better.'

62

'...dressed in white. Her... *his* hair long, blonde,' I hear Elliot say as I come through the front door after dropping Kerry off at the airport. 'I couldn't work out what was happening when this figure flew through the door.' He turns his head as I enter the lounge. 'Hey, you're back.' It's good to see my brother sitting on the sofa, looking well, almost his old self.

'Hey,' Seb says from the armchair, raising a hand.

'Kerry get off all right?' Mum asks from where she's sitting beside Elliot, leaning her head on his shoulder. I can't believe she's here. The court gave her bail, deemed she wasn't at risk of committing another offence, that it was exceptional circumstances.

I nod. 'She'll be in the air by now, has promised to message when she's back in Australia. I don't envy her that long flight.'

'I was just telling Seb all the gory details,' Elliot says. He sounds flippant, but I know it's not how he really feels. These awful events, for him, for all of us, are going to take time to come to terms with.

'Don't mind me,' I say, dropping down onto the floor near the flickering fire.

'I darted after what I thought was a woman making her way into the wood, could hear Margot yelling from behind, "Giselle, come back." My head spun. Giselle was dead, wasn't she?

'I followed the woman as she climbed up the rocky path. Out of breath, I found her on the clifftop. "Don't!" I cried. She was so close to the edge. I'd never really seen Giselle close up, only ever from a distance, but the sight of her – dressed as a woman yet, in build, the shadow shading his chin, so clearly a man – well, I felt as though I'd stepped into a parallel universe.'

I've heard all of this before. The retelling is for Seb, who is spellbound.

Mum shakes her head. 'Margot was one crazy bitch,' she says.

'Mum!'

'She was going to kill you, Annie. And not only that, she let your father die, then took away my chance to grieve.' She folds her arms. 'So I'll call her whatever I like.'

'Fair enough,' I say with a half-smile. But I do worry about Mum. She killed Margot, after all. Her solicitor says they have a good case for her defence, but the coming months are not going to be easy.

'Carry on,' I say to Elliot.

'"I was born male," Giselle said, voice low, Adam's apple bobbing. I gave him my coat, the money Margot had given me for gardening, told him to take off, and he did.'

And then it hits me. The note I found. *'Thank you for everything. G x'* Tom/Giselle had left the note for Elliot when he returned the coat.

'Margot appeared within moments, raging like some sort of banshee,' Elliot goes on. 'I felt the push against my chest before

I could say a word. Lost my footing. Stumbled backwards. And that's the last I remember.'

Like history repeating itself. Yet Fi wasn't quite so lucky.

The doorbell rings, and Mum rises and leaves the room.

We're all silent for a moment, before Seb moves forward in his seat, puts his elbows on his knees and entwines his fingers. 'There's something I want to ask you,' he says, his eyes on Elliot.

'Sure. Everything OK?'

'Good, yeah. The thing is, my workload is expanding, and I'm struggling to keep up with orders. I don't suppose you'd be interested in coming on board?'

Elliot stares at his old friend. 'You don't have to do this—'

'Elliot, I'm a businessman. I didn't get where I am today by doing anyone any favours. I want you with me. You're a talented wood carver, mate. I'd be honoured if you'd say yes.'

Elliot's face breaks into a smile, his eyes brightening. 'Then the answer is yes. Thanks, my friend.'

The lounge door swings open, and Mum appears once more, Elliot's carer following her in. 'Do you remember Michael, Elliot? He cared for you while you were—'

'And I'm so sorry.' Michael bustles in and thrusts a bunch of flowers at Elliot. He passes them to Mum, who tilts her head on one side as she fiddles with the cellophane.

'Sorry?' Elliot says.

'I take full responsibility.'

'For what?'

'It was my fault you fell down the stairs.'

Mum and I stare at him, our mouths dropping open.

'I was reading to you, Elliot, and...'

'Go on,' Mum says, her tone tense, though not aggressive.

'I'd had a bad night, felt exhausted. Turns out I was harbouring a virus – if I'd known, I wouldn't have come here.

The book was long, and it became an effort to keep reading after a while. I'm ashamed to say I fell asleep. I'm wracked with guilt. I should be reported, deserve to be blacklisted.'

Mum shakes her head and looks around the room, focusing for a moment on the photos of Dad, reinstalled on the windowsill, a wooden robin that Elliot carved shortly after our father's death amongst them, and then onto our shattered faces. Her gaze rests on Michael, whose red eyes tell us of lack of sleep and tears. 'Sit yourself down, son,' she says. 'I'll put the kettle on. I think there's been enough heads on sticks over the last week, don't you?'

63

We're sitting in the One Trick Pony, tucked in the corner of the busy bar, Tom huddled into a dark jacket, despite how warm it is in here. It's been almost three weeks since Margot died.

'Do you remember leaving me in here alone?' I say with a smile.

He nods. 'I'd seen my mother go by the window; it had freaked me out.' He sighs. 'I'm sorry, Annie,' he says, lowering his head, giving it a shake. 'Sorry that I deceived you. Sorry for what my mother did to you.'

'No, I'm sorry.' I stare at him, trying to find the Giselle I once knew, unable to find her at all, except, perhaps, in the blueness of his eyes. 'Sorry about how your mother died.'

'The woman was going to kill you.' He picks up his beer and takes a gulp. 'She left your mum no choice.'

'Are you going to be OK?'

He shrugs. 'Who knows? I mean, Christ, my gene pool isn't exactly brimming with mentally healthy family members. I'm not going to lie, I'm struggling. But I've lined up a counsellor, and I've got Joel and Jackie.'

'And me.'

'And you, and I'm grateful for that.'

'I'm guessing the funeral will be hard.'

'Yeah, I mean, let's face it, who's going to attend?' Another gulp of beer. 'I expect there will be some rubberneckers, and the press. It's been all over the media.'

'Will Joel go?'

He nods. 'He says he will. He's pretty messed up, poor bloke. Though not quite as much as me.' He laughs, but it's fake, moves the palm of his hand over his forehead. 'Christ, what a mess.'

I reach across, cover his hand with my own. 'Would you like me to come?' I'm not confident I can face it, but I will be there for Tom – my oldest friend – if he needs me.

'Thanks, I appreciate it. But I wouldn't want to—'

'I'll be there.'

We're silent for a moment before he says, 'I should have spoken out when she pushed your brother off that cliff. Should have gone to the police. But my mother would have lied, told them I did it, that I also killed Fi.' He swallows, running a hand across his throat. 'Joel respected my wishes, kept quiet too. Though we agreed we would watch over you and Elliot. Make sure you were OK.'

'Like guardian angels?'

'Something like that.' A beat. 'I'm so sorry.'

'Please stop apologising. I understand what you've been through, really, I do.'

'But I should have done more.' He lowers his head again. 'She kept me in that room for years. OK, so she gave me books to read, and I enjoyed art, and by then I had the TV and a never-ending pile of films to watch, but...' He pulls his hand from under mine, presses the thumb of one hand into the palm of the other, closes his eyes. 'Of course, by this time Fi had explained to me that I was male, and I knew she was right, even if Mother would never accept it. When she trapped me in my prison at Sycamore House, she kept my hair long; my only clothes were dresses.'

'And you never fought her? Never tried to overpower her?'

'You have to understand that she had the power over *me*, Annie. If she lied to the police, told them I killed Fi, hurt Elliot, I would go to a prison far worse than the one she'd trapped me in. As long as I kept myself clean-shaven and continued to wear the dresses she supplied, she said she would care for me.'

'But you ran when Elliot let you out.'

He nods. 'I'd got to a point by then that I wanted my freedom at any cost. So, when I heard someone downstairs, I began tapping on the pipe, hoping whoever it was would find me, and when he pulled that bolt, freeing me, I shot out, ran for my life.

'I had Uncle Joel's address. He told me a few days after I escaped that when he visited Sycamore House all those years ago, he'd sensed something wasn't right – though he couldn't put his finger on what it was. He said I wasn't how he expected. That the fact I never went out and had no friends was unnatural. That's why he slipped me his address. At the time he had no idea I was a boy.

'When I stood on his doorstep the night I escaped, my hair long and blonde, my dress white, wrapped in Elliot's coat, Joel and Jackie took me in, Joel seeing immediately what his sister had done.

'Jackie asked what I believed my true identity was, and I told her that despite being brought up as female, I'd known, even before Fi told me, that something wasn't right, and that I saw myself as male. She got me new clothes, cut my hair and dyed it brown. I didn't recognise myself when I looked in the mirror, but I knew it was the real me.'

'So, you stayed in Ridgewater. Worked in the One Trick Pony. Weren't you worried she would walk in, recognise you?'

He shook his head. 'It was a risk I had to take. I was worried about Elliot, I blamed myself for his accident. I knew I was on pretty safe ground at the bar: she had no friends, never socialised, and was never one for drinking outside her own four walls.'

My mind travels back to Margot telling me 'a friend' told her about Elliot. A lie, of course. She knew because she was the one who pushed him off that cliff edge.

'I needed money,' Tom goes on. 'Joel and Jackie aren't well off. I wasn't about to freeload.'

'Your name?'

'Name?'

'Tom Brown. You made it up?'

He nods. 'One of the nights when I was roaming in the woods, I saw you and your brother with Natalie and Seb. I watched you for a while. Later, as I walked back to the house, I heard a voice yelling "Tommy" – I guess that's where I got it from, or maybe it was the novel *Tom Brown's Schooldays*. I've read a lot of books over the years.'

I take hold of his hand, a range of feelings flooding in, from remembering my old friend Giselle, to a strange magnetic draw to the man sitting in front of me. The whole situation is confusing as hell. It plays with my mind, so God knows how Tom must feel.

'I sobbed the day I finally got away from my mother, and Joel held me for hours, patting my back gently, like I was a child, and going on and on about how he should have done more.' Tom pauses for a moment. 'I know I've accepted I'm male, but I'm still achingly confused by who I really am.'

'It will take time.'

'I guess I was programmed for eighteen years to think as a female, but I had and still have the hormones and body of a man.'

I place a hand on his arm. 'Well, I'm here for you. I'm not going anywhere,' I say.

'Thanks, Annie,' he says, his lips twitching into an almost-smile. 'I appreciate that.'

As I walk home alone, I worry Tom's got more to go through. He and his aunt and uncle covered up Fi's death; they would be accountable for that. I hope any judge or jury would allow for everything they'd been through.

64

It's been three months since Natalie thought she'd found out the truth. Since she thought Mouse raped her and left her for dead. How wrong she was.

She stares down at the crumpled body at the bottom of the stairs, lying at a strange angle. He'd hit the stairlift on his way down. She can see, as she hovers on the dimly lit landing, that the fall has snapped his neck. It's a gruesome sight, far worse than in the movies.

She struggles to move, her body frozen, but feels no guilt. Revenge tastes good on her tongue, it makes her smile.

Behind her is Aiden's bedroom, where he once tried to force himself on her. Would he have pushed things further that day if Mouse hadn't crept from his room, disturbing his brother? *'Pervert,'* Aiden had called out.

She'd asked Aiden why he called his dead brother Mouse. It was on one of her visits to the prison where the one-time king of the school lingers, lonely, wondering how it came to this, how the younger version of himself is guilty of his brother's murder. Natalie won't go again; a couple of visits to find out everything he knew was enough. She got what she went for.

He told her Tommy was called Mouse because he tittle-tattled. *'Little Tommy Tittlemouse'* after the nursery rhyme. 'Dad called him it first,' he said, 'and it kind of stuck.

'When we were about ten or eleven, Mouse told Mum he'd seen Dad kissing Caroline Blair from next door – that she didn't like it much, that she'd cried when he touched her boobs.

'It was just before the Blairs moved to the farmhouse,' Aiden had gone on. 'Dad took off to work on a shoot in the US a month later. That's when Mum divorced him.'

'And then Lance came back?'

'Yeah, for a short while when I was eighteen. He didn't stick around Ridgewater for long. Only returning to England much later when some bloke assaulted him.'

'Some bloke?'

Aiden shrugged then. 'Dad wouldn't talk about it.'

'The necklace?' She asked Aiden on another visit, sitting down opposite him in the prison's visitors' room. 'Did you leave it for me at the vet's?' This had bothered her since his arrest. If he'd left it, he must have attacked her. How else would he have it?

He shook his head, eyes narrowing. 'Necklace?'

'The one I was wearing that night in the woods. The one someone took from round my neck, when I was left for dead.' She paused, trying to find the truth in his eyes. 'A few months back someone left it for me at the vet's where I work.'

'It wasn't me.' He sounded sincere.

'Then who was it? If your brother was dead, and you didn't—'

'I've no idea, Natalie. Honestly.' His eyes widened, glistening, his hand creeping back and forth across his mouth, round the back of his neck, as it slammed into him that he got it wrong, his brother wasn't a rapist. Little Tommy Tittlemouse had simply been in the wrong place at the wrong time. He'd found Natalie after she was attacked, barely alive – left for dead. What he was doing in the woods that night she'll probably never know, but he wasn't her assailant. He hadn't put his large, gloved hands around her throat that night. Someone else had ripped off her clothes and ruined her life, and whoever it was had taken her necklace as some kind of trophy.

Natalie first suspected Lance the day Kerry mentioned Caroline Blair's diary. Her friend had seen it at Seb and Sasha's farmhouse the day she accused Seb. She told Natalie and Annie that she'd been bothered by a couple of entries from a week before Caroline took her own life. *'I'm afraid of him,'* Caroline had written. *'He won't leave me alone.'* The suicide note Caroline had left when she took the overdose had said she couldn't live with herself. Natalie knew that feeling. She'd thought about taking her own life over the years.

So it all began to add up:

Someone had raped her twelve years ago.

Had the same person raped Caroline years before?

Had it been Aiden and Tommy's father? Lance, who'd handed the necklace in to the vet's in an attempt to scare her? Had he seen her working there, maybe on a visit with his cat?

And had he attacked a woman when he was in the US and someone took revenge, shattering his legs so he would never walk again? And that's why he never talked about it.

The more she realised it must have been Lance, the more her memories of that awful night surged into focus.

The aftershave her attacker wore was the same as Lance wore that day in the kitchen. *The day I kissed him, flirted with him, all for a bottle of wine.* Lance was wearing the same aftershave when she saw him wheeling his way into the police station.

She looks at his empty wheelchair beside her. It all been so easy. The man let her into his house, up the stairs. He really thought she was going to... No, she won't go there, as she'll probably heave, may even throw up.

She hurries down the stairs. Crouches down near to the man's face and whispers into his unhearing ear, 'I said when I found who wrecked my life, I would kill him. My job here is done.' She rises, not sure how long it will be until he's found. He could get a bit pongy before anyone does.

A ginger cat purrs round her legs. She lifts her into her arms, tickling behind her ears, checking her collar. 'Well, hello there, Trixie, sweetie,' she says. 'I know a cat lover not far from here who will simply love you.'

Once out on the street, she takes a lungful of cold air.

Do I feel any better? Probably not. It might take a while. But I can finally stop looking over my shoulder. Stop wondering if the next man I see is the bastard who destroyed me.

She looks at her watch. She's late. Duncan will wonder where she's got to. They're just friends going for a drink. But one thing is for sure, she's no longer afraid. She's a survivor, and it's time for her to take a deep breath and move on with the next stage of her life.

EPILOGUE

ANNIE

It's been over three months since the world caved in around us. After the shock of everything, my mental health took a further dip. Aftershock, I suppose. But I'm pushing back, upwards and onwards, finding the strength from somewhere to rebuild, and so is Elliot.

From where I'm sprawled on the sofa, I smile at my brother sitting in the armchair, reading *The Ghost Next Door.* We're still here at Fairy Cottage. For now, at least. Though Elliot misses the Highlands, has plans to return. Seb insists if he moves, they can still make things work with the business, so we'll see how that goes. I'll miss Elliot when he leaves, but we've promised to keep in touch, see each other regularly. There's no doubting we've bonded over everything that's happened, and I feel as close to him now as I did when we were young.

He told me a few weeks back that he'd had an email from Christer. The man had heard what my brother had been through via the media.

'He was more than my business partner,' Elliot told me. And I wondered if, deep down, I already knew that. We shared sob

stories about our failed relationships, though his sadness runs deeper than mine. In all honesty, I've almost forgotten my ex, it feels like a lifetime ago that we broke up.

'I'd never felt so helpless when he walked out, leaving the shop heading into administration,' Elliot had said to me. *'I won't be replying to his email.'* Despite everything that's happened, my brother is getting through it with the support of friends and family, as I am.

I may go back to my career as a doctor when the time is right, but, for now, I'm enjoying my new job in the second-hand bookshop, filling shelves, chatting with customers about authors we love. It's where I want to be.

I stroke my cat's silky fur, tickling her ears as she purrs like a tractor. She's a stray Natalie found. My friend had her checked over at the vet's, and it seems the ginger bundle hasn't been chipped. I took her with open arms, Natalie's only condition being I called her Pixie, which is fine. 'Pixie of Fairy Cottage' has a kind of ring to it.

Lance Shaw is dead. Was found broken at the bottom of his stairs. The coroner ruled it accidental. Natalie seems happy he's a goner. She's getting there too – seeing a therapist, and Duncan is as kind as they come.

My thoughts turn to the Bancrofts. I wonder sometimes why I was never allowed in Sycamore House as a child. Was Margot afraid I might accidently see that my best friend was a little boy? Perhaps going to the loo? Or was I truly that grubby child she deemed unworthy of entering her home?

Joan Bancroft is receiving palliative care. She only has weeks left. Nobody knows who Sycamore House will go to when she dies, or even if she's written a will. Neither Tom nor Joel wants the place.

Tom's pending court case seems promising; like Mum's, the

circumstances are playing in his favour. I see a lot of him. We're good friends, though I'm no closer to knowing how either of us really feels – if there's a spark of something romantic between us. Perhaps time will tell. Perhaps it won't.

I rise, moving Pixie onto one of Mum's un-puffed cushions – she gives me a look and then curls up once more – and head for the window.

Through the glass, a two-inch fairy on the windowsill smiles in at me, flapping her wings. I blink, and she's gone – never there, perhaps, or only in my imagination.

I turn to see Elliot rising from the armchair. He winks at me.

'Just a fairy,' he says, and smiles.

* * *

ACKNOWLEDGEMENTS

I've absolutely loved working with the brilliant Francesca Best on *Let Me Out*. I feel so lucky to have such a talented and supportive editor.

A big thank you to my wonderful publishers. It's a joy to be part of such a fantastic team at Boldwood.

Big thanks too to Helen Woodhouse for her excellent copy-edit and Arbaiah Aird for a brilliant proofread. And I'm delighted by the wonderful cover design, thank you, Jane Dixon-Smith.

To my lovely friends Karen Clarke and Joanne Duncan, thank you for your continual support – this book is dedicated to you both.

Thank you, Amy Brittany, for sharing her medical knowledge about bedbound patients, and for her support. Any mistakes are my own.

Thanks to my amazing readers, to everyone on social media who cheers me on and all the reviewers and bloggers who take the time to leave lovely reviews – I keep on writing because of all of you.

Thank you to all the lovely members of Fiction Addicts Book Club, with special thanks to Lisa Bedford, Teresa Nikolic, Trina Dixon and all the other brilliant admins.

Thank you to all the lovely members of The Book Club Virgins, who are so supportive of my book journey.

To Hitchin Library, Liz Tye and Julie Anderson at Next Page

Books and Roy Allen for helping me get my books out into the world.

Thanks to Gina, Jude, Lynn and to all my friends and family for supporting me, and to all my lovely writer friends who are always so giving.

Thank you so much to Lynda Checkley, Dianne Garbis, Lauren Lewis and Jill Haine for choosing the names of three of my characters – Joan, Duncan and Agnes – in *Let Me Out.*

Big thanks to Liam, Daniel, Luke and Lucy for always supporting me – and for plugging my books! No, you can't have any commission.

My acknowledgements would never be complete without a loving mention of my mum, dad, and sister Cheryl – miss you all so much.

And finally, thank you Kev – writer's widower extraordinaire.

ABOUT THE AUTHOR

Amanda Brittany is a bestselling author of psychological thrillers including *Her Last Lie.* She lives in Hertfordshire with her husband and dog.

Sign up to Amanda Brittany's mailing list for news, competitions and updates on future books.

Visit Amanda's websites: www.writingallsorts.blogspot.com and hitchinhertfordshire.blogspot.com

Follow Amanda on social media here:

- facebook.com/amandabrittany2
- x.com/amandajbrittany
- instagram.com/amanda_brittany_author
- bookbub.com/profile/amanda-brittany

ALSO BY AMANDA BRITTANY

Now You Are Mine

Let Me Out

www.ingramcontent.com/pod-product-compliance
Lightning Source LLC
La Vergne TN
LVHW030916080826
845145LV00013B/2922

9781836171867